ONE DAY OF LUC

Andrew John E

COPYRIGHT AND DISCLAIMERS NOTICE

ABOUT THE AUTHOR

Andrew was born in County Durham, England, and still resides there with his wife and their young daughters. Andrew has worked in a private care home setting as a Care Assistant, and then as a Senior Care Assistant, for almost a decade. During this time, he has assisted in meeting the needs of residents who are sadly reaching, and have reached, the end of their lives. He has written this book to highlight awareness around Palliative, Dementia and Cancer care provision/experiences, in the aim of helping towards breaking down the stigma wrongfully associated with them.

DEDICATION

This book is dedicated to those who I have ever had, and continue to have, the privilege of providing care for. It is also dedicated to the amazing carers and nurses I have the honour of working with.

In loving memory of Harry, Doris, and Liam.

TABLE OF CONTENTS

AN UNFAMILIAR SETTING

Something isn't right. I can't quite put my finger on how or why this is, but... it just isn't.

I'm awake, without any shadow of a doubt, although I can't peel my eyelids apart to convey this. Only making matters worse, my entire body is completely locked rigid, as if it were frozen stiff within a searing block of ice. No matter how hard I try, I simply cannot move an inch - not even my fingertips will budge. What has happened to me? I can't recall feeling ill, at least not in this terrible way.

For some unknown reason, I also find myself lying in a foetal position, like a vulnerable infant, and are unable to from change this. Don't get me wrong, the bed I'm in is most-certainly warm and comfortable, but... still. A daunting possibility soon rises that I've been asleep for many months or even years, all the while helplessly immersed inside a dream-like state of total unconsciousness - a ludicrous notion, but perhaps *that* is the case? Perhaps I fell into a coma of some sort? Surely, that can't be right? I'm lucky to get four hours sleep – if that. How very strange. How very unusual.

Nothing compares to this horrid sensation, this lack of control over my own self and whereabouts. I don't feel replenished whatsoever, as one should after a lengthy rest. If being honest, I can't recall the last time I truly awoke from my dreams, if you can even call them that? I mean, aren't dreams meant to take you off into fantastical realms - places of vivid fabrication and fulfilment? Only, what I have been experiencing of late couldn't be further from that wantful ideal. Pull yourself together, Isabella Cunningham. For goodness sake, old girl! What has gotten into you? You've always been so sensible - logical, not a paranoid mess as you presently are. Lord, I've never felt so scared. This is simply awful. Calm yourself,

Isabella. Deep breaths now. Panicking will get you nowhere, will it? That's it... deep breaths. Relax.

As my frantic thoughts begin to clarify, I recollect certain images and sounds of late: strangers talking in muffled whispers, a woman quietly sobbing (and I'm sure that I recognise her), distorted waves of amber light that eerily fall into a sea of endless darkness... none of which appear remotely rational. Luckily, there's some occasional laughter thrown into the mix, which itself is received in a most-welcomed manner. However, and it continues to eat away at me, nothing seems or feels as it once did. I'm not myself usual self at all. What is this unfamiliar setting, this persisting veil of beleaguerment and utter frailty that hangs over me like Damocles' sword? Do I really want to learn these answers, for what dreadful facts would be revealed? Perhaps not. Maybe I should just go back to sleep and be done with all this confusion? I don't know.

To my instant gratitude, there is *some* respite to ease this heightened level of fear in me: I can just make out a piano playing nearby, and the piece being performed is one of my all-time favourites, Frédéric Chopin's *Nocturne, Opus Nine*. My memory remains somewhat clouded, making it difficult to be one-hundred percent certain of this delightful assumption, nevertheless this music's joyful tones quickly encapsulate my ears. I would often pretend to play an imaginary piano alongside, but my fingers are so crippled and painful now rendering this strong desire frankly impossible. Oh, what a frustrating pity. Classical music has brought so much joy to me over the years; it is my swiftest route to solace, and one I pray shall never end. How I adore this piece. This is perfect. This is wonderful. I feel a little better now.

"Should we check on Isabella first?"

"Yeah. She's had another bad night apparently, according to Hollie."

Who said that? Who's there?

Within seconds, some encroaching footsteps invade my personal space. My heart and breathing hasten together in unison against this unforeseen development, which is reasonable, given the nature of my weakened body. Goodness, *should* they turn out to be an intruder, how can I possibly fight back? I'm like a small rabbit in the headlights, nervously awaiting what monstrous beast aims itself towards them, with nowhere to run nor hide. Knowing my luck, it'll be a bloody juggernaut that comes to greet me.

Opening my eyes continues to come with little success, despite numerous attempts. They are clamped shut, each lid bound together by a burning substance that irritates the skin around them like a scalding layer of hot glue. Oh, it's unbearable - intolerable. Where *has* all my strength gone, and when did I become so... ill? So many questions, all far-too difficult to willingly comprehend. The most-important question now being: *Where am I?*

"Good Morning, Mrs. Cunningham. It's a lovely day outside - nice and sunny." declares a masculine voice, which to my dismay is completely unrecognisable. I would have jolted upright with dread, if only my tremoring muscles would have allowed for it. "How are we feeling today, sweetheart? Didn't you get much sleep last night?" I'd better act on my best behaviour, just in case he does turn out to be a ruffian. Mind you, he doesn't sound like one. "It's just Marius and Zanna, your Carers. According to this clock of yours, Isabella, the time is now 08:15am. You're well-overdue a positional change." What is this deranged fellow babbling on about and, besides that, who the bloody hell *is* he? Admittedly, this chap does appear pleasant enough and has some wonderful manners. Give him a chance, old girl. "Hey, Zanna. They did say *four-hourly* turns in handover, didn't they? I can't remember if it was two or four. Baby Amelia's kept me up for most of the night. I can't think straight." A separate and notably feminine voice mumbles something back in response. I don't recognise her either. Patience, Isabella. You *must* know who these two are? Think. "Four-hourly? I thought that was right. Poor Isabella, she never gets a moment to herself from us. I bet, all she'd like to do is just get a few hours of peace and quiet without any disturbance. It can't be helped though, can it?"

9

Marius is clearly Polish by his distinct accent. My husband, Robert, and I visited Warsaw a few years back on one of our many excursions abroad. Poland is such a splendid country, despite its sombre past. I'd love to visit Warsaw again with Robert – my Bobby - should these legs of mine miraculously recover. Hold on a minute... *Carers*? Since when have I ever required Carers? I'm in my thirties! Heavens above! Trying to grant a verbal response only proves to be unfeasible, being that my lips are clamped together in the same fashion as my eyelids are. What a ghastly state to find yourself in, Isabella. Dear me.

"Look at her eyes, Zan, they're awful – totally coated. They're not normally this bad. I wonder if they're infected again?" continues Marius, in a disheartened tone. Well, that would explain why I can't open them. Nevertheless, I'm very thorough regarding my personal hygiene and particularly with my appearance. Who knows where this random, sticky gunk has come from? Gracious, this day is so far turning out to be a nightmare. I must be still dreaming? "You will need those eyes of yours bathing at once, Isabella. We don't want you getting another infection now, do we? It wasn't that long ago when you were on some antibiotics for the same problem."

"You mean those horse tablets Doctor Kain issued?" sniggers the female associate. What was her name again? "I can't believe he prescribed them in the first place. For starters, Isabella's on a puréed diet. How Doctor Kain expected her to swallow those things was *ridiculous*." This girl is close by – too close for comfort. I can smell her breath, and she clearly enjoys strong cup of coffee. I might have some strong mints in my handbag, dear, should you care for any? I'd kindly suggest you take a couple. "It's so sad, isn't it? I hate seeing anyone suffer like this, especially Isabella. The poor woman barely got over her last infection." Did Marius say this girl's name was Zanna? She doesn't appear to be a threat to me. Neither of them do. Why I felt so nervous in their presences a few moments ago seems so silly now. Goodness, their voices are trailing all over the place, only fuelling my obvious delirium further. Marvellous. "To think, it

10

was only two weeks ago when she was chasing me down the corridor with her walking frame. That thing didn't half hurt when she'd smack it off you." laughs Zanna, albeit in reminiscence of an event I have no recollection of. Marius, the cheeky devil, laughs back in an apparent confirmation that this so-called assault did take place. Their abhorrent version of me does not sound very accurate *nor* complementary. However, with their ridicule cast aside, I am steadily growing to like them both. "I'll get some sterilised water before we get started. We'll need to hand over that Isabella's Blepharitis is flaring up again to Nurse Emerson. Don't let me forget." Blepha-what? Talk some sense my girl, or else I *will* go doo-lally. Anyway, my eyes can't be that bad to look at. They don't feel sore or infected. "Can you get the bed ready while I'm doing that please, mate? We'll help Rosa get dressed after we're finished with Isabella, before she falls out of bed again. We might get a break before twelve o'clock, if we're lucky." humours Zanna. "There's no rest for the wicked is there, Isabella?"

Bear with me, my darlings, I'm on the go-slow today. Do I really own a walking frame? I can't remember ever needing one of those things. These two are surely playing fun-and-games with me? They are clearly delusional. I'm as fit as a fiddle, or at least I was until this morning. A set of rugged fingers then gently land upon my left shoulder blade. I gather they belong to Marius, being that if these heavy digits belonged to a young girl, such as Zanna, I'd be pretty concerned for her.

"Truth be told, I'm not that worried about getting a break, Zan. We've got such a busy morning ahead: there's breakfast to serve, eight residents left to get washed and dressed, Reginald's District Nurse is due in half an hour for his Diabetes check, and not to mention all the paperwork we'll need to fill in afterwards." he pants, wearily, and I'm not surprised. Take a moment to breath, dearie. Gracious, you *do* have a busy schedule lined up.

"Isn't that just a normal morning for us, Marius?" I love how this Zanna giggles, her laughter is so rejuvenating. "We'll help to get you

11

nice and clean first, Isabella. Don't worry, we're not going to rush you." I'd bloody-well hope not. I'm still trying to wake up. "Thanks for pointing out all those things, like we needed reminding."

"Sorry. I got a bit side-tracked there, didn't I?" jests Marius, showing less melancholy in his voice now. Thank the Lord. "Before we start, I'll need to raise your bed up, Isabella. It's just so Zanna and I don't hurt our backs when we're helping you. Okay? It won't take long." In what manner will these two be 'helping' me? I dare not ask. They could assist by explaining as to what is actually going on here, although there's not much sign of that happening. "Try to be quick, otherwise Isabella might get unsettled again. She's so frail now, but there's still some fight left in her. I know there is."

"Won't be a sec, Marius." Take as long as you need, darling. I'm hardly able to sprint off anywhere, am I? "We need some more wipes and bags. I'll get some on the way back."

"Cheers, Zan." Marius now appears to be fumbling with something that is attached to my bed. He grunts a couple of times, which is hardly reassuring. "Right, Isabella. There will be a loud beeping sound and then some minor vibrations. This is just me lifting the bed up, so don't worry. You're in *good* hands. We've done this plenty of times before, haven't we?" I'll take your word for it, flower. This sounds like a whole new experience to me. Should I be excited? "I wish they'd get you a new remote. The buttons always stick on this one."

I do wish I could talk back to him. For Pete's sake, has somebody superglued my lips together or what? All that escapes from my mouth are a series of indistinguishable gargles. I'm a Doctor's Receptionist by trade and have been for a long while now. Talking is one thing of which I'm highly skilled at, admittedly under more normal circumstances. Don't kid yourself, Isabella. These are *not* normal circumstances, not by any means. Surely, this must be a dream... an extremely weird, unnatural, and terrifying one. Dreaming doesn't last forever, though. You'll wake up soon enough.

"I'll count to three before raising your bed, Isabella. Hopefully, Zanna will be back soon with the eyewash and then we can get you all cleaned up." Marius is announcing this as if it were to be some act of impending ecstasy. I'd rather just be left alone to quell on my racing emotions and dire predicament, thank you very much, not be jacked up like some worn-out car in a garage. Besides, I don't need strangers to cleanse me. I can manage that myself. "Ready, sweetheart? One...Two...Three."

I'll give him his fair dues, Marius did warn me. However, the wave of random vibrations riddling across my body at this moment are utterly barbaric. The bones in my spine are rattling against one another like coins being tossed around inside a washing machine whilst on full-spin. Strangely, I can't feel my teeth chattering together during this ordeal. How peculiar. Where'd they disappear to?

"Sorry, it took a while to find the irrigation ampoules." Ah, Zanna has returned. I would have sooner preferred a small sherry over eyewash, my dear. Beggars can't be choosers though, can they? "I'll bathe Isabella this time. I'd like to help her as much as possible before... y'know?" Before *what* exactly? "I don't think it's going to be long now." she whispers, indiscreetly hinting towards some mysterious secret. "The last few days have really played their toll on her." More riddles to decipher? Tell me, what *isn't going to be long*? Oh, why can't I speak? "We'll be gentle with you, Isabella. Please, don't be frightened. We're not going to hurt you. We're just here to make sure you're well-cared for, that's all. Aren't we, Marius?"

"That's right, Isabella. You've got nothing to be afraid of." Marius echoes Zanna's assurance, yet their message unfortunately brings little comfort to me. Regardless of my doubts, I have no choice but to submit myself to whatever act may follow. "We'll be done in no time. You'll feel so much better after a good wash."

"Howay, Marius." implores Zanna. "Isabella's starting to get flustered. The last thing she needs is to get wound up."

Zanna has such a lovely voice. She's so very refined in her pronunciations, and I immediately recognise her wonderful lingo. It's not Geordie – Lord no! It is the South Durham accent. I would recognise those linguistic tones anywhere. The first time I heard this accent was when I worked at an ordnance factory in Newton Escomb, County Durham, during the Second World War. I was one of the *Escomb Angels* - Britain's secretive, all-female, bombmaking squad. It was incredibly dangerous work for us. I even lost two friends there after some grenades went off by accident. Margaret and Elizabeth were their names and they had only just reached adulthood, as had I at the time. The other girls would often make fun of how I spoke. They'd say I was 'too posh' to be working alongside them, that I'd fit in better with the Royal Family, though it was all in good fun. We 'Angels' assisted in protecting Britain's sovereignty from Hitler's tyrannical reach, a contribution I'm still very proud of to this day. County Durham became my permanent home after the war, once Robert and I moved there from Harrogate. It has its ups and downs, like any other town, but Newton Escomb will always be our *true* home. Finally, something makes sense to me. Keep talking, Zanna. I'm feeling less anxious now.

"Be careful when rubbing over her skin with those wipes, Zan. Isabella bruises so easily. Don't you, sweetheart?" You tell me, Marius. For all I know, I could be black and blue all over. These bloody eyes of mine, I wish they'd open. "It's because of those Warfarin tablets. The slightest bump and *BOOM*, there's another bruise added." To my vagrant knowledge, I have impeccable skin – absolutely flawless. I can thank having a healthy lifestyle for that, despite its lacking use now. No artificial muck. No smoking. No alcohol. Goodness, some could argue that I've led a boring life. I don't think I have. If anything, it's been quite the contrary. Robert and I are adventurous souls, which is what makes us such a perfect pair. Where in the devil *is* he? It's not like Robert to abandon me. "We'd better check her all-over again, just to be on the safe side. That pressure sore..."

"Don't mention it." commands Zanna, in-between some retching noises. "The thought of that sore makes me feel sick. I can't believe how bad it's gotten. The creams haven't helped much, have they? We may as well be slapping butter on her for what it's worth."

"I know. We've been turning Isabella like the nurses asked us to. It's what happens when you don't eat or drink enough... the body can't recover properly." I beg your pardon, Marius? I'm a good little-eater. I adore my meals, that is, unless Robert has made them. My Bobby has a knack for cremating whatever he cooks. I've tried domesticating him, which has sadly come to little avail, and has also only caused me to suffer from several headaches. Beans on toast is the most-complex dish my Bobby can muster. He does try his best though, bless him. "It's not like we haven't tried to encourage her intake, Zan. You can't force-feed people."

"I know," whimpers Zanna, "I know. It's just so hard to watch her waste away like this."

A lukewarm, tingling fluid starts to slowly trickle over my eye lids. Then comes the patting of, what feels like, a cotton-like material across my swollen eyes and the skin below them. I shift with a countering judder, although the unexpected pleasure this sensation brings quickly removes what discomfort arose. I feel quite foolish now for reacting so uncharacteristically. Zanna is duly obeying Marius' instructions to the tee. She is being extremely careful when bathing my skin, regardless of the fact I've never met her before. So, *this* is the kindness of strangers?

"You're doing a great job there... and so are *you*, Isabella." remarks Marius, sympathetically, though in a slightly patronising way. I don't think he intended to be rude, mind you. I do get easily offended, well, according to Robert I do. "Take things nice and slow. We'll wash Isabella's back next. Make sure you clean around the site of her wound and, whatever you do, don't get any soap on the dressing."

"I won't." groans Zanna. "I think the dressing might need changing today. I'd be probably doing Nurse Emerson a favour by

15

getting some of the adhesive off." she says, with a suspicious caution in her voice. "God knows how painful that sore must be for her, and Isabella's only on Paracetamol." Oh, please don't be giving me any Paracetamol. I simply can't stand the stuff. A good tout of whiskey is the best cure for ailments, as my father would say. "Her eyes are clearing up well. It took some doing, mind."

You're correct, Zanna. I can now make out a lighter blur instead of the previous pitch-blackness. I'm trying to pretend that I'm at a spa of some sort, that Marius and Zanna are my own personal masseurs. This joyful façade *could* make things a little more bearable? This bed bath is delightful. I could easily get used to this treatment.

"Are you enjoying your bath, Isabella? I can see you're smiling."

"Of course! Isabella loves being pampered - don't you, darling?" declares Zanna, as if she is sharing in this wonderous relief with me. "Are you going to open your beautiful eyes for us today, Isabella? I'd love to see the sparkle in them again."

"She hasn't opened them in days, Zan." bleats Marius. "Don't get your hopes up."

"Yeah, but there's still a chance. *Please* open your eyes for us, Isabella. They're the prettiest pair I've ever seen."

Well, I'm not one to disappoint, particularly after being given such an endearing compliment. My eyes open wider, then gradually adjust to the various new lights and shapes now compelling them. This must be what it is like to be a new-born, when making their own anticipated appearance into our turbulent world? Although, *I* am not a child. I'm far from it. I'm a grown woman, with a loving husband and promising career ahead of me. Goodness, I can't stay here for much longer. Robert will be worrying about me. I must get out of this wretched bed!

"She opened them, Zanna! That's crazy, man." gasps Marius. What is so crazy about me doing that? "She must have heard you?" he laughs, with a boisterous bellow. "You're doing really well in proving us wrong, Isabella. I can't believe it." Since when have I become a source of such simple amusement? I do feel some guilt in

16

thinking this way, given how these two have assisted me so kindly and without any obvious compensation sought after in return. I should be grateful - not bitter. "You've made our day, Mrs. Cunningham. There they are, those gorgeous eyes of yours."

"Good Morning, sweetheart." stammers Zanna in a shocked, yet pleasant, whisper to me. Her features remain relatively blurred, however, I can tell that she is smiling back at me. Zanna has such a heart-warming expression. Lovely. "I can't wait until we tell the others about this. They won't believe us, will they? You've been sleeping so much recently, Isabella. We thought you'd never wake up."

I can distinguish Marius and Zanna features more clearly now, though only while they're leaning closer towards me. Marius looks a little like Humphrey Bogart, which is a fervent pity, since I could never stand his motion pictures. Zanna is incredibly small, in a way similar to Audrey Hepburn's petite stature. Now, I do enjoy *her* movies. Going to the Cinema is one of mine and Robert's favourite past times. I do wonder... where is he? It's not normal for my Bobby to be away from me for so long – totally uncharacteristic. Likewise, I would never part from his side (even if he does occasionally annoy me).

"We're nearly finished with your bed bath, Isabella. You'll be nice and comfy again in no time." says Marius, with some resounding confidence. "There's no resistance in her now, is there? It's so weird, Zan. I don't like it one bit."

"It's awful." grumbles Zanna. "If she could just see herself..." I'd love to, dearie. I'd love to see what I look like, but that's not going to happen, not whilst I can't move. "She'd be devastated. I know that I'd be."

I choose to ignore Zanna's last few comments by focusing on Marius' tall and muscular body instead, which (I dare confess) comes as a welcomed surprise and of no disappointment whatsoever. If I were ten years younger, I would likely consider courting him, should he be be able to withstand my affections. Zanna reminds me of myself at around the same age - late teens - with looks that could instil jealously upon any of whom would glance upon them. She has a hypnotising grin that stretches right across her face, with a pale complex that highlights her prominent-green eyes. It's settled: I like Marius and Zanna. I would still appreciate someone explaining just how we three know one another. It's not like I've got all day... is it?

"Okay, Isabella. That's your back nice and dry now. We just need to take a good look over your skin integrity further down, if you don't mind?" The very thought of being bathed by a strange man would have once horrified me, though Marius is incredibly soft-spoken for someone with the body of a Greek God (which does help to somewhat calm my nerves). I'm not too happy about having my legs washed. Where is my say in any of this? Good Lord! I can't remember shaving them. It'll be like a jungle down there, my darlings. Don't say I didn't warn you both. "I'm not looking forward to this part, Zan." Neither am I, old chap. Bathing at this moment, particularly with having someone other than Robert assisting me, is not listed under the highest of priorities. I'd rather wake up from this nightmare than for it to linger on. Plus, one of you is getting too close to my private areas for comfort. Desist - at once! "I can't imagine that her sacral region has healed much, not since we last examined her. The sore couldn't have been in a worse place. Right next to where she..."

"You're not kidding." interjects Zanna, apprehensively. You know, I'd so love to give them both a big hug, if it would stop their recurrent moping. "Let's just get this part over with. Turn Isabella towards me, then you can examine her backside... I can't do it." Well, madam. I might not have Elizabeth Taylor's curves, or Marilyn Monroe's supple thighs, but - by God - I am scarcely Quasimodo, and I most-certainly do not have any sores down there. You can leave me alone with Chopin now. I'm quite ready for another nap, thank you. Please, remove that hand of yours away from my buttocks. Now, I say! "On my count, we turn her towards me. Are you ready, Isabella?" No. I'm settled where I am. *Please*, no more rolling. "One...Two...Three...*Roll!*"

Four hands immediately clasp onto my body with perfect timing. As Marius and Zanna turn me over, against my politest resistance, a scorching pain enters every cell from where they are making contact. Oh, it's horrible! Adding to my risen dismay, they then both exhale with a noticeable shriek. This would have really gotten to me, if it wasn't for the distracting draft now flowing over my exposed skin. Please don't say that my arse is out on show? Good Heavens!

"Urgh, the dressing's come off. That sore on her sacrum is definitely a Grade Three, maybe even a Four." despairs Marius. "I can't really see from here. There's so much blood..." He exhales nervously, and I dread to fathom why. "This is bad – *really* bad. We're lucky though, the blood is only on her Kylie sheet and not on her nightgown or bed. It probably looks worse than it is, to be fair."

Blood? I can't feel anything unusual back there, apart from my buttocks feeling as if they are being placed into a bucket of cold water. What a way to treat a lady. How charming.

"Oh, Isabella." Zanna takes a turn in making some pitying noises. Neither of you are promoting my self-confidence, if anything, you're making my paranoia increase ten-fold. "The wound is a lot worse, far-worse than I thought it would be. You can see right down to the bone." Pardon? Surely, *I* would have noticed something as concerning or drastic as that? What I would give to speak again. My lips simply won't move. Never mind talking, all I want to do is scream. Get off me! Leave me alone! "There's the dressing. It must have come off from the soap? Poor Isabella. We'll make things right for you, darling." Both gasp again. I'm understandably losing that relaxing vision of being at a Spa. It's more like sitting in a doctor's waiting room, all the while, anxiously knowing that the news you're about to receive isn't good. "I'll let Nurse Emerson know when we're finished changing her. She needs a new dressing - A.S.A.P."

"Like it'll do any good?" Zanna has a forlorn look on her face. Even I, with these fuzzy eyes of mine, can see that. "We said this

19

would happen. How many times has it been handed over about checking the wound and repositioning her on-time?"

"Like I said, Isabella hasn't been eating or drinking much, Zan. Her skin is wafer thin now. There's little *we* can do to prevent it breaking down. Our job is to keep her settled, which is what we're doing. Don't get yourself down. It's not *our* fault."

The surrounding atmosphere has become as frigid as my tremoring extremities are. This isn't real - it can't be. I don't need Carers. I'm not bleeding from anywhere. These two are making me panic, but I don't think they are meaning to. Oh, my head. My skull is throbbing like something rotten. Marius and Zanna have fallen silent, which itself can't be a promising sign. I'm no longer feeling at ease. I just want to wake up, to be rid of this terrible situation. I'm so desperate to awaken from this sordid experience, only to find myself back in my Bobby's arms again. Wake up, Isabella. *Wake up*! Oh, is there nobody here who can understand me?

"I would get Hollie right away. A Nurse needs to see how bad the wound is." Thanks again, Marius. You are hardly proving to be a calming force, dear. It's a ruddy-good job that I fancy you, but don't let my Bobby know that. "You don't deserve this kind of life, Isabella. No one does."

No, I certainly do not. I don't deserve to be tossed and turned around like lettuce leaves in a salad bowl. I don't warrant a bed bath. I'm an adult. I can fend for myself. I don't need to rely on anyone else to meet my needs, I mean, Robert can surely help with that side of things? My Bobby's always been there for me, to shoulder my burdens, to be my valiant knight in shining armour. Who *are* these people, these *Carers*? Why won't they leave me be? Wake up, Isabella. Wake up! It's no use. That awful state of unconsciousness is creeping back over me, though would that necessarily be a bad thing? At least, I won't know what's happening to me in my dreams. *Ignorance is bliss*, is a phrase Mother often tells me.

"She's getting agitated. We need to get Nurse Emerson – NOW!" cries out Marius, as he quickly sprints away from my bedside.

"Isabella's pad was clean, so don't worry about changing it. She hasn't passed any urine overnight either, going off her charts. This is bad, Zan. I won't be long."

This predicament is getting better by the second. Of what interest would my pee be to anyone but myself? I'm feeling more and more like an animal caged in a zoo, trapped and lost. The only things missing are a set of iron bars around me. There's a cushioned rail running along the length of my bed that's greatly reducing my line of sight, so I'm not too far-off having some bars... am I?

"Never mind getting Hollie." responds Zanna. "I think we need a doctor to come out." Oh, it seems this girl has now become my personal advocate. I can still make my own choices, can't I? I am by no means lacking any capacity. Admittedly, I do like Zanna, since she is clearly so much like me. If something goes wrong, I've always been the first to act. Zanna appears to think the same way. Don't be cross with her, old girl. "Isabella's toes are getting colder, and the colour in her legs is starting to drain away. Poor Isabella."

Enough of this 'Poor Isabella' malarkey. There's nothing the matter with my health. Yes, I can't see very well or move a great deal, but that doesn't make me an invalid. Just listen to yourself, Isabella. Who are you trying to kid? You can't move... can't speak. Does *that* sound at all healthy to you?

"It might be a good idea for us to contact Isabella's Next of Kin? That is, if they answer their phone for once. I got nowhere last time." Stop being so bloody pessimistic, Marius. Honestly. "We won't be long, Isabella. You get some much-needed rest. Can you turn her music back up before you go please, Zan?" Where are you vanishing to now, Marius? I'm growing ever-fonder of your company. I take back those wicked words said earlier. I don't want to be left alone. I really don't. "It's not a call I'm going to look forward to, especially after my last run in with *her*." I wonder if they're going to contact my mother? I haven't seen her for a while, which itself is very unusual. My parents visit once a week - without fail, come rain or shine. Could they know that I'm here, wherever *here* is? I could really use my father's calming presence. Father always knows what to do. "I hope she doesn't shout at me this time. For someone who only visits Isabella once or twice a month now, she has a lot to say about her care." My dearest Marius. Mother is a stubborn old bird, bless her, but she's good at heart. There's nothing wrong at all with being feisty. "See you soon, Isabella."

"You'll be okay, sweetheart. See you in a bit." Oh, great. Zanna is leaving me too? Isn't this the peace *you* wanted though, Isabella? You can't exactly complain. They *are* doing what you instructed of them. "I'm coming, Marius. Don't wait up for me." Zanna! Please, don't leave me in this unfamiliar setting. I don't recognise anything. I'm so scared. Come back! I beg you. "I hope it's not Doctor Kain who comes out to see Isabella today. He was a waste of time the..." Zanna's voice suddenly trails off, only leaving me to guess what her last few words were.

"It's not our place to argue with him. Just, see how things go." assures Marius, his own voice now barely attainable. "Hollie is good at standing her ground. She'll fight Isabella's corner..."

Marius and Zanna disappear without any further word to me. In a sense, I'm already missing them. It was better to have some companionship, albeit unrequited, than to have none whatsoever. I do recall knowing them both, but I'm not sure how. Other, far-clearer, memories start flowing into my immediate thoughts during this haunting period of solitude. Robert and I have children – two, I believe. We had a son first and then a daughter. I'm certain of this, although, I can't quite remember their names. Oh, God. Doesn't that make me an awful parent? What kind of mother forgets her own children's names?

I openly welcome the resurgence of sedating darkness like an old friend. It swiftly takes a powerful hold over my waking eyes and brings with it a sense of peace and ease to this tormenting melodrama, this drama which is apparently now... my life. I'm not always this miserable, I'd like to add. I'm the life and soul of parties, a positive person, someone that never gives up on anything or anyone... no matter how hard the task may be. What has happened to you, Isabella Cunningham? Wake up from this wicked fantasy. Wouldn't that be perfect? Wouldn't that be wonderful?

BLENDED EGGS AND TOMATOES

There's an overwhelming and utterly disgusting scent of sulphur trickling through my nostrils now, which alone awakens me back into this surreal existence, this place of daunting uncertainty. I twitch my nose a few times in a vain effort to ascertain where this pungent aroma is coming from, whilst also praying that it is not some passed wind caused by myself. Now, that *would* be embarrassing. The reason being? I'm cautiously aware that I could still be playing host to some less-familiar company i.e. Marius and Zanna, my 'Carers'. Speaking of which, where *are* those two mites? I can't have been napping for all that long, surely?

Chopin's *Nocturne in E Flat Major* is about half-way through playing. It's a marvellous piece and, quite frankly, is the only thing keeping me sane at this moment in time. Oh, Lord. I'm still incarcerated within this wretched bed of mine. Every now and then something moves beneath me, raising itself eerily like the waves of an ocean during a turbulent storm. Still, things could be worse: I could be stuck in an unfamiliar place, with complete strangers watching over me like vultures, and have my arse out on show for the whole world to glare at. Oh, yes. That *is* my current situation. How delightful.

"Hey, Isabella. It's just me again. Sorry if I've woken you up." Well timed, Zanna my girl. There's no need for any apologies. As a matter of fact, I was beginning to worry that you'd never return. It's a terrible feeling, you know, to be so lonely. I'm not used to it. "Nurse Emerson won't be long, sweetheart. She's going to check you over before your doctor comes, okay? I'll help with your breakfast while we wait for them." Breakfast does sound like a marvellous idea. I do hope Zanna has brought me some poached eggs on toast, or a greasy English fry-up? Mind, in saying that, I'm not really that hungry. I seem to have somehow lost my once-insatiable appetite. "I've got your favourite: scrambled eggs and tomatoes. It looks and smells yummy." Hardly, my dear, but that does explain the awful pong, and I guess it'll do. I'm not exactly in the position to argue, am I? My fragile vocal chords continue to defy the orders I'm giving them. For goodness sake. "Let's put your serviette on first, shall we? We don't want to make a mess."

An irritating, crunchy noise then replaces the ambient tones of Chopin in my ears. A *serviette*? It feels more like a baby's bib being placed around my neck *and* it's made of paper. I've never been a messy eater in all my life – goodness, no! I have impeccable table manners. Get this bloody thing off me at once.

"Stop squirming, Isabella." laughs Zanna. "The longer it takes me to put your serviette on, the longer you'll need to wait for breakfast."

Sure enough, an intense wave of sickly egg fumes soon moves closer towards me, along with the blurred image of a teaspoon. My mouth slightly waters in anticipation, curious to taste what is in store for me. Those eggs better be seasoned correctly, my girl, or I shan't be best pleased. If only I could lick my lips, I would.

"I've only put a small amount on the spoon for you, Isabella." assures Zanna, as she awkwardly motions the spoon closer. "Please, *try* to eat something today. You've gone too long without any food, darling. You won't get any better, you know?"

Like a well-behaved infant, I pry open my mouth to take in the gifted food on offer. If being honest, I'm quite anxious to take in this generous serving from Zanna, rather than to be excited. First, there is a salty hit that almost makes me wretch, and then comes a butter-laden coating across my tongue that makes me instantly gag. Gracious me, Zanna! This is all so... sloppy. What on Earth are you feeding me - bloody *baby* food? That wonderful expectation I had of receiving a breakfast fit for the Queen herself quickly diminishes, along with what minute appetite had arose.

"Are you not fancying any breakfast?" sighs Zanna, with a disapproving frown on her face. "It'll be the fifth day in a row. You won't get your strength back if you don't eat anything." Would *you* wish to eat this gelatinous gruel, my dear? I certainly don't. I'd prefer chewing on an old leather belt instead. At least, that way there'd be something to sink my gums into. "To be fair on you, I don't think I'd be able to stomach this either. We'll give it a miss, yeah?" *Please*. Lord have mercy on me. I couldn't be happier as Zanna removes that dratted teaspoon and its rancid, puréed contents away from me. I think I'll pass on breakfast, darling. "Shall we try you with a nice cup of tea, Isabella? You can't start the day without having a good cuppa to help warm you up." Now, that is a much more appealing offer. My mouth slowly begins to water again. I do love the odd cup of tea, especially with some fluffy crumpets on the side for picking at. Could you be so kind as to make me some of those, Zanna? "Milk and two sugars, just how you like it. I think it'll be cool enough now to drink." I could be mistaken for a young child celebrating their birthday at this point: excited, elated, jittery, and all over a little cup of tea. Gracious, Isabella, you always have been so easy to satisfy. Come on, my girl, there's no time to waste! I'm looking forward to this. "Okay, sweetheart. Here you are..."

That ruddy teaspoon makes an appearance again. Oh, where *are* my spectacles? I can't see my cup of tea, and that spoon (which I'm rapidly growing to detest) is getting closer again by the second. Without any further warning, a tepid yoghurt-like substance presses against my upper lip. I poke out my tongue defensively, checking that this isn't those dreadful eggs again, then retreat it as fast as I can physically manage. It tastes like tea, but it's all gloopy and bitter. Bloody hell. What are you playing at, my girl? What *is* this catastrophe?

"Is it too cold?" questions Zanna, with some level of sympathetic remorse. I'm not all that fussed by it being less than piping hot, which is how I usually prefer my tea, but rather deflated. Since when have I required baby food and thickened fluids? Saying that, I still can't find any teeth in my mouth. I do wonder, have I been in some sort of terrible accident? I brush my teeth twice daily and I've never

26

had any concerns raised to me by my dentist. "Should we try once more? I'll put less on the spoon this time." If you so-dare press that ghastly spoon against my lips again, Zanna, I shall scream. That I can promise you. "Never mind. I'm not going to force you, not if it's going to cause upset." There's a good lass. My faith in Zanna has been fully restored. If only Robert would do as he's told like this girl. Speaking of which, where is the stubborn old goat? "I'll go see where Nurse Emerson is. She should have been here by now." comments Zanna, in a concerning voice. "It's almost ten o'clock. I don't know, Isabella. You can't rely on anyone these days, can you?"

As Zanna gracefully leaves my bedside, I focus again on Chopin's enlightening performance - his virtuous arrangements that I shall never grow tired of listening to. The piece playing now is called *Fantaisie Impromptu.* It was this very composition that encouraged my interest - my keenest devotion – to become a world-renowned pianist. Sadly, that dream never came to be. I first heard this composition being performed in a local chapel by my Aunt Edith. She is a magnificent pianist, a true maestro. From around the age of seven, all I wanted to do was play Chopin and Beethoven as well, and as perfectly, as my aunt. It took some time and a great deal of practice, but I eventually got there. I often frequented the local church halls and Women's Institute meetings to perform Chopin's illustrious works, though never the grand halls of London or Milan as I had so dreamt of doing. Robert insists on me playing Mozart more than Chopin, since he somehow finds the latter 'far-too depressing' to listen to. On the contrary, I find Chopin to be utterly enchanting - enthralling. I'll win my Bobby over one day. He won't even know it, bless him.

"Hello, Isabella." Zanna's voice has dropped dramatically, and she somehow sounds South African now. The poor girl must be falling ill herself? "It's just me, Nurse Emerson. I've brought one of our Senior Carers to help me with your dressing." Fantastic. More strangers to become acquainted with, to no doubt glare upon my weakened state. "John, can you do me a favour please and fetch a dressing pack over from inside of Isabella's cupboard? I ordered more last week, so there should be some left."

"Yeah. No worries." This chap doesn't sound remotely like Marius. I do hope that he's just as pleasant and dashing. I've already had enough disappointment to deal with today. "Good morning, Mrs. Cunningham. How are you feeling? I see that you're not wanting your breakfast again." John too has a South Durham accent, like Zanna. How lovely. "It was only a couple of weeks ago when you flung your dinner plate off the back of my head." he snorts, however only amusing himself (I might add). Where these people are getting this wrongful impression, that I'm aggressive, is well beyond me. "It might sound daft, but I miss you doing those things, Isabella... even if they *did* hurt." That's your prerogative, my dear. *I* can't remember throwing anything at you, or at Zanna, or at any beggar else for that matter. I can't even move from this foetal position. "Found one, Hollie. Marius said something about Isabella's pressure wound possibly being at a Grade Three to Four. I hope it's not - it shouldn't be, not with all the precautions we've taken."

"I'll take a look in a sec, John." says Nurse Emerson, with some apparent reluctance. "Let's get our gloves on first. Have you washed and dried your hands?"

This 'John' fellow is standing right in front of me now, and I can just make out what is written on his name badge: John Davidson - Senior Carer. He doesn't appear old enough to be a Senior of anything. Still, age shouldn't come into things, should it? He's wearing a long, white tunic with burgundy lapels and looks like a football thug with his shaven head. If it wasn't for John's feminine voice, I'd be feeling rather concerned with having him care for me. You should never judge a book by its cover, Father used to say. It's a saying I firmly agree with.

"These aprons are nightmare to put on." chuckles John, as he fights against a thin layer of white plastic to strap it around his torso. "I can never get them on first-time. You might need to help me,

Hollie?" he grimaces, then sighs in relief. "Sorted. Man, that was a struggle. Thanks, Hollie."

"Okay, Isabella." interjects Nurse Emerson. "Now that John has finally managed to get his apron on, we'll need to take a little look at your bottom." Stay well-clear away from my rump, if you both know what is good for you, my dears. I *must* have been in an accident, surely? I mean, why else would I be in a hospital? This nurse looks a little like Judy Garland, only happier. "Can we roll Isabella towards you, John? I'll be able to examine her lower back better from this side." Here we go again. Toss me like a pancake, bare my arse for the whole world to see. It's not like I can stop you. I wish I could. "Try to stay calm, Isabella. We're not going to hurt you, darling. It'll only take a minute." Listen to your nurse, Isabella. Settle down and stop being so frightfully rude. It isn't going to get you anywhere. "I wouldn't be surprised to find if Isabella *does* have a Grade Four. Her skin is so dehydrated and thin. The lack of adequate intake won't be helping..."

"We've been trying Isabella with thickened fluids to see if that helps." explains John, his voice clearly defensive and fearful. "Isabella's intake has been getting worse over the past week or so... since the T.I.A." Tee-Aye—What?

"The doctors weren't exactly sure whether it was a T.I.A or if she had a seizure, John. Doctor Hewitson thought that Isabella might have just had a fainting episode. Without a proper hospital scan, it's difficult to say. She's hardly able to go for one of those, not in her condition. Just transporting Isabella to the hospital would be such a huge strain on her."

T.I.A? Now, where *have* I heard that abbreviation before? Didn't Mother have one of those? Isn't it like some sort of mini-stroke? Believe it or not, I find this news quite settling, as it would explain why my memory and mobility are now so poor. Mother fully recovered from her mini-stroke, so why shouldn't I? This is fantastic news, although still somewhat worrying. Be quiet, Isabella. You're talking gibberish again. It's a good job nobody else can hear you.

"We've been doing four-hourly positional turns for her, as well as popping in every chance we get to see how Isabella's doing. We're trying our best, Hollie. Honest."

"I'm not insinuating neglect on you or any of the other Carers, John. I know it's hard." assures Nurse Emerson. "Doctor Kain is due in shortly, by the way." Goodness, she has a great deal of underlying dread in her voice announcing this said doctor's visit. Hold on, my doctor is called *Appleton*, not 'Kain' or 'Hewitson'. I've never had a particularly good relationship with doctors, not after Father's completely avoidable Pneumonia and resultant death. Oh, my! I forgot... Father died. What a terrible daughter I must be? Oh, Father. I didn't mean to forget about you. "Doctor Kain is due in at about Eleven o'clock. We'd best get Isabella's Care Plan ready for him. It's going to be a long morning, John. I can't wait for this day to be over."

"Same here." replies John, almost instantaneously. "Have you managed to contact Isabella's Next of Kin?" he mutters, with a wearisome groan. "I tried both her home and mobile numbers, and *still* didn't get an answer. It's lucky that we're not trying to phone about anything major, isn't it? Oh, yeah – we are."

"John," simpers my nurse. "Behave yourself. I know, as relatives go, she's not always the most-approachable, but you've got to stay professional."

"She's... alright." counters John. "I just wish she'd answer her phone more often."

Robert must be at work. Maybe, that's why he hasn't visited me? Mother could be out shopping, which could explain why she mustn't have been able to answer your calls, John? Keep trying, my boy. I do so greatly wish to see my Bobby - I'm desperate. We've never been apart for this length of time before, and I don't want his absence to continue. Please, find him for me.

"On the subject, I've had more success than you, John." Chuckles Nurse Emerson, faintly. "I managed to contact her before coming up here to see Isabella. It wasn't an easy conversation." There is some underlying dread in her voice, but why? Mother and Robert are gentle souls, and they'd never be rude to anyone. "She can't make it here until this afternoon. We discussed a few things over the phone... I've been given verbal authorisation to put a DNACPR in place, which is better than nothing." *DNACPR*? What in Layman's terms does that stand for? I wish these folks what talk sensibly. It's insufferable. "Let's take a gander and get this dressing sorted. I've got Maybelle's annual review in half an hour. Her social worker is already waiting for me downstairs."

Despite my staunchest will to resist, I'm rolled over again onto my opposite side. I try to stretch my legs out, believing this movement may have freed them up, but can't. God, they're cramping terribly now from this effort. One good thing, within all this chaos, is that gut-wrenching eggy smell is beginning to waft away. However, it's quickly replaced by another, sickly-sweet pong. What's happening back there?

"Oh, John." Nurse Emerson's responsive gasp only instils a greater sense of fear in me. Nobody has a pretty backside, Nurse. What makes mine so horrifying to behold? "It's definitely a Grade Four. You can see part of her lower vertebrae." *Pardon*? How has that occurred? Who has done this to me?

"Can I take a look?" questions John, clearly in a state of panic himself. "Christ, her wound wasn't this bad a couple of days ago. I'll go and get some silver packing." You're not going to pack anything in me, whether it's silver or likewise. What is going through this boy's head? You're not sticking anything up there, you hear! "Will that help with the smell, Hollie?"

"It's worth a try. I wish we had some of those charcoal dressings left, they'd have been far-more effective." Nurse Emerson sounds as if she's starting to cry, the poor woman. Rest assured, I honestly can't feel any pain back there. I'm pretty sure that I'd notice protruding bone before anyone else? Really, they're getting in a tiz-waz over nothing. "Can you fetch some sterilised saline solution as well, please? There's not much we can do but to keep her wound

31

clean now. Isabella's not getting any calories, so there's nothing to aid the healing process. This will only get worse."

A few more tense moments pass, where all three of us are held within a mutually-awkward silence. I'm concentrating harder on Chopin, but Nurse Emerson's persistent whimpers are drowning out his wonderful music. Do be quiet, my dear. Enjoy this delightful composition. Forget any woes that are present... and *stop* staring at my backside, while you're at it. I bloody-well know you are, and it's not *that* fascinating.

"Here you go, Hollie." John hands across what looks like a test tube to Nurse Emerson, which I can see has a clear substance inside of it. "I forgot I had one in my pocket... the seal's not broken. I'll keep Isabella steady."

"Thanks, John. This might take longer than I first thought it would. There's a lot of exudate to wash away before renewing her dressing."

"Exudate?"

"The green stuff..."

Another pair of masculine hands rest upon my tender skin, just like before, although they're not as large as Marius'. John's rubbing his thumbs up and down in a gentle fashion across my left shoulder blade and thigh, which I find to be *very* relaxing. I do hope Robert doesn't come in to witness this scene. For one thing, he'd be fuming with me, and would probably have a few choice words for John. In contrast to this pleasant massage, Nurse Emerson's hands seem to be nervously wandering along my spine, counting down each lump and bump towards my little rump. *Ouch!* What is she poking at back there?

"The wound is ten centimetres by eight in diameter. It's twice the size it was a few days ago, and deeper too. There's tracking at least a couple of more inches inside, from what I can make out. Poor Isabella." There's not any buried treasure down there, darling. I would really appreciate it, and I can't emphasise this enough, if you could just kindly *sod off* now, the pair of you. I'm not a bloody pin cushion for you all to play with. Would you be so generous as to put those covers back over me? It's freezing cold where you're standing, Nurse Emerson. If I still had teeth, they'd likely be chattering now. "I'll start by giving it a small rinse with the saline..."

A wave of fire instantly tears across my lower back and buttocks. I want to scream, I really do, but can't. Whatever my dutiful nurse is pouring on me now feels like boiling water or even acid. I try to reach around, hoping to stop this present torture by clasping onto Nurse Emerson's hands, but still... I can't. Every small movement requires my fullest exertion of strength. I can't shift more than a few millimetres, despite these valiant efforts of mine. Oh, I'm so helpless. When did you say Mother was coming?

"She's getting distressed, Hollie." Well observed, John. *Of course*, I'm getting distressed. This treatment of yours is horrific, regardless of you claiming otherwise, and there's little sign of it ending anytime soon. "Have Isabella's sedatives come in yet? I'm sure we requested some last week?"

"No." mourns Nurse Emerson, with a glimmer of disdain in her delivery. "She was still at such a high risk of falls when the request was made. I'm hoping that Doctor Kain will be more understanding, when he visits today. Who knows what he'll decide to do?"

This is incredibly unorthodox. I can feel Nurse Emerson tugging away at my skin, as if she's merely prying open an envelope. What is she doing to my perfect body? She's stuffing, what feels like, some cotton around my tailbone, although it's evidently more coarse and rugged. Oh, this is excruciating! Please, I beg you... STOP!

"The wound's packed nicely now, John." gleams my nurse. "Can you hand over the gauze and dry dressings, please? We're almost done." You don't sound too pleased with your handywork, Nurse Emerson. Thank you, by the way, for turning me into a stuffed turkey. I'm very-much obliged. "Won't be a minute, Isabella. You're doing so well – you're so brave. You've got the patience of an Angel." I'm not doing much though, I am? I'd make a fantastic life-model. Now, *there's* something I've never done before. I love trying out new things. "Maybe try Isabella with another cup of tea, John, before you go back to ground floor."

"Sure, it's worth a shot." John has a funny smirk on his face. He's either being hopeful or else knows that this will be a wasted endeavour. "How many scoops of thickener does she take again?" None. Heed my words, John. No more gloopy tea! I couldn't bear another mouthful of it. "Three? Cheers, Hollie. I'll catch up with you after the review."

I'm left to my own devices again. Oh, Chopin. Your sweet music will get me through this wicked trial, I know it will. I'll try moving my legs again, as perhaps they'll shift this time? Lord, they simply just won't move, and neither will my arms. Am I destined to be imprisoned this way forever, to be trapped as a prisoner within my own body? At least, I can move my fingers a little more now, which is one promising development. It'll be so nice to play the piano again, even if it *is* just an imaginary one.

"I'm back, Isabella." boasts John as he hastily returns with, what I pray is, a regular cup of tea. "Now, I'm not the best brew-maker going." Neither am I, flower. I couldn't care less how it tastes, so long as it's not thickened again. "Shall we have a try, before Doctor Kain turns up? Between us two, I won't be making that miserable git one." Your secret's quite safe with me, John. I can't say that I'm looking forward to this doctor's visit, either. "Here you are, sweetheart."

Like a dire re-enactment of Zanna's failed attempt earlier, my drink is once again thickened into a vile, custard-like substance. Why does it also have a sandy texture? Not even two sugars could make this abomination palatable. I've just enough strength to spit out the ghastly drink and push away the nuisance teaspoon with my tongue. Thankfully, John takes the hint. There's a good lad.

"Sorry, Isabella." he laughs. "I know it might feel weird, but that's how we need to make your drinks now, ever since you had that choking fit a few months back." John carefully places the mug of tea on a bedside cabinet situated next to my bed. My eyes seem to be improving. An electronic clock sits next to where John placed my cup, which has red numerals showing 10:50am on its face. Goodness, this morning is flying over.

"I wish I had a magic wand, you know?" laments John. "What I'd give to see you running down the corridors again... chasing me with your walking frame." There he goes with more of that make-believe, reminiscent tosh. I'm the most laid-back person you could ever meet, and I don't need a bloody walking frame. "I miss having our little chats and listening to Chopin with you. You've got a great taste in music, Isabella." Yes. Yes, I'd say that I do, my dear. However, Robert might not agree with you on that. "Would you like me to read one of your books, Isabella, while I still have a minute to spare? You always loved having your books being read to you." That's a very generous offer and is one I'd happily accept. Books are a gateway to imaginary realms, places I'd gladly visit, people I'd love to meet, and perhaps some reading might help to somehow remove me from this awful setting? That would be wonderful. "Which one should we read today? We finished that Wilbur Smith novel, didn't we?"

I can't see where John has disappeared to, the sly minx. There are some loud rustle sounds nearby, and I'm sure he's knocked something fragile over (a muffled curse word from John is what confirms this to me). What are you up to, my boy?

"Right, Isabella." smirks John, as he pops his head up next to me like a meerkat. His cheeks have gone all red. What have you done? "I'm *really* sorry, sweetheart. I've only gone and knocked over a picture of your sister. God, I'm so clumsy today." Ah, my sister - Agnes. How could I ever forget her? I'm certainly not *that* fortunate. We're total opposites, Agnes and I, and have rarely gotten along since early childhood. You've done me a favour, John. No apologies are necessary, not in this instance. "I'll get this glass cleaned up, and then we can have a good read together, Isabella. This'll probably be the only chance I'll get to spend some quality time with you, before I need to start my meds round, which is in half an hour. Shi..."

Whilst John diligently cleans up the mess he made, I try to remove Agnes from my present thoughts. Goodness, that does sound like an awful thing to say, doesn't it? I know one shouldn't think ill of their siblings, however Agnes is a firm exception. You see, Agnes: ruined my favourite Sunday dress by throwing it in a puddle, constantly stole my expensive perfumes, would embarrass me in front of my friends, and not to mention she tried it on once with my Bobby at our local dance hall. Luckily, for Robert's sake, he shunned her affections - and quite politely. Mind you, there were some good times between Agnes and I, albeit they were few. Agnes did help me a little to care for Mother, when she got Cancer. Hold on... Mother died too. My lovely mother has passed from this life, from my physical grasp, just like Father. How could I have forgotten her death as well? It's all coming back to me now. I was in my late forties when Mother passed away, wasn't I? Doesn't this mean, that I'm *not* in my thirties, as I thought I was? Isabella, you utter fool. Don't you know anything anymore? What age are you really at?

"You've got a canny selection of books here, Isabella." grins John, with a child-like level of merriment in his voice. "Agatha Christie, Jane Austin, Charles Dickens... how about one of your Catherine Cookson novels? Should we go with *Tilly Trotter*?" A wise choice, my dear, very wise. I love reading about the early twentieth century, as it reminds me of my grandparents, God rest their souls. They were simpler times, where money was scarce in my family, but our love was everlasting. That's what mattered most, and still does. It's a pitiful shame that other folks don't realise this manageable feat. Money isn't everything, especially if it only leaves you on your own. "We don't have long, Isabella." moans John, whilst fleeting his eyes across towards my clock. "I'll do my best to read through the first chapter. I like this book as well, between me and you. I've got a soft spot for Catherine Cookson, but I wouldn't admit that to the others." There's no shame in being a fan of a great author, my boy. Although, if you do wish to keep this a secret between you and I, then I'll happily stay hush. "I hope you're comfortable, Mrs. Cunningham? Let's begin..."

John has an immensely soothing, yet somewhat monotonous, reading voice. It has a guttural quality, much like my father's when he would read to me as a young girl. Within a few pages or so, I start to feel my heavy eyelids closing again. Along with Catherine Cookson's exquisite writing skills and Chopin's musical serenity, I soon fall back into a carefree state of unconsciousness. I'm only left to wonder at how long this fantastical existence will endure this time, and how long will I remain pain-free? I begin to picture myself nestled safely within a small cottage's garden, the very-same peaceful setting of which I dreamt of earlier. There's no fear in this place, only tranquillity. Oh, this is perfect. This is wonderful.

PLAYING DOCTORS AND NURSES

I've not yet mustered the strength necessary to reopen my eyes, but I can tell that there are some strange figures leaning over me again, each one encroaching on what precious, personal space remains. Not that I'm an introvert or anything, if that, I'm quite the opposite. I just despise the fact I'm utterly powerless to stop their intrusion. Honestly, what awful acts have I committed in life to warrant this awful fate? I for one don't think I've been bad. Others may disagree, although I haven't made too many enemies during my short life, at least not that I'm vaguely aware of. It's all so much to take in, and it's not something which I particularly want to dwell on. I mean, who in their right mind would?

Chopin's music has been abruptly quenched, only adding a further disappointment to my debilitating circumstances. What lingers on thereafter, like the foulest of stenches, is a haunting and claustrophobic atmosphere of which I yearn to be quickly released from. Keep your chin up, Isabella. You're not one for letting things get on top of you. Goodness, I've survived German air raids, Scarlett Fever, and not forgetting my Bobby's horrendous driving skills. Stop being so bloody pedantic, old girl. You're an *Escomb Angel*, you're as proud as can be! You're meant to be strong, bold and defiant. You shouldn't be sinking into a pit of self-pity, as you presently are. You're steadily becoming an utter disgrace - a complete shadow of your former self, Isabella Marie Cunningham. What *would* Mother and Father say? I couldn't care less what Agnes might think.

Never mind all that, there's a sudden rustle of papers nearby and then the sound of fingernails tapping against my bedside. Oh, I do wish these visitors would leave me alone, even if it would mean being left to fend for myself in this dreadful limbo. Gracious, the tapping is getting faster – frantic even. What's happening now?

"So, *this* is Mrs. Cunningham?" questions a man, another of whom I have not yet grown accustomed to. He sounds very formal and not at all friendly. This chap is also giving off a militaristic quality with every syllable performed. Maybe he's a Sergeant Major? He most-certainly comes across as being one. I of all people should know. I met a few soldiers when working at the ordnance factory, though they were a great deal politer and more courteous than this fellow appears. "I examined her a few weeks ago, didn't I? Wasn't it for a bad case of Blepharitis, or something along those lines?"

"Yes, Doctor." I recognise *this* voice to be Nurse Emerson's. Her presence creates a deep sense of relief in me. However, my nurse doesn't seem at all happy and, if anything, she is coming across as apprehensive. "Isabella has deteriorated rapidly over the past few days, Doctor Kain. She has been refusing oral intake and isn't responding to our current pain relief program. We're getting very concerned about her wellbeing." How kind of you, my dear. Apart from you poking at my backside a few moments ago, all is well, fine and dandy. I'm in ship shape, as Robert would say. There was no need to contact a doctor on my behalf. Doctor Kain doesn't say much, does he? I can't even hear him breathing. "We're worried about Isabella's level of frailty and the fact we have nothing stronger to give should she become more distressed. Could you...?"

"I know exactly what you're going to ask of me, Nurse. Before saying anything else, you *are* fully aware of Isabella's medical condition, aren't you?" This doctor is hardly giving off any tell-tale signs that he gives a single dollop of muck about me. First impressions count, you know? Still, one should not always go off first impressions. That's what I'm telling myself anyway. Mother and Father would be so very proud of me, for reacting as such. Patience has not always been my strongest point. What was it that Father and Mother used to say to myself and Agnes: *give people a chance to flourish, even if they come across as idiots to begin with*?

39

In all honesty, I've never followed this motto to the tee, only because my gut instinct is usually correct. My gut instinct at present doesn't seem to favour Doctor Kain, not by any means. "You can't possibly expect Isabella to be prancing around like a teenager." sniggers Doctor Kain. To my frustration, Nurse Emerson merely holds her tongue in response. Get him told, my girl! "She currently has Paracetamol and Codeine in suspension form - yes? Are these being administered at a regular level, four times daily?"

"Well..." hesitates Nurse Emerson. "The thing is, Isabella's Codeine caused her to suffer from severe constipation. We haven't been giving her any for a few weeks or so. Not to mention, she's not managing any of her oral medications, as I've already stated." she says this meekly, like a child being scolded. "We were instructed by Melissa, the Advanced Nurse Practitioner, to just keep on trying. We have, and things obviously haven't improved."

"I see. Well, that's a pity." replies my doctor, within a lengthy yawn. Am I that boring, dear? "On Isabella's notes, it states that you can administer her medications covertly. Are you?"

"We've tried several ways to administer her meds..."

Why is Nurse Emerson being so subservient? This man is no different from you or I, even if he does hold a title. Robert had a dreadful saying which would sum this up perfectly: *we all crap out of the same hole, even the Queen does.* I'll tell you this much for free, should Doctor Kain continue to be rude towards my nurse, I shall gladly intervene. This broken body of mine will not stop me.

"Ah, yes. I can also see from Isabella's records that an ANP, Melissa Goodheart, has visited last week and discontinued the Codeine. You mustn't have received the corresponding fax?" Doctor Kain pauses, no doubt to sharpen his tongue for a further assault. "Might I ask, how do you know if Isabella *is* in pain, or are you just assuming this?"

"Isabella can express her pain physically, and these episodes are becoming more and more frequent now. Even when she did accept her medications, they seemed to have little effect. We requested a pain relief patch, but it was deemed to be unsuitable. I believe, given how quick the deterioration is progressing, Isabella may need something stronger now to help alleviate her distress." That's my girl. I admire your resilience, Nurse Emerson. I'm not in any pain, mind you. "I believe..."

"What *you* believe, with all due respect, is frankly irrelevant. I need solid evidence to justify an authorisation for a stronger prescription. I hope you understand this?" Why must you talk to her like that, Doctor? I say - what a Cad! Surely, Nurse Emerson is only acting in my best interests? She clearly knows more about me than *you* do? "I can gather that Mrs. Cunningham has deteriorated from my last visit..." *But*? I know there's one coming. "But that does not mean we should be doping her up to the eye balls, as you are insinuating." *See*? Told you so. "That would constitute abuse and you know this. I'm not going to sedate this poor woman for no reason."

"We're not asking for you to *dope her up,*" seethes Nurse Emerson, through gritted teeth. "We just want Isabella to be pain-free – to be comfortable. I fully understand the implications of what you're saying, but can't you see where *I* am coming from? With all due respect..."

"Well, if you are one-hundred percent positive that she is in such discomfort..." snarls Doctor Kain. I'm swiftly getting the impression that he's in the wrong job. Doctor Kain comes across more to me as being a Tax Man. Lord, he's certainly as popular as one. "I'll discontinue Isabella's Hydroxocobalamin injection, Lactulose, Memantine and Warfarin - seeing as there's little use for them now and given her current presentation." Why must certain medical professionals use these ridiculous terms; names that no ordinary person can recognise? What is Memantine and Hydrox—acob—mina - whatever the bloody hell they're called? Remarkably, I do know what Lactulose is, and the last thing I desire are laxatives. I'm as regular as clockwork. You can set your watch by my bowel movements. Never mind *doping me up*, I already sound like a drug addict from what he's apparently putting a stop to. Gracious me.

"With the greatest respect, Doctor Kain." Go on, Nurse Emerson, show him who is the boss here, and teach him some bloody manners while you're at it. "Isabella might appear settled to you, but overnight she has been very distressed, more so than we've ever seen. I'm adamant, without any doubt, that she is in a considerable amount of discomfort. When she squints her eyes, as she is now, it's a big giveaway. Please, trust me on this. I've cared for her for long enough to know the signs." A daunting silence then follows between us three, like the prelude in an Opera that builds up towards a truly epic climax. All the while, I'm lying here like a mute prisoner, against all resistance, and it worsens with each passing second. Oh, I wish I could help you, Nurse. I really do. I'd do anything to speak.

"I *do* trust in your clinical judgement, and it's nothing personal, Nurse Emerson. I'll examine Isabella first and then decide on what to do about your request. Are you happy with me doing that?" Doctor Kain, aren't you such a caring gentleman? You really know how to woo a lady. Believe me, Nurse Emerson and I are quivering in our boots on account of your charismatic personality. I wonder if he understands sarcasm? "Hello, Mrs. Cunningham. I will need to check you over now." A marvellous chat-up line, my dear, but you'll need to do better than that. "I'm going to take your blood pressure, okay?" Go ahead by all means. "There will a tight feeling around your arm, though it won't last for too long. Nurse Emerson, can you help to keep her still while I do that, please?"

"Yes, sure I can." submits my nurse, quite reservedly. "Try to stay still, Isabella. It's very important that we give you this little check-over. We'll be gentle."

I soon hear the irritating sound of Velcro pulling apart, then comes a clammy hand that wraps itself around my wrist like a serpent snaring its prey. The next thing I know, there's a freezing-cold material placed around my arm, nestled just slightly above the elbow. A proceeding, vice-like grip then slowly begins to crush into

42

me at this very point. I didn't realise medieval torture was still permitted these days? Robert, where *are* you, my darling? Get this horrid man off me! Bobby! BOBBY!

"Her pulse is reading low, though it's not too concerning." Doctor Kain gradually removes his torture device away from me, and then reaches down for something else. I can just see through a small opening in my eyelids. What's he up to now? "Shall we see how your SATS are doing?" My - what? "Let's take a look at your oxygen levels."

A small machine, which feels unnervingly like a stapler, is then clamped onto one of my fingers. In a pleasant sense, it reminds me of a Yorkshire Terrier that Robert and I once owned - Winston. The little tinker would often nip at my fingers in the very same manner, especially when he was hungry. Sadly though, we lost dearest Winston in a road accident a few years back, not long after I turned forty. I do miss him at times, particularly when I've got no one else to talk to. He was a far-better listener than Robert, as he never gave back any cheeky responses. Thinking about it, I could have ordered Winston to sink his gnashers into Doctor Kain's ankles, if he were still here. Now, that *would* have been amusing.

"Her reading isn't very good, is it?" stammers Nurse Emerson. Honestly, dear, you're meant to be keeping calm in wake of Doctor Kain's present experiments. What's worrying you now? "The lowest oxygen level I've seen Isabella reach was at 92%."

"Well, her oxygen is currently at 84%; however, we must take into consideration Isabella's COPD diagnosis. 88-92% would be accepted as an average rate for someone with her condition. Still, it *is* somewhat on the low side." Well, this is one for the books. Doctor Kain himself now appears to be showing some empathy towards me. I do believe he has gotten his wires crossed somewhere, mind you. I've never been diagnosed with having COPD before. He's as muddled up as I am. "Isabella's Care Plan states: avoid hospital admission wherever possible. I'm sorry, but this greatly limits what we can do, regarding any further action. My advice, and I suggest you take it, would be to continue with Isabella's present level of care here and not in hospital. I'm afraid there's nothing else that can be done."

"Is there a chance that she might have another chest infection? Isabella's already had three bouts of Pneumonia this year alone." Nurse Emerson is showing a great deal of resurgence in her resolve again. Good show, my girl. You're doing me proud. Although, I can't remember ever having Pneumonia either. The odd cold – yes.

"I would stay along the lines of COPD." states Doctor Kain, firmly. "Her temperature is falling in range. If she is not systemically unwell..."

"Personally, I don't trust those laser thermometers." quips Nurse Emerson. "We know that she has COPD, but Isabella could still have an underlying infection as well, couldn't she? There's a terrible rattle in her throat..." A notable pause from Doctor Kain follows where his cogs must be going into overdrive, although I can still hear him grunting on like an ignorant swine. "Would another course of Flucloxacillin be viable?

"Given her test results – no. The rattling noise appears to be upper-respiratory to me. You're not positioning her correctly." replies Doctor Kain, in strong defiance. Goodness, how I'd love to wipe that smirk from his face. "I don't think it would be in Isabella's best interest to prescribe more antibiotics, let alone examine her chest again. Doing so would only cause further and totally unnecessary distress. You were meant to have received a separate fax about the scans over a month ago. Have you, might I ask?"

"Yes." sighs Nurse Emerson. Her forlorn expression speaks louder than any words, and portrays a clear sense that things aren't going to plan. "So, there's literally nothing else you can do?"

"Mrs. Cunningham does not warrant further tests; they are too intrusive and would not be of any benefit to her. I presume, without coming across as credulous, that you've informed Isabella's Next of Kin about those results? They do have a right to know."

"Yes. Of course, I have." Nurse Emerson sounds as depressed as I'm rapidly becoming. It doesn't take a genius to work out what these 'tests' were for. Mother had Cancer, and it seems that I too now have it. I wonder how long I have left, and at what stage I'm at? Why isn't my Bobby here to share in this awful news, to comfort me? Does Robert even know about my illness? Good Lord, it'll surely break his heart? Oh, Bobby... "Isabella's Next of Kin are due in later today. I'll go over the diagnosis' again with them then, if they want me to. It's a hard subject to talk about."

"Not an easy task at all, I can imagine?" replies Doctor Kain, passively. "Can I also ask, has Isabella passed any blood overnight?" Thanks again, Doctor. You're really helping to keep me calm. I bloody-well hope I haven't passed any (pardon the pun). "I'm only asking, because our ANP mentioned something last week about this issue." Oh, really? What an eventful life I now lead. "If so, how frequent is Isabella passing blood, and at what consistency? I'd appreciate some accurate amounts, if possible?"

"There have been some occasional episodes, though nothing significant. Just a few small droplets of frank blood have been reported over the last couple of days. Melissa *did* examine Isabella but, because it was just a few sporadic episodes, and given her current condition, she didn't take any further action. It seemed like the right thing to do at the time. I still agree with Melissa on this."

"It is to be expected, given Isabella's prognosis." explains Doctor Kain, as he ruffles through some more papers. My eyesight is clearer now, though regrettably not enough to see what he is reading. I wonder what is on those papers? "I'm still not overly convinced that anticipatory drugs are necessary. See how things go today. If you need any further advice, or visitations, just call the Surgery's bypass number. Our receptionists will be able to sort out another visit, if need-be."

"Well, there is one other concern which I need to raise with you." grimaces Nurse Emerson. "We've been given verbal authorisation for a DNACPR to be put in place by Isabella's Next of Kin." she says this sharply, as if sickened by the very topic. "If you won't prescribe any stronger pain relief, or drugs to settle Isabella's distress, then can you at least authorise this request? It'd be appreciated."

Give me a moment, my dears. I'm trying to fathom out what a *DNACPR* is. I've heard of the 'CPR' part somewhere before. Doesn't it involve resuscitation – the kiss of life? In all fairness, if I were to 'clock-off' now, I'd rather not be brought back into this confusing mess of a world. Another wave of silence emerges from those two, which is only broken when more footsteps enter my room.

"I'll go back to the clinic and have a think about it. As I've already emphasised, I *must* justify my actions. There are strict protocols and laws we must all follow. However, writing up the DNACPR shouldn't be a problem."

"Good morning, Doctor." John? I'm dismayed that you never did finish that first chapter with me although, in this instance, I shall graciously let you off the hook this time. "I'm John, one of the Senior Carers here. We've met a few times before, Doctor Kain." he states proudly, and with a much firmer voice than Nurse Emerson. John obviously knows what he's up against. "I've helped to look after Isabella during her time here as a residential client, before she was turned over to Nursing. I hope you don't mind me getting involved?" I for one don't mind, dear. Here comes the cavalry, I say!

"I welcome any rational input, John." replies Doctor Kain, apparently taken aback by John's unexpected arrival. "If it is in relation to anticipatory drugs, however, Nurse Emerson and I have already discussed this topic. They are *not* necessary. Isabella is stable, from what I can gather." Well, there's an understatement, if there was ever one. "I think we're jumping the gun a little, don't you?"

"Just... leave it, John." implores Nurse Emerson. "Doctor Kain is going to sort out Isabella's DNACPR. There's nothing else to discuss."

"Doctor," John's voice dramatically deepens. Oh, this is very exciting! I wish I had some chocolate to munch on. "Isabella is getting weaker by the minute. We've tried all avenues with her, relating to intake and pain relief. The last thing we want is for this poor lady here to suffer. Can you not prescribe something stronger to help?"

"John!" gasps Nurse Emerson. The poor boy's only trying to help me, darling. Heavens above. Cut the lad some slack. "Please, remember your place. Doctor Kain knows what he is talking about. He is doing what is in Isabella's best interests." I greatly beg to differ, Nurse. The man's insufferable. "I've explained our concerns to him, John. It's probably a good idea for you to go wait outside, at least until he's finished with his examinations."

"I'm more than happy to listen to what you have to say." mutters Doctor Kain, with an obvious essence of condescending snobbery. "But, like I said to Nurse Emerson, your personal opinions do not matter. I need hard facts, not emotional responses. The NHS is under a lot of pressure nowadays and a great deal of public money is wasted on wrongful decisions being made by professionals, such as myself. I cannot go throwing prescriptions around willy-nilly, just because people yourselves ask me to. Can you not see it from *my* perspective?

"Look at her, man!" snaps John, portraying his point across like a furious beast. It's like watching two heavyweight boxers start their first round together in a ring. I'm rooting for you, my boy. Don't you dare let me down. "She's in obvious agony. I can't believe..."

"*Please*, John." interjects Nurse Emerson, despairingly. "I know you care a lot about Isabella... we all do. Regardless of what we might think, Doctor Kain has a valid point and it's something we can't argue against. We must respect his professional decision. We're only here to do as we're told, not to question those above us. I've had this chat with you previously."

"We've spent more time with Isabella then *he* has, Hollie." continues John. I'm impressed by his passion, though I still haven't the foggiest clue who he is or how he knows me. Not that it matters anymore. "*I* can tell when she's in pain, and she is!"

"I admire your passion," says Doctor Kain, in a pitiful attempt to alleviate these risen tensions. "But *please* see it from my perspective. I have a variety of denominations to consider when prescribing medications. It's not as simple as you may think it is. There are protocols to abide to, and I'm not prepared to defer from them. I have a reputation to uphold."

Does this doctor not realise that I'm not a government statistic? I have feelings and rights still, don't I? I've fought for this bloody country *and* pay all my taxes on time. Don't those things mean zilch? God, I wish that I could just say even one word back at him. I would be so very polite, make no doubt about it, but also incredibly firm. What ever happened to compassion – to empathy? What has become of this great country, if people like me are thrown aside because of money or political problems? Where did it all go wrong, I ask?

"Please, both of you, *calm down*." speaks the voice of reason, Nurse Emerson. "We're not solving anything by acting this way. Poor Isabella shouldn't have to listen to us lot rambling on about these things. She needs peace and quiet." Thank you, my dear. Yes – I do. That would certainly be most-welcomed. "This is getting us nowhere. Isabella's DNACPR is getting sorted and, if she's not being prescribed any new medications, we should leave it at that... for her sake."

"Look," groans Doctor Kain, whilst wearily rubbing away at his sweat-riddled face. "If Isabella's Next of Kin wishes for a DNACPR to be put in place, then I will go ahead and authorise this request without any further argument. However, I simply cannot..." Oh, it looks like we've made a breakthrough, my fellow comrades. Doctor Kain seems to be seeing sense! There *is* a heart in that dogmatic body of his. "Fine! I may as well prescribe some anticipatory drugs while I'm here, if to save myself another pointless visit. But - and I mean but - they are only to be administered if absolutely necessary...

PRN." He's using that militaristic tone again. Still, a breakthrough is a breakthrough. Crack open the bubbly, my darlings. "Please ensure that you adequately document any future concerns, just so that this prescription, if need be, can be amended. Next time, *should* there be another problem, please contact the Surgery's Advanced Nurse Practitioner first. Our ANP can deal with Isabella from now on. I've enough on my plate to deal with today." How very considerate of you, Doctor Kain. Saying that, I have no inclination as to what anticipatory drugs are, or why I need any. Regardless of this revelation, these medicines can't possibly make my condition any worse... can they? Keep on telling yourself that, Isabella. Just keep telling yourself that.

"Th-Thank you, Doctor." Nurse Emerson exhales lengthily in relief. Good show, my girl. Bravo! Both you and John have worked wonders this morning. You've earned my utmost respect, which takes some bloody doing. "We wouldn't have called you out if we didn't have any justifiable concerns, Doctor. At the end of the day, we just want Isabella to be comfortable." My faith in humanity is unequivocally restored. I'm not in any pain, for what I can tell. I just feel a little out of sorts, that's all. Discovering that I have Cancer doesn't help too much. Oh, I do wish Robert was here. I miss him dearly. Where are you, Bobby? Wait until I get my hands on you!

"It's settled." declares Doctor Kain, reluctantly. "I will write up a Card-Ex for Morphine, Hyoscine, Levomepromazine and Midazolam. Please ensure that you collect these medications from Isabella's pharmacy as soon as possible. Thank you for your time and goodbye, Mrs. Cunningham. It's been a pleasure to see you again." The pleasure is all yours, Doctor Kain. Mind you, I *can* understand what stress he must be under, and sort of feel remorseful for being so uncouth against him. It mustn't be easy to have the lives of others resting on your shoulders every day? One can only guess how awful that level of accountability must feel. "Thank you for your assistance, Nurse Emerson. Take care, John. Goodbye."

A set of footsteps soon dwindle off into the distance, and then some rustling and panting noises arise nearby. I don't believe that John and Nurse Emerson have left me. They've gone terribly quiet though.

"You could get in a lot of trouble for going on like that, John. What if Doctor Kain puts in a complaint about your conduct with him?" comments Nurse Emerson, again with that fearful tone. John tuts back in response, apparently unphased by this supposed threat. "I'm not being funny or trying to upset you. I'm just saying, you shouldn't put yourself in a predicament like that. Think of your wife and Baby Lucy, John. It's not worth losing your job or jeopardising your career over something like this."

"I know. You're right as always, Hollie." replies John, after a few distinguishable grunts. "When push comes to shove, we're just showing how much we care about our residents. The likes of Isabella can't speak up for themselves, so it's our job to do it for them. You know, it's a bloody shame that others can't see it the same way we do. How is it Isabella's fault that the NHS is on its knees?"

"It's not, but what right do we have to contest a doctor's decision?"

"We've got every right, haven't we?" counters John, in dismay. "We look after these residents both day and night. Half of our time is spent on caring for them. We know when something is wrong, yet that doesn't seem to matter. We're their voice when they can't be heard. I'm proud of that, and I don't give a toss if it offends anyone – especially Doctor Kain... the knobhead."

"Shush, John. He could be still outside the room, and Isabella might still hear what you're saying." emphasises Nurse Emerson. As curse words go, that one John used is quite tame to what I'd like to throw at Doctor Kain. "There are ways to make your opinions heard without jeopardising your career. I don't mean this nastily, but you've still got a great deal to learn about working in this profession. I'm saying this as a friend, John. I'm saying this, because I don't want you to get into trouble."

"I know."

"Don't let him get to you."

There's a further period of awkward silence and then more footsteps. They're both walking away from me now, aren't they? Finally, it seems, I'm left alone in solitary confinement yet again. It's clear to grasp that Nurse Emerson and John have left me in a frantic manner, possibly to retrieve those fantastical medications? Goodness, they've forgotten to put Chopin back on before leaving. Oh, Lord! This dreadful white-noise is far-worse than having to listen to Doctor Kain's incessant ramblings. It's like I've been locked inside an air-tight bubble, completely robbed of air and any ability to escape. It's dreadful, I tell you. Being lonely isn't any fun. I miss my Bobby. Where in the devil, is he? My husband has a lot of explaining to do.

From what I can make out, the clock on my bedside cabinet now reads 11:15 a.m. Gracious me, this day is now being insufferably drawn out. I'm *still* waiting for a decent cup of tea, as well as some edible food. Is that seriously too much to ask for? I'll just lie here, like an infant in their cot, waiting helplessly for someone who truly loves me to turn up. Where are you Robert Francis Cunningham? I'm using his 'Sunday Name' now, which only means I'll have a few choice words to say to him, at least, when he does show his face. My husband is so much trouble, particularly when I catch up with him.

"Hello, Isabella." Woe is me. Who is *this* new stranger with this incredibly high-pitched voice? They don't sound anything remotely like Zanna or Nurse Emerson. Actually, I think they're Cornish. "I've brought some things along for you, sweetheart. Goodness, it's such a lovely day outside. It's a shame we can't have a look to the duck pond, like we used to."

Oh, what an invigorating accent! Bobby and I visited Cornwall once, back in the fifties. We found it to be an idyllic vision of paradise, despite the tedious eight-hour bus journey involved to get there. Perhaps this woman will remind me of happier times, those precious moments I shared with Bobby back then. Let's see, hey?

51

"It's just Kelly, your Activities Co-ordinator. Sorry I'm late. I didn't want to bother Doctor Kain while he was here seeing you." What's an 'Activities Co-ordinator' on a cold Sunday morning? The only activity I'd like to willingly participate in right now is to enjoy a lovely nap, or to have Chopin's music put back on. What I would give to hear one his Etudes. Oh, it would be simply divine. "I've brought some sensory toys for you, Isabella. There are some squishy ones, bumpy ones, scratchy ones..." Is there anything you don't possess on your persons at this moment, my dear? You don't happen to have a decent meal in your back pocket, do you? "I hope you'll still find some fun in playing with these toys again? I've brought along all your favourites." This girl is very giddy and loud. Admittedly, I'm growing to like her. Kelly is a welcome change, especially after Doctor Kain's morbid visit. She has a joyful personality which is uncannily alike to Joan's – my best friend. I wonder how Joan is doing these days? I can't remember the last time we spoke. "Here, Isabella. Try this one."

Kelly places something squishy and wet into my arthritic hands with the greatest level of enthusiasm. I'm initially repulsed by the weird texture of this toy, though I do soon discover an unusual enjoyment from it. I squeeze the rubbery balloon with all my might, and without any shame pretend that it is Doctor Kain's scrawny neck. Oh, Isabella, how naughty of you to think such thoughts. Nevertheless, it is *very* satisfying, albeit immature of me.

"Do you like that one, Isabella?" chuckles Kelly and presumably to herself, since I can't exactly respond. It's alright, I guess? "I like that one too. It's great for stress-relief. Would you like to try another toy now?"

Kelly gently removes the squishy object from my hands, only to replace it with a firmer, more tweed-like material. This toy somehow reminds me of Robert's favourite trousers. He constantly insists, against my repetitive pleas, on always wearing the same make of trousers, and they're an absolute bloody nightmare to iron. I discreetly allow for this toy to fall away from my hands. What a shame.

"Oh, do you not like that toy anymore?" Kelly sounds so deflated, bless her. I didn't mean to come across as rude. Try something else with me, my dear. I'll happily play along with this game of yours, if it means not to offend you. "You're doing really well, Isabella. It's okay, darling, we'll just try something else instead. I've got lots of toys here." Aren't I a tad-too old to be playing with toys, Kelly? That said, I do enjoy board games such as Monopoly, but without my spectacles... "How about if I read some more of this book to you? John didn't get very far with it, did he? You've got a great selection of novels. It's like you've got your own little library on this bookshelf, Isabella." Oh, yes! Please, do indulge me with more of Catherine Cookson's wonderous imagination. I shan't argue with that kind offer. Take me back to rural Northumberland, to Tilly Trotter's cottage, to a place surrounded by birdsong, a place where all my troubles can vanish. I must get out of this bed sometime today. I guess, at least for now, these dreams of mine will have to suffice? "It'll be lunchtime soon. We might manage a few pages by then, or *even* finish the first chapter? That would be nice, wouldn't it, sweetheart?" It would wonderful, my dear. Utter bliss. "Hmm, let's have a look. I've got Dyslexia mind, so bear with me."

After a few pages or so, I find Kelly's reading voice to be as soothing as any musical masterpiece. My eyelids close again, feeling even heavier now than before. My breathing becomes slower and less difficult to manage, although it is still - what you might say - raspy. My rigid bones begin to ease, and those terrible cramps I had earlier in my legs and arms are starting to ware off. The odd electrical shock continues to course along my spine but, nevertheless, this is simply perfect. Lovely.

The Northumbrian cottage soon comes back into vision. It has a traditional thatched roof, and a beautiful garden lain outside of it. Some yellow roses are strewn throughout the cottage's vast garden and are truly awe-inspiring, even breath-taking. There's a majestic and mystical feel about this place, and it's creating a sense of total peace in me which I hope shall never fade. I don't need 'doping up' at all. *This* is serenity. I'm in a realm of purest perfection, where nothing can annoy nor ail me. The only features now missing, to complete this marvellous utopia, are Robert and our two children. Oh, to be with my family again. That would be perfect. That... would be wonderful.

A RIGHT TO REFUSE

Good Lord, did I doze off again? It's becoming a regular habit of mine, and not one I'm overly proud of. Mother would call me lazy, if she were still here. You see, I was raised to be a hard-working and obedient early-riser. My sister, Agnes, on the other hand was always the shirker; she's never held a job for longer than a month, though mostly through her own choice, mind you. *Get up with the birds if you wish to be successful in life*, was one of Father's favourite sayings. I couldn't have possibly wished for a kinder, more loving dad. I've been blessed in that one sense, at least. I have no right whatsoever to moan.

Other memories come back to me now, although they are not necessarily welcomed, I might add. Father died of something else other than Pneumonia, didn't he? Think, Isabella – THINK! Didn't Father pass away from some form of Dementia? I remember now, though I don't particularly want to. By the end of his illness, Father was like an infant himself: helpless, oblivious to his surroundings, and totally dependent on others to care for him... just like *you* are now, Isabella. It was so awful to watch Father suffer through those last couple of weeks in hospital, with little-to-no dignity or sympathetic care granted. I don't want to remember those awful days. Get these terrible images out of your head at once, Isabella. Remember all the good times you had with your parents, for there were so many of them, weren't there? Hold on... Father passed away when I was in my early fifties, not long after Mother. I'm getting all mixed up here. My head feels like a ticking time bomb, only moments away from exploding. Surely, I'm not in my *fifties*? All this sleep can't be doing me any good. That's what it is. This oversleeping lark is what has caused these delusions to rear their ugly heads. Focus on the good times, old girl. Focus.

"Hi, Isabella." Zanna? I'd rather not endorse your company at this moment. It's nothing against you, my dear, just I'd rather you let me dwell in self-pity for a little-while longer. Lord knows it, I may as well. "Sorry, sweetheart. Marius and I need to reposition you. Can you jot down the time on Isabella's charts for me please, mate? 12:35pm."

"Sure." My Greek God, or should I say my Polish God, has returned to raise these failing spirits of mine. Marius' presence is most-certainly welcome, being that his deep voice reminds me of Robert's. Goodness, my Bobby still hasn't visited me. I'm starting to grow impatient with him. I wonder what excuse he'll come up with? "Should we put Isabella on her back, seeing as it'll be lunchtime soon?" You have such a dreamy voice, Marius. Carry on talking, my dear. "Do you reckon she'll even manage to eat anything? If Isabella won't though, I'm not going to force her. No chance."

Oh, gracious. I'm praying that they won't be treating me to any more of that detestable, mushy food. A small portion of fish and chips, with some generous lashings of salt and vinegar, would go down nicely. Although, I can't see *that* happening, not given the disaster that was my so-called 'breakfast'. Marius is scribbling away on some paper beside me. Goodness, it's awfully irritating. It's like a set of fingernails being scraped down a chalkboard.

"It'll be a miracle if Isabella eats her dinner." dismays Zanna, though with a faint glimmer of hope in her voice. "Doctor Kain said himself: if she doesn't accept intake, then we're to only give mouthcare. *Please* eat your lunch, Isabella. It's the only way you'll get your strength back. Try to have even just a few mouthfuls... for me and Marius."

Such a request is very humbling, but the outcome shall greatly depend on what food will be offered. I must say, what have I done to deserve such unequivocal devotion from these two? I shall try my hardest to stomach whatever is thrown at me, so long as it is not that bloody baby food again. If not some fish and chips, a hearty bowl of Mulligatawny soup would definitely suffice, or some apricot jam sandwiches. Oh, and by the way, don't forget that cup of tea I've been waiting for, my dears. I'm still hanging on tender hooks for one.

"I wouldn't count on Isabella managing any food, Zan. She looks weaker now than she did only a couple of hours ago." Marius, darling, don't be so disheartened. Have *some* faith in me, like I do in yourself and Zanna. "Would you want to be on a puréed diet, if you had a choice? Christ, I wouldn't."

"No way." Zanna's response is staccato-like and resonates perfectly with my own stance on this matter. "I'd rather starve to death, mate. It looks horrible." I'll admit, the food earlier smelled... fine, but the consistency was anything other than pleasant. "Some people don't have a choice though, do they? I guess, you *could* get used to it over time? What gets me though is, Isabella used to be such a good eater; she could easily manage more than me, well, once over." I'm not surprised, dear. I can't honestly see where you'd put it all. There's not a morsel on your tiny body, Zanna. I'm quite jealous. "The worst thing about this job is how useless it makes you feel at times, especially when it comes to this stage of the illness."

"We knew this would happen to Isabella one day." Now Marius is displaying a futile melancholy in his voice. For pity's sake, what has made me so important to them? Have I become royalty overnight or something? "She's in *God's waiting room* now, after-all. Man, I hate when people say that, but they're not far-off being right, are they? We always knew Isabella wasn't going to improve, but it's still hard to watch." How incredibly charming of you, Marius. I despise waiting rooms, by the way. I'm not the most patient individual going, nor religious. My current placement is clearly not a suitable one. "Should we put some music back on for you, Isabella? I bet you're sick of listening to Chopin and us two babbling on?" I will *never* grow tired of my dearest Frédéric! And, quite frankly, I don't mind listening to you or Zanna. The pressure is on you here, Marius. You'll need to make a very wise choice here, my darling. Chopin's music is as vital to me as consuming any sustenance you may offer.

Tread carefully and try to avoid Debussy, if possible. "You aren't half making some funny noises there, Isabella. I think she heard me, Zan." laughs Marius, possibly realising the magnitude of his mistake. "Pass the Beethoven CD over, please. You need a change from Chopin every now and then, Isabella. Vary things up a little." You're always thinking in my best interests aren't you, my darling? "Cheers. It's a good CD, this one."

Thankfully, I am impressed by what begins to resonate in my ears some few moments after. The piece now performing is Beethoven's *6th symphony*. I'm instantly taken back into that wonderous dream I was having earlier, before being rudely awoken. I'm at the cottage in Catherine Cookson's novel, sat on a small deckchair, with an interesting book in hand, and my Bobby is stood smoking one of his cigars nearby. I've never really seen the fascination in smoking myself; it's an expensive habit and in more ways than one, although I've always found Bobby's cigar plumes to be somewhat relaxing. Perhaps it is because my father used to smoke a pipe, therefore rekindling some fond childhood memories in me? Particularly the ones where Father and I would both sit by the fireplace, each making up ridiculous tales about faeries and pirates, and munching on scones with jam and cream. Who knows?

Anyway, back to my dream. There's a gentle flutter of birds flying overhead, then afterwards comes a peaceful silence that removes any previous anxiety once instilled. There's a wildflower meadow which lies just beyond the cottage's rose garden; its enticing scents soon rise into my nostrils, filling them with the most-wonderful aromas. What a beautiful setting this is. In the heavenly field are two small children, and both are quite cheekily chasing one other around in circles. It's such a delightful thing to witness, and I recognise the little boy and girl... my children. David, my first-born, and my daughter, Caroline, appear just as I remember them to be. They look so happy and carefree, just as any doting parent would wish for. This is perfection. This is simply wonderful. Oh, I love it here.

"Isabella. I'm really sorry, but we need to check you over again."
Can you just wait a minute please, Zanna? I'm currently immersed
within a fascinating vision, one that I don't ever want to cease.
Caroline and David are running towards me now, and in response I
open my arms willingly to welcome them. Come to me, my darlings.
Mammy is here for you. "Turn Isabella towards me on the count of
three, Marius. One...Two...*Three!*"

I'm immediately rolled onto my righthand side, but I'm not
bothered in the slightest. My dream presses on regardless. David
runs towards me, tripping a little along the way, but his smile never
leaves from him. He's such a handsome little boy, is my son. David
is the spitting image of his father, unlike his sister. Caroline inherited
a lot from me, such as: my features, my embarrassing laugh, my
auburn locks, my stubborn temperament...

"How's Isabella's bottom looking?" Oh, Zanna, *really*? Here we
go again with my arse being put out on show for inspection. Should I
start charging you both for this privilege? "Is it as bad as John said?"

"Yeah." Marius! Kindly remove your wandering hands away from
my hips! What *would* my Bobby say if he were to see you doing
this? It's so un-gentleman-like. Mind you, I would hope that some
lingering jealousy would arise, as often seen in those romantic films
I used to enjoy. Your so fickle at times, Isabella. Do behave
yourself. "That's a Grade Four, alright. The dressing has come a way
a bit on one corner... easy put back. John wasn't lying. Jesus." I
swear, if I hear *one more* person say that... and less of your
blasphemy, Marius. It doesn't become you. "I'll just sort the
dressing out. Give me a sec, Zan."

"We'd better press the nurse call and get Hollie, mate. I wouldn't
touch that wound if I were you. A Nurse needs to check it." Thank
you, Zanna. It's nice to know that my backside is now a source of
such concern. "She'll be doing her meds round. Fingers crossed, it
shouldn't take Hollie too long to get here."

A piercing beep then overwhelms the transient tones of
Beethoven's symphony, something which I adamantly detest by

grunting back a little in response. *More* footsteps enter my room. Nurse Emerson, perhaps? Another set of tremoring fingertips soon fondle over my exposed back and intimate parts, and with only the subtlest of warnings given. I'm trying to knock them away with my hands, but they just won't shift. These arms of mine are glued to my side, despite all attempts made to slide them away. Goodness, Isabella. What a dire predicament this is.

"Thanks for making me aware." states Nurse Emerson, evidently still held in a nervous disposition. I can feel her rubbing her fingertips along my clenched buttocks. Even my Bobby never paid *that* much notice to them. "I can't see Isabella's wound getting better any time soon. These dressings are useless." She's tutting on like a demented woodpecker. It's hardly reassuring, dear. "Apply some barrier cream around the site when you're both finished cleaning her. Hopefully, that should keep Isabella's skin nice and moist, and might also help to stop the damage from spreading." I can't stand that word 'moist', being it always comes across as something dirty. Yuck. Who would want a 'moist' bottom, I ask? "Keep a close eye on her. Isabella's wound could quickly turn septic... that's all she needs." There's a further awkward pause, and then... "I've got to dash. Let me know if Isabella accepts any intake, and can you please change her nightgown while you're at it. There's some blood droplets where the dressing slipped off."

"I hope she tolerates us doing that." whines Marius, with a humorous undertone. "Only, Isabella used to kick off with us when we'd try to put her socks on."

"Howay, Marius." chortles Zanna. "Isabella hasn't lifted her arms up in days. I doubt she'd be that bothered, bless her."

"I was joking, Zan." emphasises Marius. "You need to have a laugh now and then. Isabella doesn't need a bunch of people standing over her, moping on and crying. Do you, sweetheart?" Certainly not, Marius. Thank you, dear. "There's that smile again. You have a beautiful smile, Isabella."

Please, Beethoven. Enchant my ears with your calming influence. Remove me from this weird environment. I want my Bobby. I want my children. I want them all to be here with me. I'm becoming desperate - frantic. I don't know why I need these dressings or creams. I don't know why I'm here. Go back to sleep, old girl. Let your worries drift away. Relax.

"See you soon, Hollie. We'll sort things out." says Zanna, as a set of footsteps quickly move off into the distance. "It looks like she's been incontinent of urine, Marius, but only a very small amount. Can you pass over the wipes and a clean pad, please?" *Incontinent*?! We ladies can often suffer from the odd bout of 'pittle-spittle'. That's normal, isn't it? Admittedly, I have suffered from the occasional accident when coughing or laughing. Peeing yourself is a common side-effect from giving birth, or so Mother warned me. Bringing my David into this world was like passing a cricket ball through your earlobe, however, I most-certainly do NOT require incontinence pads because of this feat. They're for the elderly, the infirm... aren't they? I don't fit into either of those categories. Some rotten beggar must have spilt a drink back there. Yes, that's what it is. "Cheers, mate. Can you do the honours, before she gets anymore wound up?"

There's a ghastly, dragging sensation coursing between my legs now; it's slithery, cold and quite frankly humiliating. I didn't even realise it was there. Another thing: when did I start making a habit of wetting myself? Oh, this is intolerable.

"She hasn't passed much urine, Zan." I beg to differ, given the density of what just slipped between my legs. "We'd better tell Hollie about that as well. In fairness, Isabella hasn't drunk much over the past few days. You can't expect her to void much if there isn't anything going in."

"Our Isabella..." sighs Zanna, whimsically. "What *are* we going to do with you?" Well, Zanna, there are several replies I could offer in answer of this. The most-prominent answer being... oh, why bother? I have no idea what is going on anymore. Do you what wish with me. I'll stay quiet for you both. I'll just keep on praying that Robert will turn up at any moment to save me from all this embarrassment. He'd better show his face soon. Lord help him, if he doesn't. "I wonder if they'll put up any sub-cut fluids? It'll be nearly three days since she last drank anything, from what I can see in her notes."

"Nah, I don't think they will." Marius seems very confident about this. "It wouldn't be fair to drag out her suffering. Anyway, can you see Doctor Kain authorising sub-cut fluids? I can't. You can go a long time without food... but not water."

I agree with you, Marius. I cannot see Doctor Kain doing many things, especially if they were to benefit me in such a way. I shouldn't really moan. Not all doctors are the same. The majority do care. It would be so very wrongful to pile them all into the same dirty basket. Trust me to get landed with such a miserable oaf as Doctor Kain, though. My mother and father's practitioners were brilliant - incredibly compassionate. I could trust everything they said to me, even when they gave their terminal prognosis'. I was held in denial for a great many days, but I still trusted their advice. Our world has sadly moved on it seems, with money now overruling the precious gift which is 'life'... so long as it is permitted.

I remember when the NHS was first created. It gave a new lease of entitlement to those who had been previously deemed unworthy of existing - the poor. My family could have easily been classed as paupers; regardless, we were still proud of where we came from. We loved one another and our lifestyle, even if we only had one hot meal every few days or so. Blood is thicker than water. Blood is more precious than any man-made currency. Being allowed to live should not revolve around the amount of cash one has in their pockets, or of what fruitful social status they possess. How times have changed since those days, and not necessarily for the better.

"I'll get you cleaned up, Isabella... won't take long." assures Marius, with some obvious reluctance. "The wipes shouldn't be too cold. I'll be gentle with you, sweetheart."

"Be careful when wiping around the dressing, Marius. The soap in those wipes will sting like merry-hell." How very considerate of you, Zanna. I can't imagine they – OH MY! She certainly wasn't telling fibs! A searing surge of pain sweeps across my buttocks. Lord, it feels like Marius has ran a hot iron across them! What kind of soap are you using, old chap, battery acid? "Be careful, mate. Isabella's wincing pretty bad there."

"Sorry, Isabella." Apology accepted, my dear. But, please can you stop rubbing that dreadful thing over me? You may as well be using sandpaper. "We can't have you getting any sorer than you are. I'm so sorry if I'm hurting you." Don't be remorseful. I know you're doing this deed to help me. My only wish is that you'd be quicker in finishing this present act of torture. "Can you pass over the barrier cream please, Zan? I just need a small amount."

There's a fleeting moment of respite, where only the surrounding air makes contact with my body, and then comes a freezing deluge of gloopy grease that's quickly spread by Marius upon my lower back and tailbone. Oh, it's *disgusting*. Whatever this cream is meant to be, it has the texture of margarine – *repulsive*! After a few more seconds of understandable disgust, the burning sensation dwindles as the cream gradually seeps into my skin. I don't mind it so much now, although it's not something I'd like to get used to.

"You're doing really well, Isabella. We're almost finished." Praise be, Zanna. All I want is to be left alone with Beethoven and his exquisite symphonies, the releasing impact of Catherine Cookson's picturesque landscapes, and the promise of my family being reunited with me. That would be so wonderful. "I'm gonna have a chat with Hollie about these positional turns, Marius. It's not fair on Isabella being put through this carry on every few hours." Good girl. I like you even more now. You've gone right-up in my estimations. "She's getting too distressed. Her breathing sounds different from when we first came on shift, doesn't it?"

"Yeah. I didn't want to mention anything, though." Marius, you're making this melancholy of yours into such a filthy habit. I'll be back to my normal self in no-time. Just you wait and see. I'm full of surprises, I am. "Where's Hollie at? The buzzer's been going off for a good while now."

"Who knows? Isabella should be Hollie's top priority." comments Zanna, sharply. Being so uncouth doesn't suit such a spritely girl, if my honest opinion matters? Nurse Emerson will be undoubtedly busy? She doesn't come across to me as being a shirker, anyway. "We've still got all the charts to write up. There's not enough time in the day to do all the things asked of us."

"All you can do is try your best, Zan. You cope better than I do." The pair chuckle and then, within a daunting air of tension, both take turns to raise my arms up into the air. "Let's get this new nightgown on for you, Isabella. You'll be comfy and snug in no time."

'Comfy and snug' sadly do not come into fruition over the next three minutes that follow, believe me. Before I know it, my upper half is exposed for all to see. Gracious, I do hope that I'm wearing a bra? It doesn't feel like I am. The muscles in my arms have evidently seized, making it near-impossible to straighten them, which is what Marius and Zanna are desperately trying to do. The new nightgown feels icy-cold on my skin, and my arms won't stop trembling from the exertion wrought on them. How much longer must this go on for? Is there any need?

After another polite warning from Marius, I'm carefully repositioned onto my back, now fully clothed and utterly shattered. Beethoven's music once again takes precedence. Thank the Lord. I can no longer hear Zanna or Marius, only some frantic scribbling sounds nearby. One of them turns my music's volume back up, then returns to whatever they're scribing. Oh, this is fantastic. Beethoven's Moonlight Sonata soon enters my ears, and I'm again transported to a dream-like plain where nothing can bother me. This is perfect. This is wonderful. This... is all I desire.

"Nearly done, Isabella. I just need to comb your hair." says Zanna, seemingly from a distance by her diminutive voice. A series of thin barbs are then harshly run along my scalp, as if in attempt to remove every strand of hair from it. Bloody hell, Zanna. Are you using a fork to comb my hair, girl? Ouch! "You've got such a good head of hair, Isabella. I'll be back shortly with your lunch, darling. You enjoy your music in the meantime."

What if I don't want any lunch? What if I don't want your help? What actual choice do I hold on these matters? As my consciousness starts to recollect more clearly, I ponder as to what influence I still hold over my own life, albeit a decimated one. For some strange reason, I'm reminded of when Robert would occasionally discuss the horrific scenes he had witnessed back in World War Two, during his time spent in liberating the Bergen-Belsen concentration camp. What a dreadful memory to recall, though what an even-worse memory for my husband to hold onto... and he did.

My Bobby rarely spoke of what he saw at that abhorrent place; it was far-too traumatic for him to relive, especially when sober. I never pressed Robert for his sorrowful insight but, now and then, he would willingly grant me a small glimpse into the evil he had contended with there, in that pit of Hell, in that lowest depth of human travesty. The scenes Bobby would describe were far-more gruesome than anything a Hollywood director could imagine: men, women and children, most starved and robbed of what rights they once possessed, all incarcerated within a state-led campaign to tear away their God-given gift to exist - to be free - to have a will of their own. I'm in no way suffering as those unfortunate souls did, but I can relate to their helplessness and their reliance on a fading scrape of hope. My body has become such an entity of internment, given it no longer answers to my wantful desires. This is simply awful. This is not living.

I fleet my half-open eyes across the empty room lain ahead, searching, yearning for any sign of my husband and our two children. Where *are* they? Have they forsaken me? Do I deserve to be forgotten? I'd even welcome Agnes' company now, which is bloody saying something.

"I wouldn't worry too much about Isabella's dressing." assures Nurse Emerson, appearing again out of the blue. When did she come back? "There's little chance of her wound healing. So long as the dressing is covering the site of her wound, then it should be fine."

"Thanks, Hollie." mumbles Zanna. I thought she and Marius had long gone? "Isabella's due some lunch. I went to get it, but Irene needed the loo. I'll go and fetch it for her now."

"Okay." whispers my nurse. "If Isabella doesn't accept it - don't worry. I need to go myself, Zan. I've still got half a med's round to finish off. Let me know how things go, and don't worry."

Nurse Emerson and Zanna leave without any further word. However, Zanna soon reappears with something clasped in her hands; it's a bleached-white bowl, and God only knows what contents lie within it. I flicker my eyelids subserviently, again like an infant willing their mother's providing bosom towards them. I'm holding out on the small and ever-unlikely chance that Zanna has brought me those fish and chips, which I so do desire. Come on, my girl. Appease this renewed appetite. And for goodness sake, do NOT give me anymore of those sloppy eggs you offered earlier.

"Here's your lunch, Isabella." I'm getting excited, my dear. What delightful meal do you have in store for me? "It's puréed Hot Dogs with mashed potatoes and carrots... one your favourites."

HOT DOGS? I swipe my face away in refute, which itself takes some doing, and I'm not bothered in the slightest if this causes any offense to poor Zanna. I have a right to refuse and plan to implement this to its fullest extent. Like you, my sweet-sweet Zanna, I'd rather starve to death than to eat this abomination. As if she can't take the hint, Zanna eagerly presses the mushy meat against my lips. In response, I splutter my tongue against the intrusive teaspoon, wishing to cast it far away and never to return. Eventually, after a few more attempts, Zanna seems to have accepted my disapproval of this vomit-inducing meal. She moves away from me with a look of upmost despair, a look I shan't forget soon. Oh, I feel terrible now.

I'm so very sorry, petal. Honestly, I am. Although, I'm afraid you won't be able to change my mind on this matter. I can assure you that nothing will convince me to consume that disgusting food, at least, not while it's in that present form. To refuse is the only right I have left. Fall asleep, Isabella. Take yourself back to that serene cottage in Northumberland, where Robert and your children are waiting for you, where you can be free. Wouldn't that be perfect, old girl? Wouldn't that... be wonderful?

IN THEIR HANDS

Gracious! What *was* that dreadful bang? It sounded as if my bedroom door had been deliberately slammed shut. As well as being frightened by this sudden racket, I'm also very annoyed and for two specific reasons. One: I wasn't given enough chance to fall back into a deep and meaningful sleep. I was so hoping to find myself back at that lovely cottage again, with my children and Robert. Two: it certainly came across as being a malicious act. When others have visited me today, none of them entered or left with such pomp and circumstance. Goodness, can't people see that I'm trying to rest here, to regain my strength as duly instructed by Nurse Emerson? The rotten cretins. A little peace and quiet is all I ask for.

"Here we go..."

"Urgh, it reeks of piss in here. Doesn't it smell like a filthy litter box?"

Little, if anything, is given away to reveal who the perpetrators of this startling development are. All I can hear are some snapping sounds and the occasional shuffling of feet. In any civilised society, this would undoubtedly be considered as being most-rude and uncourteous. Don't these two know basic manners? My only solace lies in Beethoven's continuing support, though even his music now appears to be falling silent. I'm becoming scared again, an emotion usually foreign to me, well, at least before today it was.

"It's alright for Zanna and Marius to have a break, isn't it? What about us two? We're always covering for them lazy gits." A man with a surprisingly high-pitched voice says this, at least, I believe this person to be a man. It's very difficult to tell.

"Yeah, the *A-Team*! Don't talk to me about those skivers... Hollie's 'perfect' carers. It makes me sick how she insists on working with them all the time, instead of us. Who does Hollie think she is? Just because she has a pin, she thinks she knows everything. I've being doing this job for longer than Marius and Zanna. *I know what I'm doing.*" This response comes from a woman, I think? My observation again proves difficult to tell, since she sounds a great-deal more masculine than the other chap and is obviously a heavy smoker by her give-away crackles. Goodness, I can smell her stale tobacco from here, and *they* had the gaunt to say my room smelt of filth!

I try to open my eyes, despite some reluctance in wanting to discover who I am now faced against, but they seem to be sealed shut again. What's the chance of these charming people cleaning them up for me? I don't believe the odds are in my favour on this one. Prepare yourself for the worst, old girl. This is going to be an uneasy ride.

"Do you reckon it was Marius who put this crap music on?" sniggers the fellow. By what is he referring to in such a horrendous manner? Surely, he doesn't mean *my* choice in music? I have an impeccable taste. "It's so depressing. I'm not putting up with that while we're seeing to her. It's going straight off." My good sir, Beethoven is *not* rubbish. Don't you dare turn this Sonata off! You hear me? "Let's put some proper tunes on, yeah? Stick the radio on 99.5 FM. The 'Trance Hour' should be still on."

My ears immediately come under fire from some deafening white noise and then comes another, far-more offensive, sound. Beethoven's tranquil cellos have been sinfully replaced by a relentless, fast-paced drum and some girl wailing the same bloody words over and over again. *Hold me, Baby. Touch me, Baby. Yeah-yeah-yeah.* What utter tripe is this? Music these days has become so simple and boring. *This* is crap, my dears. Turn it off at once! I beg you.

"Thank God for that. I nearly slit my wrists there, mate. Who would want to listen to that Classical shit all day?" declares the gruffly-spoken woman. What a surprise. This day just keeps getting better. "This tune reminds me of when I went to Ibiza a few years

69

back. You can't beat dancing to some Old School tunes with a few, sly Vodkas on the go. You get me?" Her proceeding laughter grates on my nerves even more so than this torturous song does. Imagine rusty nails being dragged along a thin sheet of metal and you *still* wouldn't be close. This is excruciating! How am I meant to rest with all this dreadful noise? "Keep the radio's volume low, just in case one of the others walks past. There's plenty of snakes in the grass working this shift today. I've already been called into the office once this week. You're not allowed to have any fun in this place, are you?"

"What did you get called in for?"

"For having an 'abrupt attitude' towards other staff members and residents - *apparently*. It's a load of bollocks. I've done this job for twenty years. I could run this place blindfolded, and there'd be a few Judas' facing the sack if *I* were in charge."

"I'd best watch myself around you for now on." humours the chap. "Phwoar! That smell is getting worse, isn't it?"

"Let her fester in her own dirt for a little longer." orders the woman, presumably in reference to myself? I'm not... incontinent. I really don't know where that smell came from. Perhaps the drains outside are playing up? "It can make up for all the times when she attacked us, can't it? That's what you call 'Karma'. It's not like she's going anywhere, and it's nice how she can't whinge on at us anymore... the snobby cow. I could never get away with that posh accent of hers."

"Oh, yeah! She talked like Julie Andrews, didn't she?"

"Aye, all 'prim and proper'. But we know what she's really like. There's nothing upper-class about *her*."

As much as I have already grown to detest these new acquaintances of mine, it would have been nice for them to show *some* pleasant acknowledgment towards me. What are their names? Are they Carers, or are they just some scoundrels who have been sent here to drive me utterly bonkers? By the looks of it, I've become invisible as well as being an invalid now. Thankfully, they've turned the music down a slight tad, though it's still bloody torturous. Oh, my head. It's throbbing terribly.

"We need to turn her onto the right-hand side. You know, I honestly don't get why people make such a fuss over Isabella now." And I don't like where this is going, although it is some relief to hear my name being mentioned. So, I *do* exist. "She's been nothin' but a pain in the arse since she first arrived. How many scars have you got from her? I've got a beauty on my left forearm where she bit me last year."

"Too many!" snaps the beastly woman in response. Seeing her is inconsequential, believe me, as I can easily gather that she has a cold heart. Who would willingly want to look upon a monster if they had the choice not to? However, I can imagine that this was not always the case. People aren't born to hate, they simply learn that over time. I bet she's an ugly so-and-so, mind you, as it would perfectly reflect her wicked personality. "We don't get paid enough for the beatings we get, mate. You need frigging 'danger money' or better training to do this job. It's a joke, and we're the daft muppets who put up with it." Really? You're hardly working in a war zone, my dear. I'd have loved to have seen you do one of my shifts back in the ordnance factory – then moan. That was *real* dangerous work. I'm hardly going to explode in your face like a grenade, am I? Lord knows it, I wish I could. "We've put up with her aggression, for how long now? Ever since Isabella's gotten worse, everyone's taken a sudden liking to her. Bunch of hypocrites. *We* know what's she's like, don't we? She'd better not pull any funny moves on me today. I can't be arsed for any of her usual tricks."

"It would be our luck, wouldn't it?" interjects the weasel-like fellow. "You watch, I bet she'll give us a good slap or two. Leopards can't change their spots, and Isabella knows what she's doing."

The pair of you, *please*, relinquish your scorn. For one thing, I haven't got an aggressive bone in my body. I'd never lift a finger to anyone. Nevertheless, what I *would* like to raise with you is this subtle conundrum: if your job does involve caring for others, then does that not also involve dealing with their emotions, their personalities - both good and bad? When I worked at the ordnance factory, myself and the other girls were under an immense amount of pressure. It was very stressful work. Most of us would feel like crying, and sometimes we'd regrettably take our frustrations out on one another. We were at war, after-all, and war plays havoc on one's ability to cope with everyday tasks. Regardless, we still held an innate respect for each other, and those debilitating feelings were quickly turned into positive ones. Above all else, we 'Angels' understood that you had to take the easy days with the hard. Look, what I'm trying to say is: to be able to show empathy towards another human being, who is suffering, is one the greatest skills to possess in life. I believe this is something you should both strive to understand, my dears. It would certainly change your lives for the better, if not improve my current treatment whilst in your hands.

"She's grunting now - *see!*" sneers the whiny man. "She's still got that nasty streak in her! Watch yourself."

"You know what the answer to that is, don't you?" declares the woman, with a cackling voice similar to that of an old hag. Is it a Full Moon today? Only, I'm sensing some lunacy here. "We'll do what we've got to do with her – and quick. No messing around – *right*? I'm not pissing about with putting any cream on her either, I mean, what's the point? That wound of hers is never going to heal. Isabella's hurt us plenty of times before, so now *she* can suffer to make up for it. Like I said, it's only *Karma*."

Dear me. I can't see much hope in my lecture being acted upon. It doesn't matter where life takes you, old girl, there's always someone there to put a bloody damper on it. Don't bother opening your eyes. Pretend to sleep. Maybe then they'll disappear? Where have Zanna and Marius vanished to? Where is John and Nurse Emerson? I could do with their kind words and actions at this moment. I could really do with my Bobby being here.

"Have you got the wipes ready?"

"Yeah."

"You hold her hands, just in case she lashes out again."

"You give me all the good jobs, don't you?"

"Shut it! Get the covers off her and get started. I want to get a break at some point today. I'm gagging for a cigarette."

"I thought you'd quit smoking?"

"Doing *this* job... no chance."

Aren't they going to talk to me at all? Out of nowhere, an unexpected and extremely cold draft tears across my lower body. The bedsheets have been ripped away from me as if they were aflame, and without any warning given by these so-called Carers. What are they doing to me? Do they get some kind of twisted enjoyment from treating me this way? The freezing breeze is then added onto by an equally frigid pair of hands, themselves forced against my tender skin in a manner akin to a butcher casually preparing their slaughtered meat. I'm suddenly cast over onto my side. I can't fight back, no matter how hard I try. There's a ripping sensation upon my exposed hip, and then comes a deafening wail from the wicked woman.

"God, she *has* shit herself. You... *dirty* old woman, Isabella!" I'm not sure which is more offensive, being called *dirty* or *old*, because I am neither. I categorically do not suffer from incontinence. How many times must I say this? Anyway, your foul language and approach are a great deal worse than any bodily function I could present to you. What vile human beings you both are. Leave me alone. Leave me alone, I say! "Pass the wipes over, mate. Bloody hell, she stinks like a wet dog."

"Phwoar, Isabella! You're ramming, love." giggles the man, as he cruelly throws a sodden set of cold tissues upon my thigh, only adding to the discomfort and embarrassment already felt. They're laughing at me, I know they are. How could this possibly get any worse? Oh, Isabella. What have you done to deserve this? "How's her dressing?"

"There's a bit of dirt on it, but it won't need changing." snorts the woman. I'm starting to see humanity's worst side in these two, and I can't wait for it to end. "Hollie can sort the dressing out later. Isn't that what she gets paid extra for? Hand the pad over..."

Another pair of hands clamp onto my ankles and arms, restraining me against all further resistance. Again, without any forewarning, I'm cast over onto my back. An instant, agonising wave of pain ripples throughout my spine and extremities. The pain somehow enters every cell within my body, soon leaving me with a sickening sensation to then dwell upon. Lord, this is unbearable. How much longer must I endure this evil for?

"Drag her up the bed a bit. I want to get this pad on before she shits again... the dirty bitch." Sticks and stone, my dear. You might want to look in the mirror, yourself? "Sod using a slide sheet, we haven't got time for that. Hurry up with getting her pad."

"Give me a sec!" retorts the man, hinting at some unease in his squeaky voice. "I think we'd better use the slide sheet, mind. Isabella's skin is proper thin now."

"Never mind using that stupid thing, just get on with it!"

"Okay..."

In a single movement, and without any obvious consideration, I'm swiftly reminded of my infant-like state again by these two morons. The malicious creatures raise my legs up high into the air, rolling me further onto my shoulders and neck, just like a baby having their nappy changed. The pressure on my upper spine immediately renders my pain receptors into overdrive. Oh, this is awful. This is not living. Get off me, you *beasts*!

"Howay then, pull 'em up!"

"Hold on! I don't want to catch her. She's wriggling all over the place!" A good wrestle is the best I can do. Lord knows that I'd like to manage more in my efforts. "Stay still, Isabella!"

"Hold onto her tighter! Do I have to do everything for you?"

"I don't want to catch her with my nails... or get done for restraining her."

"It'll stay between me and you. Grab her hands... I'll sort the rest out."

74

A sweet moment of vengeance is now granted to me against these two serpents. One of them motions a slithering hand against my fingers, apparently to intensify their restraint on me, and I jump on this opportunity like an excitable fool. With all strength that remains in my wasting muscles, I grip onto their plump flesh and then drive my nails hard into it. There is some resistance but, by Jove, I *will* make my displeasure known. Take that!

"Isabella!! Get her off me!

"Stop it, Isabella! *Stop* it!"

"She can't be that ill, can she? Not if she can do this to me!"

"Get your hands off him, you little bitch! How'd you like it?"

"Jesus! You've cut me, Isabella!"

It was certainly worth your valiant effort, old girl. You got the lad. Although, sadly, not where it hurts most. Let this be a lesson to yourselves. You are not superior to me. We... are equals. You may be in a position of power, where I in comparison am trapped within a fortress of vulnerability, but that does not give you any right to force your will upon me. I am truly remorseful for hurting you, my boy, though your wound shall soon heal, whereas the mental scars I've received today shall likely not.

"There!" The woman crushes and then cracks my fingers to pry them off, sending another surge of agonising pain throughout this broken body of mine. "We don't get paid enough for this shit. Stop moaning, Isabella. It's your own fault! I had to do that." she cackles again. "Who knows, this might just teach you a lesson for being so nasty to us over the years, mightn't it?"

They are tossing me around on this bed now like someone kneading bread dough. Gracious, how can *this* be classified as care? Is *this* what I have amounted to, a soulless vessel, a person not worthy of any sympathetic care? Am I just another nuisance, another burden to add onto their busy schedule? I don't know. Within my mind, I perform a piercing wail at the very top of my lungs, but only the faintest murmur leaves from my parched lips. They're laughing at me still. Just give up, Isabella. Stop fighting, old girl. Your feelings and quality of life don't concern them in the slightest. Nothing does, it appears, so long as it involves *you*. Where is Robert? Where is my darling husband at? Save me, Bobby.

"She's took a canny chunk out of my hand." whimpers the man. "There was no need for that, Isabella."

"Don't just stand there gawking, bring the pad over so we can get finished. Hopefully, we won't need to see her again after today." That's a mutual feeling, dear. I can assure you. "You're only bleeding a little bit. Stop being so soft."

A pair of papery undergarments are then forcefully thrust up and along my legs, which are followed by a new and overwhelming pain. You know, these 'Carers' are so very different to the others, to those who have shown only kindness to me. Not everyone is bad, though these two are certainly proving to be an exception.

"You've caught her leg... for Christ's sake!"

"I didn't mean to!"

"*Shit*! There's blood everywhere!"

Something warm begins to trickle down my left thigh. It's wet and is spreading across my knees like a viscous stream. Don't say...

"How are we going to explain her getting a skin tear? IDIOT!"

"I didn't *mean* to do it! She's squirming all over the place. She's slashed my hand! What else was I meant to do?" Shouldn't you be apologising to me, my dear boy, for causing such a terrible wound to myself? No, you just worry about how this will impact you and your friend here. I'll carry on pretending that nothing has happened, that you have treated me with the greatest of respect and dignity. Lies are quite foreign to my usual nature. However, if lying will get shot of you, then I will gladly play along. "We'll tell Hollie that we found her this way, *right*? Isabella's been known to scratch herself when agitated."

"It's not the best excuse, but it'll have to do. Come on, let's get out of here before anyone hears her groaning. Don't forget to turn the radio off. Put some of that crappy Chopin music back on."

76

The next few moments of silence come as a total relief. I'm not too concerned by the wound upon my leg as, maybe, it will draw back some nicer strangers, people who will remind me of humanity's more loving side? Wouldn't that be ideal? I do hope Zanna and Marius return, my doting saviours. I really miss them.

There's a cautious knock at my door, then more footsteps. Lord *please*, with all your mercy, don't say it is those horrid demons coming back to taunt me some more?

"Isabella? It's just me again." John? Thank goodness! I was getting rather worried there for a moment. "I need to have a look at your leg, sweetheart. *Apparently*, you've been scratching at it?"

Lies, my dear! They've been telling you beastly lies! Oh, Isabella. Speak! Try to form even a coherent whisper, it'd be better than nothing. John *must* be told of what they did to you. He comes across as an intelligent man. He will see through their twisted tales, surely? John will know that you wouldn't do something so silly as to scratch yourself. You can trust him, old girl.

"We found her that way." Oh, that bloody woman! Shoo! Be gone! "She was distressed when we came in to reposition her. Hasn't Hollie got Isabella's chill-pills yet? She needs to pull her finger out, doesn't she?"

"Isabella wasn't this distressed when Hollie and I left her." John sounds like he's scowling. He must be seeing through their fibs? Good lad. Teach that horrid wretch a lesson or two. "By *chill-pills*, you mean Isabella's Midazolam? Marius has gone out to collect her anticipatory drugs a few minutes ago, instead of going on his break."

"Oh aye, *Mr. Perfect*?" sneers the woman. "He can't do anything wrong, can he? Marius is nothing but a bloody brown-noser. You need to watch yourself around him, John. He's the one who grassed me up to management."

"If you have a problem with Marius, then you'll need to take it up with Sally. Personally, I can't see how him giving up his free time to get Isabella's medications is brown-nosing." You tell her, John.

"Anyway, let's have a look at this skin tear of yours, Mrs. Cunningham."

In comparison to those horrific moments earlier, John removes my duvet cover with the gentlest of swipes. He peels it away as if he were disarming a bomb, whilst showing only empathy and consideration towards me. Oh, how I miss those glorious days when I worked at the ordnance factory. John would have made such a good technician, without any question.

"It's pretty bad, isn't it?" remarks the woman, quite calmly. Doesn't that say a great deal about her character? "I swear down, John. It was like that when we first looked at her."

"That's a very *significant* tear." scowls John. "It's going to be difficult knitting the skin back together, from what I can make out." John appears angry – seething almost. I couldn't be more grateful for him being here with me. That awful wave of anxiety is starting to ease off. Breathe, Isabella. You can relax now. "There's not a cat-in-hell's chance that she has done this to herself. Isabella can barely move, for one thing. Are you honestly telling me the truth? If you've caught her, just tell me."

"What are you implying?" shrieks the repulsive witch. "Are you saying that *we* did this?"

"It doesn't matter what I think or say, just wait until Hollie takes a look. That's more than just a little scratch, as how *you* described it to me."

"You can put a dressing on, can't you? I thought Seniors could?"

"Yeah, I can, but I'd prefer for Hollie to see it. Do me a favour and press the emergency call button, please. I'd suggest you stay here until either Hollie or Sally arrive. You might have some explaining to do." There's a lengthy pause between my Carers, where only their frantic breaths endure. I can only imagine what terrified thoughts must be going through that woman's mind. You reap what you sow, my dear. "Now's the time to think about what has *actually* taken place here. Hollie will want to know exactly what has happened, so make sure you get your facts right."

"I'm not lying! Christ, I've given up my own break to help her out, y'know? I'm gagging for a fag."

"You can go for a cigarette break after Hollie's seen Isabella. I'd seriously suggest you wait here until she comes."

Bravo, John. I can hear that woman's breathing getting louder and more desperate. Perhaps now she may realise the errors of her ways? Actions have consequences. Karma is a... well, I'm not one for swearing, you get the picture. A soothing, warm tissue is then pressed along my leg, gradually easing the burning torrent that continues to linger there. I'm presuming that it is John doing this kind act, as I'd doubt that dreadful woman would dare come near me now. He is cleaning what blood has been spilled with such diligence and is doing a bloody good job of it. I don't feel any discomfort at all from his wandering movements, unlike the rough swipes made by those other two creatures. There is always good where there is bad, Isabella. There's no need to drug me, Nurse Emerson. I feel so much better and more relaxed now, simply on account of John's empathetic display. This tenderness *would* have persisted, if it were not for that loud ringing noise. Goodness me, what *is* that terrible racket?

"I'm here!" pants Nurse Emerson. "What's the problem, John? What's happened?" Another of my guardian angels has arrived to save the day. Nurse Emerson approaches me with a sickening yelp, cementing into my conscience that this wound must be worse than I had first assumed. "What the... what has happened to you, Isabella? Are you okay?" Not really, but we all have bad days now and then, don't we? "Was it you that pressed the emergency call button, John?"

"I asked Brenda to activate it. I'm not comfortable about dressing such a serious wound. Sorry." John sighs and then kneels himself beside me, clasping onto the cushioned bed rail and my nearest hand as he does so. As an unexpected virtue, it seems that the tears which have formed in my eyes, during those terrifying moments earlier, have helped to remove whatever glue sealed them shut. I can open my eyelids fully now, and I do so with the swiftest of effort. I allow for the blurriness to settle over a few seconds, then focus on the sorrowful expression John now shows across his face. It's not a pleasant experience to be surrounded by such a high level of sorrow, although, I can sympathise with him.

"Don't worry." assures Nurse Emerson to John, with an endearing smile. "It's my job to help Isabella with her dressings. Do you know how this injury happened?"

"No. I haven't had a decent explanation as to how Isabella's received this tear, in all fairness. *Apparently*, she 'scratched herself', according to Brenda." John lifts his eyesight to glare at someone stood behind me. From the responding silence he receives, it is easy to gather that this person must be 'Brenda', the same monster who did little to prevent my injury. Silence can speak louder than any words, my darlings. Guilt always seeps through the most-convincing of lies.

"I'll speak with you later, Brenda. You can leave now." declares Nurse Emerson, in a bitter and concerning tone. Again, there is a silent response from that vile woman. If what she and her friend have done to me makes them change their ways, then I shall be very glad indeed. That way, at least, my present discomfort will not be suffered in vain. "This is bad, John. Can you go to the clinic and fetch back some wound strips, sterilized water, gauze and dry dressings for me, please? I'll get Isabella cleaned up in the meantime."

"Sure. Thanks, Hollie."

Nurse Emerson, like John, is taking every precaution to reduce my displeasure, which is not a simple feat by any given means. My faith in humanity is being restored once again, though only just. I still don't know how or why I've ended up in this predicament. I've still not seen any sign of my husband or beautiful children. Hold on, Isabella. Think this one through. They're all grown up now, are your children. Gracious, where did *that* insight come from? It's like trying to piece a jigsaw together, and the more I complete this puzzle the more I wish I hadn't. It's certainly a harrowing game you're taking part it in, old girl. Maybe you should just stop arranging those pieces and go back to sleep? Rid yourself of this awful existence. I'm too scared to do anything.

"I've got them, Hollie." says John, enthusiastically.

"Thanks." Nurse Emerson carries out her duties immediately, and with very delicate precision. I instantly grimace on her pulling the torn fragments of skinfolds back together, her own sordid jigsaw game. Nurse Emerson knows what she's doing. Don't panic yourself as such, Isabella. That tugging *is* bloody awful! Oh, dear me.

After my unusual massage finishes, comes a sealing strip of sticky fabric that my nurse carefully knits the wound up with. I can't see this action but, by golly, I can feel every action made. "There's not as much blood here as I thought there'd be."

"Really?" comments John, aghast. "Saying that, Isabella has barely drunk anything over the past couple of days. There can't be much fluid left in her body?"

"You'd be surprised." adds Nurse Emerson, as she completes her embroidery work. "Can you pass me the gauze and dry dressings over, please. I'm almost done."

All this talk of blood today is making me utterly nauseous, regardless of whether it is my own or not. I've never been any good at coping with such things. When my son, David, was just a boy, he fell from his bike one day and grazed his knee something rotten. Robert had to see to our child. I simply couldn't bear to look at the injury, or at how upset my David was. Goodness, I felt so guilty about being such a coward. As his mother, it should have been me tending to David, but I just couldn't. I learned a valuable lesson that day. I learned that I'm not as strong as I once thought I was, especially during my stubborn teen years. I'm not strong at this precise moment in time either, though I pray this ailment will pass. Mother and Father didn't survive Cancers, God rest their soul, though maybe I will? Nature works in mysterious ways. Come on, Robert. Where are you, my beloved?

81

"What should we do about this situation?" John sounds terribly nervous, and I don't see why. He hasn't done anything wrong to me. "Isabella hasn't hurt herself, Hollie. Those two..."

"I'll speak with them once we're finished seeing to Isabella." comments Nurse Emerson, meekly. "I might need to call the Safeguarding team about this. As a matter of fact, I think I will." she sighs. "It's clear to me, what's happened here."

"I've warned Sally before about Brenda and Carl." implores John. "It's proving they've done things that's the problem. I doubt they'll get away with it, at least not this time."

"There are procedures to follow, John. Trust me, I'll make sure the facts come out." Nurse Hollie then gently pats at John on his shoulders, clarifying some agreeance with his concerns. I wish I could do the same. Perhaps, if I try to smile at them, they'll notice? "I'd really appreciate it if you could keep a close eye on Isabella for the rest of the day. I'll know then that she's in good hands with you, Marius and Zanna."

"We try our best," laments John, "but it's not always easy. By rights, one of us should be staying with her all the time. It's horrible having to leave Isabella alone in this room. We just don't have enough staff on today to manage that."

"Pop in as often as you can. I know you've got a lot on this afternoon."

All this fuss being made over me. I don't want to get anyone into trouble - Lord no. I'm a staunch advocate in forgiving others for their wrongdoings. You can't be completely bad, just like you can't be completely good. What are you saying, Isabella? The way those demons treated you...

"As if Isabella needed a skin tear to add onto everything else that she's going through right now. At least her wound is all cleaned up and dressed now, thanks to your skills, Hollie. You've done a smashing job. You've knitted the skin back together so well - I'm impressed!" Oh, John. You're going to make me sick, my dear. I'd rather you didn't discuss the wound anymore, if being truthful.

"You're listening to Chopin again, Isabella?" smiles John. "Would you like me to turn it up for you?" Why certainly, my dear fellow. Chopin's music is the greatest medicine you could offer me. "How about one of his preludes? They're the best ones, aren't they?"

Music has become my only form of escape; a method of coping through this persevering madness, especially now that this body of mine no longer works as it once did. Chopin is a wonderful elixir to my ailments. Lord, I'd even settle for Mozart or Debussy, if their graceful tunes could take me away from here, away from this staggering purgatory. Close your eyes, Isabella. Drift off again and dream of that lovely cottage, of your family. Those beautiful images shall soon rescue you from all this. Ignore the searing torment of your new wound. Ignore how those wicked Carers treated you. Wouldn't that be perfect? Wouldn't that be wonderful?

MI-DAZZLED

I'm engrossed within a dream-like state again, but not at the wonderous cottage setting as I had so greatly desired. I'm back home. This is the house where Robert and I first moved to, once we made the decision to live in Newton Escomb, after the war. I'm sat at our kitchen table. The smell of beef stew cooking initially overwhelms my senses, although it is soon replaced by the faint waft of Robert's cigar smoke nearby. Where is he? Where is my Bobby?

I follow the trail of burning tobacco, which eventually leads outside into our little garden. It's starting to rain. Where *is* my darling husband? Suddenly, there's a terrible feeling in the pit of my stomach that something isn't right. I look across to where Robert always grew his yellow roses, only to find him nurturing our son, David, in his arms. I remember now. David was awfully sick that day, and instead of resting he had decided to get some fresh air.

"Isabella," says Robert, with a haunting look in his eyes. "Why were you not watching him?" I stutter to a point where no words can leave from my mouth, utterly compelled by shame and remorse. David was asleep, at least he was, the last time I checked on him. "He needs his medicine, darling." I turn sharply to run back into our kitchen. There, on the countertop, sits a small bottle of pills. I clasp the bottle tightly in my hands, and then return to my fever-riddled son. "Give him two tablets, Isabella. He's burning up." David's eyes swoon from left to right, clearly under a veil of delirium. Oh, my beautiful boy. Mother's here. Take your medicine, it will make you better. "Be firmer with him. He *must* take his medicine, Isabella. The doctor said so."

David clamps his lips shut. I try desperately to force even just one tablet into his mouth, but my boy resists all attempts made. I begin to despair, knowing that if David continues this way he will only deteriorate. Be a good boy. *Please*, take your medicine. Mammy couldn't bear it if anything were to happen to you. Robert simply remains silent, leaving me to dwell on what fate my lie in store for only son.

I glare down upon the bottle of pills with a look of pure disdain, though Robert stares at it with nothing but a glimmer of hope. I know in my heart that David recovered from this illness, despite Bobby and I fearing the worst for several days. I've never been a fan of taking medications, usually because I always end up suffering from the 'rare' side-effects. All those drugs Doctor Kain stopped for me, what were they for? Did I really need so many?

Without warning, I start to hear some music playing and then, almost instantaneously, I am taken back into reality. The piece being performed is Debussy's *Clair de Lune*. Who in their right mind put Debussy on? Sadly, he's not one of my most-favourite composers, but I'd rather listen to this than that God-awful dance music those two brutes forced on me earlier. It was worse than water torture, that was.

"You've slipped down the bed again, Isabella. That's three times today." scolds John, though humorously. It's not my fault if this bed has been placed on a slant. Why don't you do something about it, my dear? "For someone who is immobile, you certainly shift about a great deal, Isabella. How'd you end up in that position?" Why is he chuckling on like an asthmatic pig? You shouldn't moan, Isabella. We don't want another tense atmosphere to arise now, do we? "She's still got some fight in her...hasn't she, Hollie? I wouldn't want Isabella to be any different. It wouldn't be right."

"Would you want to be stuck in a nursing bed all day?" replies Nurse Emerson, sympathetically, and with a gentle snigger. I like this joyful side to her. This makes a pleasant change to how else things have been today. "It can't be comfortable, can it?" Not particularly. But, please don't replace my mattress. I'm fairly comfortable, despite how I may come across. "Shall we get you back into a comfier position, Isabella?"

A weird, slithery feeling soon shifts under my entire body. The next thing I know, John and Emerson count to three and then slide me gracefully up the bed. That was quite a ride, I dare say. Within some matter of seconds, like when a magician removes their mystical cloth from underneath a set table, the plastic sheet beneath me is swiftly taken away. What a peculiar experience – and quite fun.

"That's better, sweetheart. Your new slide sheet certainly did the trick, didn't it?"

"Right then, John." interjects Nurse Emerson. "First, we need to sterilise the area of skin where this butterfly needle is going. We've got the syringes ready; the drugs; the Kardex..."

NEEDLES! Stick them in yourself, my dear. I don't need any needles *or* drugs for that matter. I'm very settled listening to Debussy – really – I am! I wouldn't dare lie to you, would I? Where is that cup of tea I was promised? I'm absolutely famished, not to mention sick of these experiments you're trying out on me.

"What are those medications for again, Hollie? I haven't been a Senior Carer for that long. I'm still getting used to all the names." mumbles John, bashfully. "I have an idea, but can you explain them to me?"

"Of course, John. I don't mind doing that at all." gleams my nurse, like a wizened tutor. "The Midazolam will help to settle Isabella's agitation, and Hyoscine is for her secretions..." SECRETIONS? What exactly am I secreting? It's bad enough with you randomly wiping my arse - *now what*? "It should help to alleviate the build-up of mucus, and to reduce the likely risk of aspiration. The only problem with Hyoscine is it can increase the risk of dehydration, something which Isabella is dangerously close to. However, the rattling in her throat is getting worse by the hour. We'll need to remind the other Carers to keep Isabella off her back, and to ensure that the bed is elevated properly." A drawn-out pause then follows. "It's not looking too good, is it? Bless her. The speed of Isabella's deterioration is unprecedented." I'm rapidly falling out of favour with you, Nurse Emerson. Are you trying to make me panic or even vomit on purpose? You're not far from achieving this. If I do become sick, be wary that you are in the direct-line of projection. "The Levomepromazine is for anti-sickness, but she doesn't warrant any yet." I'd beg to differ, darling. Just keep talking about these things and we'll see. Where is Robert at? He should have been here by now. If I *am* sick, my Bobby can help me with some good old Bi-Carb and milk. There's no need for any drugs. I assure you. "Morphine is for... well." There's that awkward pause again. "You know what Morphine is for, don't you?" John muffles something back, amongst a nervous burst of laughter. For a burly fellow, he has such a feminine chuckle. "These make up Isabella's anticipatory drugs. I'll explain more about them when we finish. Can you do me a favour and make a note of the time on Isabella's Kardex, please? 15:30pm."

I am being, albeit legally, turned into a bloody drug addict, aren't I? This is all I need. I'm *not* in pain or agitated... am I? Pull yourself together, Isabella, you're rambling on like a buffoon again. John and Nurse Emerson have worked wonders on you so far. You *need* to trust them. You must not allow for that awful experience earlier to make you so paranoid. You don't want to end up in some lunatic's asylum, do you? You're in their expert hands now, as David was in yours that dreadful time.

"Should I roll Isabella towards me?" queries John, in a startled fashion. I can already feel his hands wandering over my fragile skin in preparation. Mind my legs, dearie, they've already been torn once today. "You'll be putting the butterfly on her lower back, won't you?"

"Yes. It's to stop Isabella pulling it out, for one thing, and to also reduce any possible discomfort. The needle will rest in her subcutaneous tissue – her fat." Nurse Emerson! I have always maintained a lean and slender figure. You'll have a right-old job on your hands to find any fat on me. I bid you the best of luck. "The main issue we're faced with here, is the problem of Isabella having barely any body fat. I'll need to be careful." I told you so, didn't I? Don't say that I didn't warn you, Nurse. "We'll roll her towards you on three, John. One... Two.... *Three*."

Over I go onto my opposite side, like a sausage being fried and tossed about in a pan. What a ridiculous comparison to make, Isabella, really. Saying that, are you much different to an old banger? Your muscles *are* as mushy as sausage meat and locked within a thin layer of skin which you presently have no control over. I've never liked sausages... bloody disgusting things.

"Her respiratory rate is going up, Hollie." comments John, himself forever being the bearer of reassuring news. "The Midazolam will help with that, won't it?"

"It should do." Nurse Emerson wipes something warm and wet across my lower back. A few moments afterwards, she then dries me with a softer material that feels a little like cotton. It's lovely and, in a welcomed sense, reminds me of tending to my infant children many years ago. *I'm* just like a baby now, aren't I? It's so awful being this vulnerable. I feel so sorry for anyone else who is immobile. To move freely is an ability that, until now, I've taken for granted. You don't know what you've got until it's gone, they say. "Try keep her as still as you can, John. Otherwise, I might just stick the needle in you." Oh, that would be a pity, wouldn't it? Give and share alike, I say. "I'm going to place the needle in now. Where on Earth has that plaster gone to?"

"I've got it here, Hollie."

"Thanks."

I attempt to grind my teeth together in anticipation of this dreaded needle, although I stupidly forget at this point that there aren't any teeth in my mouth. What an utter shame this is, as I'd ensured that they were always well-cared for. All those years of brushing and flossing – wasted. I do hope that Robert will still kiss me, despite this unexpected change in my appearance. He better had. I carried on loving him after he lost an eye during the war. It never bothered me in the slightest that one eye constantly looked the other way. I even scolded others for mocking him. *In sickness and in health – 'til death do us part.* I shall never forsake our vows, Robert, and neither should you. Life can be so strange at times, but love conquers all trials. God help me if you won't.

"Will the needle hurt her?"

"It shouldn't do, John. The needle we're using is tiny. To be fair, Isabella must be in a considerable amount of pain already? I doubt that a little prick would do her any further harm." I can name a few 'little pricks' that have wrought me some pain over the years, my dears. Agnes, namely, being the prime suspect. Oh, do behave yourself, Isabella. You were never the best at comedy, not like Robert or David. Saying that, laughter *is* the best medicine, or so I've been led to believe, regardless of how useless I am at it.

On a more sombre note, I remember when Mother was placed into a hospice, not so long after her Cancer prognosis. She only found out about two weeks or so prior that the disease had spread from her lungs into her lymph glands, and that it was also an aggressive form... incurable. This revelation was a shock to all of us, especially me. I grew up with the naive notion that my parents would never die, like any other child protected by their innocence. Besides, no one else in our immediate family had suffered with Cancer, so why did my loving mother need to? Nobody on this planet deserves to go through what she did. Hence, why I'm not as religious anymore. Why would God allow for such a terrible disease as Cancer to exist? I don't know.

Agnes and I were completely beside ourselves, since neither of us could willingly accept nor comprehend what was taking pace. The peculiar thing was, our Father continued to smile and tell his corny jokes regardless, even when Mother couldn't laugh back at him anymore. One day, out of the blue, Father explained himself as we walked to Mother's hospice. It was on a dreary, November morning; it was a day of which I shall never forget. Father said: 'In life there are happy moments, as well as sad. If you only focus on the bad times, then where will that leave you? Your mother needs us to be strong for her. The last thing she would want is to see her precious darlings cry, so don't. We need to be the light in her darkness. We must be her pillar of strength. I am here for the both of you and always will be. We'll get through this together. As you may know, your mother's condition won't improve and there's nothing that can be done about that, no matter how much we pray. We need to make these last few days as enjoyable as possible for her. Smile, my girls. Be grateful for the blessed times we've shared together. I love you both so very much. Be strong, and please... do not cry in front of her.' A lengthy lecture, yes, though one that shall remain on my conscience for all-time. I still say to this very day, that Father died of a broken heart, and not from Pneumonia or Dementia. It *is* plausible. I know that, technically, he passed away from those illnesses, but it was definitely losing Mother that caused my father's early demise to occur. Thinking about it, Father was fortunate in a sense, in that he had a major heart attack before his mental health could worsen. I remember it clearly now. Agnes and I continue to smile, regardless of our differences, just as Father told us to. It isn't always easy, mind you. Nobody said it would be.

"The needle's in." Nurse Emerson exhales with relief. "I'll place this plaster over the butterfly to help prevent it from coming out. Thank you for your help, John, and thank *you* for being such a good patient, Isabella. You're a Saint." I'm hardly anything holy, my dear. I'm not anywhere close to being Joan of Arc, am I? "Such a brave lady. We're so very proud of you."

How strange. I didn't feel anything invade my body, let alone pierce my skin. Nurse Emerson is proving to be a master of the evasive arts, it seems. Either that, or I've got one heck of a pain threshold. The worst amount of agony I've ever felt was when I gave birth to my daughter, Caroline. I had to stay in hospital for two weeks after popping out that ten-pound miracle. She was worth those fourteen hours of gruelling torture, well, until her late-teen years at least. Caroline became such a stubborn little so-and-so not long afterwards, much like her father, when she turned sixteen. 'Sweet

Sixteen' my backside. I think we fell out over something – a petty, little argument of some sort. I can't for the life of me remember what it was about. No, Isabella, these memories can't be right? Why would I not speak to my own flesh and blood over such a fickle thing? Your only daughter, your own personal reflection, your darling princess. Oh, Caroline.

"Her breathing's faster and shallower than before, Hollie. I hope those drugs work fast." Calm down, John. Take in some deep breaths. I'm not panicking, well I don't think I am, especially not over that little needle. Honestly, my dear, it's barely noticeable. I need to know why Caroline fell out with me - *that* is what's causing my current upset. Believe it or not, it's far-worse than having a small piece of metal lodged into my skin. I wish I could somehow explain this to you. "I hate the later parts of this illness; it's so cruel, and never gets any easier to watch. It only feels like yesterday when Isabella first came to us. You know, it's probably one of the hardest things in life to watch those you care for deteriorate. My grandad was diagnosed with Vascular Dementia not so long ago." John pauses, and then glances directly into my eyes. I wonder if I'm a terrible foreshadowing of what his poor grandfather will encounter, in the sense of my own obvious frailty? Oh, what a ghastly burden I've become.

"I'm sorry to hear about your grandfather, John. How are your family coping with his illness?"

"Well..." John momentarily pauses again. Despite my unreliable eyesight, I can clearly make out some tears forming on his face. Don't hide them, petal. It doesn't make you any less of a man to cry. "Most are in denial. They just can't accept what the doctors have said. Working in this environment has been a blessing for me, in a sense, because I know what's coming: the immobility, the incontinence, the mood swings... the lack of dignity. It's weird though, because at work I can usually switch off and not get too close to what's going on. It's different when your own family are affected. Grandpa Murray is more like a father-figure to me than anything else. I don't want what's coming. I just can't process it."

"Oh, John." sighs Nurse Emerson. "You'll manage. I know you'll be fine."

"I'm not too sure about that." remarks John. His expression has fallen dire, and his voice no longer has that hopeful tone to it. "Grandad said a few years back, that if he did end up getting ill, he'd want us to put a bottle of whiskey and some tablets in front of him. He really upset me at the time, saying that, but perhaps it would be a kinder thing to do for him?"

"Isabella's respiration rate has gone up again." John's personal issues appear to be a touchy subject for my nurse. However, the lad does have a valid point. Shouldn't it be up to the individual if they want to end their life, instead of becoming a shadow of their former self? What I would give for a bottle of whiskey and some pills right now. Yes, I *have* come to that awful conclusion. Only Robert's emergence could make me think otherwise. "I know what you mean, John. That's why, particularly at work, it's vital that you remain professional. There is no harm in caring for your residents, just don't cross the line to a degree where it affects you personally."

"You weren't here when Isabella was admitted were you, Hollie?"

"No. It'll be one year in March since I started nursing here." she replies, whilst rubbing a gentle palm over my wrist. "It's an inevitable stage that Isabella's at now. You will get used to it... eventually." Nurse Emerson then tugs at whatever is presently attached to my lower back. This pulling sensation is soon followed by a cold and streaming flow of electricity that courses right through my entire body; it's like being dipped into a bath full of ice. What is happening to me? Are these drugs meant to make me feel like a balloon being inflated? "That's Midazolam and water are in now. Let's leave Isabella alone for a while. Give her some much-needed time to herself – to rest."

92

"I don't know if I can get used to this." simpers John. "You wouldn't let a dog suffer with the same problems. It's wrong how people like Isabella are expected to."

"That's not for us to decide though, is it?" whispers Nurse Emerson. "Our job is to keep the residents as safe and comfortable as possible, which we are. Don't think over it too much. One thing you need to learn about this this job is: you're going to care for a lot of people who will be suffering in the same way as Isabella, so you *must* learn to keep at a distance, John. If you don't, carrying out your duties will become almost impossible. Trust me, I know. I got too close to a client when I first became a Nurse, and it still haunts me to this day. The patient's name was Evangeline, but she preferred 'Eva'." laughs Nurse Emerson momentarily, with an underlying display of sorrow in her voice. "Eva had Parkinson's. I had to watch her lose every ounce of independence and personality she still had. It was heart-breaking to watch but also humbling, as it made me appreciate life for what it is; short, unpredictable and filled with trials."

"I know you shouldn't have favourites, but I've really grown fond of Isabella." comments John, fondly, as he looks into my eyes again. "I miss getting the odd beating from her." I'm NOT aggressive! Dearie me, John! Where are you getting this impression from? "You can't help but get close, can you? We spend so much time caring for our residents; they're like a second family."

"And that's my point, John. Don't get too close. You'll only end up getting hurt... like I did."

One of them tenderly rubs a hand along my forearm, then comes the unnerving sound of footsteps shifting away. They've left me alone, presumably to enter a drug-induced state of permanence? Have they done this to me because I *have* been aggressive towards them in the past? I've never been violent, and I've never taken drugs before (unless you can count the odd sherry on my birthdays). You're starting to panic again, Isabella. Stay calm, old girl. Take your own advice: breath deep, relax, and close your eyes. Fall asleep. Go back to that wonderous cottage in Northumberland. Lose yourself in the tranquil surroundings of Mother Nature. Be with Robert. Be with your children, at least before Caroline grew to hate you. Why did she fall out with me? Oh, Lord.

Debussy's *La Mer* is now reaching its climax. The jubilant build-up of French horns resonates strongly within my ears and troubled thoughts. Are those drugs starting to have an effect on me? Are *they* causing me to hear this music in a slowed-down manner? It certainly feels like I'm inside a dense and never-ending pool of darkness. I'm so conflicted. I want this surreal existence to end, but where *am* I sinking to within this threatening void?

The music abruptly ends, thus leaving only a trail of awful white-noise in its wake. My anxiety is made even worse by the lack of company, namely by Nurse Emerson and John leaving me. I haven't a single clue as to what is really taking place, or as to what is happening to my crippled body and scattered mindset. Everything is slowing down - not just the music. *I'm* slowing down. My breaths are fading, as are my heart beats. Rest, Isabella. Yes, fall asleep again. I could likely manage this, if it weren't for a set of unnerving grunts that now echo around me. Are they mine? They sound like a rampant animal's! They sound like...

"Isabella."

Whatever just spoke slightly roared as if it were a lion, I'm sure of it! You're losing the plot, Isabella. You're going bloody cuckoo. Lions can't talk. Gracious, why would there be a lion here in the first place? Just listen to yourself.

"Open your eyes, Isabella."

Should I? What if I *do* open my eyes, if I even can now, for what will I see? In response, I clench my eyelids firmly shut, praying for this delusion to pass by in a swift fashion. Funnily enough, I don't

94

find the growling to be all that scary; it has a gentle, calming undertone. Maybe this is a pleasant lion, one that won't see me as their next meal? What *are* you going on about, Isabella Cunningham? Have you heard yourself? Do you really think there is a wild animal resting in your bedroom alongside you?

"You do not need to be afraid of me. I am not going to hurt you – I certainly don't wish to eat you."

Like I am going to take the word of an imaginary creature as gospel? Go away! Shoo, I say! Leave me be. Allow me to enjoy this lovely music alone.

"That's not going to be possible, I'm afraid."

Hold on... the lion heard what I thought! Perhaps it would be a good idea to open my eyes, to see what exactly I'm dealing with here? Go on, Isabella. Count yourself down like your Carers do. Be brave as Nurse Emerson said you are. One...Two...*Three*!

"Thank you. I must say, your eyes are indeed beautiful. Your Carers were not lying."

Should I reply with *you're welcome* or *thank you* to this beast? Oh, this is so very unorthodox. Before having any further time to consider my limited options, I'm faced with the blurry image of a male lion. The creature is resting its chin upon my near-side bed rail, and has an unnatural smile spread far across its face. When will this madness ever end?

"Forgive me. I am weary myself, and your bed is incredibly comfortable. Would you not agree, Isabella?"

I'm glad you think so. I believe my Carers have placed me onto an inflatable mattress. It's a bloody nightmare trying to get settled on this thing, and I'm not helped in any way by the constant whirring noise coming from underneath it. Add a lion resting itself beside me and you have a recipe for disaster. How do they possibly expect me to relax in these conditions?

"The whirring noise is air in your bed; it is to relieve pressure from you, Isabella. You're in good hands. Trust me. Like your Carers, I am here to look after you."

It's quite unnerving how this lion knows my name, knows who I am, and without even introducing itself to me. If this is a side-effect of those drugs, then I'd better pass on the next offering. Nurse Emerson has a lot to answer for. Besides, how can a cat offer any aid to me?

"Azrael. My name is Azrael, if it is so important for you to know? We are not strangers, Isabella. I've been watching over you for a long time. Believe me when I say this: we are well acquainted."

Nonsense. What a load of tosh. I've never acquainted myself with any animal, other than my little Winston. Go to sleep, Isabella. The lion will go away. It's only a figment of your over-active imagination, anyhow. Oh, for Pete's sake, I can still hear it panting on... it's still there.

"Whatever has happened to your manners, Isabella? I explained that my name is Azrael. If my voice is displeasing to you, I *can* change it?"

Azrael is as loopy as you are, old girl. *Change his voice?* I'd rather it changed into Roger Moore, if possible (he is such a dish). Now, that *would* be impressive.

"Is this particular voice more pleasing to you?"

Oh, my! It's just like having Roger Moore sat beside me. I am most-impressed by your skills, Azrael. Without meaning to cause any offense, I'd rather you weren't here though, dear. Close your eyes again, Isabella. Pretend you're at a gorgeous ski-resort with Roger Moore, lost in his twinkling eyes and sensual voice. That would be lovely.

"Continue with those thoughts of yours, Isabella Cunningham, and I shall change my voice to that of Christopher Lee's. I am trying my best to please you. Stop being so difficult."

I didn't realise how much of an utter spoil-sport you are, Azrael. Fine. I shall keep my eyes open, and my thoughts will remain clean from now on. Seeing a huge lion stood next to your bed is perfectly normal, isn't it? It's a good job Agnes isn't here, because you'd only add fuel to her taunts against me. Might I ask, why *are* you here, and why *have* you been watching over me? On the subject, where is my Robert?

"So many questions, Isabella. You should be resting. Don't concern yourself with such earthly troubles. I can assure you that they are now completely irrelevant."

You mean, my asking where Robert is? You're being intolerable, Azrael. Above everything else going on, I just want to know where my Bobby is, and if he's alright. I cannot believe - I *will not* believe - that he has willingly left me to rot in this pit, to be comforted by ridiculous hallucinations such as yourself. Don't get me wrong, you do have an angelic quality, though conversing with yourself surely means that I have now fully lost my marbles. What would Bobby think of me?

"Robert is safe and well. You don't need to concern yourself with his wellbeing or whereabouts. This is your time to relax before taking your next step in life. My presence here is meant to be reassuring for you. I can see now, that this is sadly not the case."

I didn't mean to offend you, Azrael. I'm so very sorry if I have. If being frankly honest, I need to tell someone what I'm thinking and, it seems, you're the only company here that can understand my thoughts. I'm scared, Azrael. I'm utterly petrified. I don't know why my body won't work anymore, why I have strangers caring for me, why my family are still yet to visit, or why on God's good Earth *you* are here.

"I am embedded inside your conscience, Isabella. Your family *will* visit you. The answers you seek *will* be made clear. For now, close your eyes again and rest. Go back to that lovely cottage and enjoy the moments felt there. I shall grant you more time, but I *will* return. Whether you like it or not."

A sudden flash blinds my vision, which then falls into a blurry veil of darkness. The lion, Azrael, has seemingly vanished, leaving me alone to dwell in solitude once more. I slowly close my eyes as duly instructed, then play out more of Chopin's serene music in these racing thoughts of mine. My brittle fingers pitifully play along to *Prelude No.20 in C Minor*. The piece is slow and sombre enough to calm my raging nerves, or it could be just the Midazi-whatsit kicking in?

Oh, Isabella. Hasn't it occurred to you yet that if your parents have passed, and with your children being the age you remember them to be, that you must be in your sixties now? That *could* explain why my fingers feel so tired and arthritic? This day couldn't possibly get any worse, old girl, that's one thing for sure. This day will long be remembered as being the weirdest and most terrifying, at that. Sleep, Isabella. Who knows, you might just wake up normal again? Wouldn't that be perfect? Wouldn't that... be wonderful?

A BITTERSWEET CONTRITION

A timid voice, one clearly laden with fear and sorrow, awakens me from my pleasant dreams, and I'm quite certain I know who it belongs to. Surely, it can't be though?

"How has she been? God, she looks so frail now." The woman continues to whisper, making it barely coherent to understand her sombre words. I have witnessed a great deal of pity aimed towards me of late, although whoever this is seems to be inflicted the most by my dilapidated condition. I might be mistaken, I mean, they could be just another Carer or Nurse of whom I have not yet made an acquaintance with? "She's changed so much. I should have come sooner..."

"The last few days have been touch-and-go, but we've thankfully managed to alleviate Isabella's distress and discomfort to a tolerable level." assures Nurse Emerson, though with some inner-conflict present. "I'm afraid that she's no longer accepting any oral intake. Doctor Kain visited Isabella earlier today. We tried to contact you, but we couldn't get through."

"Sorry about that." sniffles the woman. "I've had a lot of things to sort out. My phone hasn't stopped." she laughs, awkwardly. "I've had a stonking headache since getting up this morning. I don't know where to start."

"It's fine. Honestly, don't worry about it." replies Nurse Emerson. "Doctor Kain has prescribed the anticipatory medications we discussed. I can't imagine what you must be going through, hun."

"Hell." remarks the woman, with a very strong emphasis. "It's been an absolute nightmare, Hollie. For starters, her payments haven't been going in correctly, so I've had all that to sort out, and not forgetting all the phone calls I've had to make to our family and friends today." Who *is* this woman? I'm certain that I recognise her.

100

"It's not really appropriate for me to be talking about those now though, is it? Christ, you can see from here how big the tumours on her chest and arms have grown. It was only a few weeks ago when I last saw her." The poor lady starts to whimper, and heavily. Goodness, I wish I could comfort her in some way, even just a little. Bloody Nora, my eyes are sealed shut again. I'll just have to take her word for it, regarding these apparent tumours. Oh Lord, please make my illness end swiftly, as it did with Mother and Father. Have mercy on my family... and on me. I've grown tired of being a burden. Make this all end. "Why didn't I come sooner? I've been putting it off for too long. I should have..."

"Don't blame yourself like that." implores my nurse. "There's nothing that could have been done to stop Isabella's frailty deteriorating. You did your best, that's all that matters. There's no need to feel guilty whatsoever. It's *normal* to feel how you are now. You can talk to me about things; that's what I'm here for."

Really, who *is* Nurse Emerson talking to? I was having such a lovely dream, though I can't precisely remember what happened in it. I believe this time, it again wasn't set within that lovely Northumbrian landscape. No, it wasn't. From what I *can* recollect of this dream, I was boating with Agnes and Father on Lake Ullswater, in Cumbria. Oh, that was such a jolly weekend away. I was about ten years old, and Father was the only man who mattered in my life, well, during those earlier years... before I met Robert. Agnes was very jealous of my taking Father's attention away from her. Agnes wasn't as close to him, but that wasn't *my* fault. Father and I always had so much more in common, like our sense of humour and taste in Classical music. It was a glorious summer that year: searing heat, perpetual sunny skies, and as much ice cream as Father could afford. What a wonderful memory to live through again. If only I could have stayed there for little while longer.

"Thank you for everything, Hollie. You've done an amazing job in caring for her." says my new company. "You're coping better than I ever could."

"It's our pleasure to look after Isabella - and stop putting yourself down." comments Nurse Emerson, in both a polite and forceful voice. "She has been a delight to care for, well, apart from her occasional tantrums. I bet you've heard about some of those?"

Both start laughing, however I am not so amused. I'm overjoyed that the depressing atmosphere is being lifted somewhat, but I'd love to know where they're getting this offensive impression of me. I've only ever once fully-lost my temper and, unsurprisingly, it was with Robert. He had promised to take us to Edinburgh for a weekend break, not long after our wedding. We barely made it to the Scottish border when his car ran out of fuel, leaving the pair of us stranded somewhere near Hadrian's Wall - the middle of bloody nowhere. It took us four hours to find the nearest garage and, it's safe to say, when we did arrive at our hotel, my Bobby spent the rest of the night on a sofa. I couldn't stay mad at him for long, mind you. We soon made up, only after he treated me to some luxurious chocolates.

"She was a whole-lot worse at home. Trust me." states the woman, in a frank and bitter tone. "At least you have those little blue tablets to give her. She wouldn't let me anywhere near, especially when she had soiled herself. God knows how many times I had to change the carpets because of her accidents."

The woman's sobbing breaths are getting louder and louder. Honestly, if I'm not being disturbed by strangers with needles, or talking lions that sound like Roger Moore, I'm being confounded by someone wailing over me. Please, my dear, let me go back to my painless dreams and less-excruciating existence. Allow me to drift off with Chopin's serene Nocturnes. Actually, now I come to think of it, don't go away. It's so dreadful to feel alone and vulnerable, as I do now. Let me share in your suffering. Perhaps, we can get through this difficult time together? A burden shared is a burden halved, they say.

"The Lorazepam was only used a few times, believe it or not. We try to offer reassurance and distractions to our residents first, before having to use sedatives on them. No one really wants that." explains

Nurse Emerson. Would you be a darling and care to explain the chemicals floating around my body to me again, dear? I'd greatly appreciate that. "In fairness, I haven't witnessed *that* side to Isabella too much. I've always found her to be very chatty and sociable." Thank you, Nurse. It's about time someone spoke some more truths about me. "You do understand that those behaviours were just a side-effect from the illness, don't you?"

"Yes, but..." stammers my new friend. "I don't know much about it. Sally gave me a leaflet to read through, but that just ended up in the bin. Sorry."

"Don't worry about it," dismisses Nurse Emerson. "I've looked after many patients who, prior to their illnesses, wouldn't have uttered a single curse word or hurt anyone. It's all to do with what part of the brain is damaged."

"I understand that, Hollie. I just can't accept it."

"*Hello?*" Another intruder! Thankfully, this appears to be Zanna, and she's tapping away at my door like a shy child. What a pleasure it is to have you back, my darling. Make yourself at home or, even better, go fetch Marius to also keep me company. You all know me so well, yet I barely know any of your names. It's so very strange, and quite embarrassing. "I hope you don't mind me popping in? I just wanted to come and see how Isabella is doing."

"Not at all, Zan." snuffles my melancholic guest. I do wonder who she is? It's really starting to bug me now. They seem so familiar, but in some irrational way. They sound a little... like me. "Hollie and I have just been discussing what the doctor said. Things aren't looking too good, are they?"

"Oh, *Doctor Kain?*" Zanna might be trying to hide it, but you can plainly sense her disdain towards my GP. Good girl. A little honesty never harmed anyone. "He wasn't in for long, I know that much. Did he sort out the anticipatory drugs for Isabella?"

"Yes." replies Nurse Emerson, with a sharpened emphasis. She obviously has a professional obligation to follow the advice from those above, but you can also gain a strong feeling of resentment towards my doctor from her – just from saying this one word. "I've administered Isabella's first dose at around half-past three this afternoon. The drugs should be starting to kick in by now. Isabella appears a bit more settled, despite her pulse being a little high still. We'll be keeping a close eye on that."

"Thanks. She looks so peaceful when asleep, doesn't she?" Well observed, my unexpected acquaintance. I look asleep because I *am* or, should I say, I *was* until you folks rudely woke me up. "You're doing a brilliant job – all of you. I tried to cope with her at home the best I could, but it just got too much for me in the end. Things got even harder when she kept seeing invisible animals and insects. She often had me chasing them around the house with a broom, for God's sake. That's no way to live... not for either of us." To whom exactly are you referring to, my dear? Surely, you're not on about myself here? I'm that stir-crazy. "I could sort of manage the incontinence. It was pretty weird at first, having to clean up after her, though I eventually got over that. The last straw came when she tried to hit my cat, Tiddles, with a hammer. She thought it was a bloody lion."

I'm starting to decipher who this woman is, and I don't know if that is necessarily good or not. Keep your eyes sealed, Isabella. Let them talk about you, over you, and forget that they're even here. This awful time will pass. Robert will be here to collect you soon. He will come to rescue you from this wretched situation.

"Give yourself some due-credit; you've done a lot for Isabella, more than most people would have. It may come as a shock, but we have residents in here who've never had any visitors come to see them. You've visited Isabella constantly, even when she kept telling you not to. You really need to stop putting yourself down." No matter the situation, Nurse Emerson holds an ability to calm even the most-anxious of souls. I'm still somewhat trembling in my boots about this realisation, however. Don't say it is... "Honestly, you've done everything possible to make sure Isabella is being well-cared for. The past few weeks have been really difficult for you and your family, with everything else going on, so it's completely understandable why you couldn't visit. You don't need to explain yourself to us, Caz." Please... stop talking, Nurse. You're only confirming my greatest fear, an emotion that I never thought would be felt in the presence of my own daughter, my Caroline. I love Caroline with all my heart and always will, though I do remember us falling out over something. Oh, I despise that nickname of hers - *Caz*. It's so common and un-ladylike. Focus. Breath, old girl. What if Caroline still hates me? Goodness, how do I possibly counter that? There is no book in this world that could answer the predicament I now find myself in. Oh Lord, help me. "I'll go make you a nice cup of tea. We'd best give you some time alone with your mam. Do you still take two sugars and milk?"

"Yes. Thank you, Hollie." Caroline, my sweet child, do stop crying. I can't tell if these are tears of sadness or of anger. Those bloody drugs aren't working. I'm absolutely petrified. I'm scared of how my own flesh and blood will react with me. Oh, how did it ever come to this? "Hiya, Mam. I know you can't talk back anymore, and once over I wouldn't have been bothered by that. God, what an awful thing to say. Sorry, Mam."

What was it. Think, Isabella – THINK! Why did Caroline disown you, or was it the other way around? Dearie me, I can't believe I'm even saying those unthinkable words. My bed is suddenly knocked, which in an instant sends a rapid wave a numbing pain throughout my entire body. I'm assuming, from this disturbance, that Caroline has sat herself beside me. Should I open my eyes, for what will I see? I'd rather have that ruddy-big lion reappear, than to watch this abhorrent scenario play through. Caroline, my only daughter, my own image, please be gentle with me. I am weak. I am lost beyond words. I have failed you as a mother. *Please*, for mercy's sake, stop crying. You will only make me do the same. No parent wants to see their child suffer, particularly if they can't do anything to stop it.

"You're so tiny now, Mam. You're half the size you used to be." Thank you, darling. I've not been eating much of late. Besides,

losing a few pounds won't do me any harm. "You look so... old."
That's not as flattering, but I'll let you off this time. "You're wasting
away to nothing." she sobs, heavily into her hands. "I should have
come sooner. Why didn't I?"

My daughter gasps loudly as she places a tremoring hand over
mine. This physical contact only seems to ignite her sorrow further,
yet it brings to me an intense surge of euphoria. I don't know what is
going through Caroline's mind at this moment, heaven forbid it, but
my own thoughts are taken back to when she was an innocent child,
one free of all the troubles that now burden her... including me.

Caroline, until she was around the age of twelve, could often be
found attached to my side. We were inseparable – so alike. It's such
a pity that wonderful phase didn't last. Nothing lasts forever though,
Isabella. She grew – you grew. You both became distant, though
neither yourself or Caroline truly wanted for that to happen. Keep on
repeating this fantasy, old girl, but just remember that you were
never any good at lying... not even to yourself.

"I've always been a let-down haven't I, Mam?" I don't think so,
sweetheart. If anything, I've always been very proud of you. "I'm
nothing but a trouble-maker, an alcoholic, a total pain in the arse. All
I've ever done is let people down, especially you and Dad."

Why so much guilt and remorse, Caroline? If I have wronged you
so badly, then why not just abandon me? Simply leave your terrible
mother to rot in this unfamiliar environment. I will manage. I've
been through far-worse times. Why don't you ask your brother or
father to visit me instead? I do wish to see Robert again, more than
anything else. Speaking of Bobby, shouldn't he be here with us,
uniting us, telling both you and I to cast aside our stubborn ways and
to make up? Robert was always such a good mediator. It must have
driven him crazy at times, all those countless instances where he had
to stand between Agnes and I? Where is your dad, Caroline? Answer
me, darling.

"Can you remember when I was a little, when we baked that
'special' cake together for Aunt Agnes?" Oh, yes. That was quite a

memorable occasion, I dare confess. "You placed a five-pence in the mixture to wind her up. It was so funny watching Aunt Agnes spit it out across your dining table. According to you though, it was meant to bring her good luck. She wasn't very impressed, was she?" A faint hint of laughter leaves from Caroline, though it sadly remains hidden amongst her pressing anguish. "Agnes was so mad, but all you did was just laugh back. I really miss those days. I miss baking with you." As do I, my love. At least, Caroline sounds a little brighter now. I wasn't too bad of a mother, was I? A terrible sister – yes. Lord, I'll gladly admit to that. There's no love lost between Agnes and me, mind you, we wouldn't have a bad word said against the other. You can choose your friends, but not your family. "Can you remember when you taught me to ride my first bike, to read, to laugh at the daftest of things? You were the best shoulder to cry on, Mam. You did so much for me." Caroline pauses, then inadvertently knocks my bed again. I try to stop myself yelping from the pain, for I don't want it to distract my daughter's growing joy. Not one bit. "What thanks have I given to you in return? Nothing! You gave me everything you could, and all you got back off me was grief." I did all those things because *I love you*, Caroline. I still do, regardless of what has taken place to separate us in this dreadful way. Do stop crying. *Please!* "How *did* I repay you? I helped to make your life a misery, took your savings, added more pressure onto you and Dad... what kind of daughter does that? God, I hate myself."

It's starting to come back to me, little by little, all those sordid last encounters between us. I wasn't upset by you taking any money, or by the way you would swear at and belittle me; I was upset because you were drinking yourself into an oblivion, Caroline. I watched you lose all that weight and sense of self-worth, *that* was the worst part of it all. Your father and I tried so hard to get you some professional support, but you point-blank refused our guidance at every turn. We simply couldn't understand why. What was it that made you so desperate to forget things, to shut yourself away from the world around? Why can't I remember something as important as this? Think, Isabella – THINK!

"I made all the wrong choices, Mam. You and Dad were the only ones who could see that. I lost you, lost my husband, my huge house in Darlington... drinking was just the easiest way to cope. I'm sober now and have been for the last year or so. It's been a struggle, but I've gotten there eventually. What I would give for you to know that achievement, Mam. You'd be so 'very' proud of me, wouldn't you?"

I've always been proud of you, and so has your father. There is nothing to forgive, nothing whatsoever. Life has its many challenges, Caroline, and it is up to us on how we should face them. Everyone has their darker days. I so desperately wanted to be the light at the end of your gruesome depression. It is *I* that has let you down, not the other way around. Please explain why we stopped talking. I'm begging you, darling. It must have been an act so utterly cruel - unspeakable? What tore you away from my bosom?

"It was Doctor Hewitson's counselling that helped me the most. It's taken twenty-two years, but I'm now finally starting to accept what happened..."

Don't leave me on such a suspensive pause, Caroline. Hold on, *twenty-two years*! That's a long period of time to forget, old girl. The bond between a mother and daughter should be infinite – unbreakable. Put an end to my woes, sweetheart. Tell me everything. *Speak* to me.

"Losing him was hard on all of us. It was just so... random. He was only thirty-seven years old. I still can't understand how you kept that straight face, when you told me our David had prostate cancer, that he wouldn't have long to live. Jessica was twelve years old when she lost her dad. Even that small bairn coped better than I did." Wait a moment, my dear. Allow me to get a word in. My son... "David was my big brother *and* my best friend. That's why I turned to drink. That's why I became such a huge disappointment to you and the rest of our family. Nothing can justify me saying that you were a bad mother, and that... it was your fault he died. It *wasn't* your fault,

Mam. I just said those things out of spite. I'm so sorry. If only I could turn back time to make things right again, to spend those precious years with you both again."

Oh, Lord in Heaven! My beloved son. My sweet-sweet, David. I'm beyond words that I'd forgotten your passing. Caroline *was* certainly correct, in her saying that I'm a terrible mother. Surely, it's this Cancer that has riddled my brain with intrusive tumours, the same of which that are now mercilessly wiping away such terrible memories? I'm beyond the harshest level of grief that I too forgot David's little girl, my precious granddaughter, Jessica. I *do* remember now, my son of gold. I can recall everything: the day you told me about your wicked illness, the look on your father's face when he found out, the harrowing expression of utter confusion on little Jessica when she learned of it. Such a thing was understandably hard to accept, even during your last days on this earth, although I found peace in that you were happy and content. You had Jessica to thank for that, didn't you, David? Jessica has your piercing eyes, your warming smile, your ridiculous musical tastes, and your positive outlook on life. *She* is your living legacy. Gracious me. This is more agonising than any physical torment, than any of the humiliation or pain I have felt today. I can't take this anymore. I can't bear this torture for another second!

"Mam? MAM! Nurse Emerson! Come - QUICK!"

What is Caroline bleating about? She's gone from being pitifully subdued to totally frantic. The poor dear. Oh, I feel dreadfully sick. I can feel a horrid, burning sensation rising from the very pit of my stomach. That awful wave of anxiety is returning, and with it comes an overwhelming sense of doom and futility. Find Robert for me, Caroline. Find your father and bring him here. I simply must see him again.

"What's the matter, Caz?" cries out Nurse Emerson. She is standing close by again and sounds just as concerned about me as my daughter does. "Is everything okay? What's going on?"

"Mam's breathing is getting faster... and what's with that rattle noise coming from her throat?"

"Isabella needs more Hyoscine." states my Nurse, somewhat in shock. "She is too weak to cough up all the horrible phlegm that's building up inside her lungs; that's the rattling noise you can hear. Don't worry though, Caz. I'll get John, and then we'll give your mam some more of her anticipatory drugs to help settle her. I'll go get him right-away."

"Hurry! I can't bear seeing her like this. Oh, Mam..."

Well, that was a conversation I wouldn't fancy listening to ever again. There are probably more drugs flowing through my veins now than water. Is *that* a way to live: to rely on medications to extend one's life? I know this Hyo-sini-whatchya-makeallit is meant to alleviate my discomfort, but will it? Until Caroline and Nurse Emerson openly started to discuss my nauseating presentation, I had no clue as to how poorly I've become. I feel like one of those innocent monkeys being tested on in a lab: prodded with needles, helpless to fight back, submissive to what fate lies in store, oblivious to what purpose they truly serve in surviving for another day.

I force my face harder into the soft pillow beneath it. The action nullifies Caroline's persistent sobs, though it also shrouds Bach's beautiful Concerto which is now playing quietly in the background. Music has always been my chosen method to cope with life's hardest ordeals, however, it's doing little to help me at this present moment. What kind of mother would want to endure their child's inconsolable misery? Not me. I'm nothing but a coward. I realise that I should be doing more to ease my daughter's helplessness, but it's just too difficult for me. The saying in Chess would be *Checkmate*, I believe. We're in quite a pickle, aren't we, Caroline? If only David and your father were here. They'd knock some much-needed sense into us, wouldn't they?

"Hi, Isabella." John? Hello again, dear. Have you brought me my latest fix, my unrequited remedies? "We've got your mam's Hyoscine and some more Midazolam, Caz." That answers that

110

question, then. "Would you mind waiting outside please, just while we administer the meds? I don't think you'll want to watch us using needles, will you?"

"God, no." replies Caroline, in a shuddering voice. "That's fine by me, John. Besides, I've got a few more phone calls to make. I'll wait outside until you finish."

Caroline? Don't you dare leave me, my girl. You're the only one who has bothered to visit. I don't care if we've had a falling out, you simply must stay! Caroline, *come back*! You come right back here this very instant, missy! You're not too old for a smacked bottom, you know? "Won't be long, Mam. Behave yourself while I'm gone. Don't be getting up to any mischief."

"Isabella's not a bother, Caz." comments John, in a passive tone. The cheeky devil appears to be telling a white-lie here, going off what he and the other Carers said about me earlier on. Aren't I on my last legs? There's been too many mixed messages today to comprehend. "We'll only be a few minutes – tops. You do what you need to do, Caz. Isabella will be fine, we'll make sure of it."

Stop telling such blatant fibs, John. You know, it forever astounds me why folk feign the truth like this. Why gloss over the undeniable, albeit horrifying, details? I have Cancer. I am dying. I'm not going to recover anytime soon, and no amount of so-called 'miracle drugs' are going to cure that. Be honest with my daughter, John. She is so very fragile, but she's not a fool. Tell-her-the-truth. In the long-run, it will be less of a burden to bear for the both of you.

"Doctor Hewitson and Melissa the ANP are on their way, John. I've requested that they amend Doctor Kain's Kardex. The doses aren't nearly enough to manage Isabella's level of deterioration. The last thing we want is for her to be in pain *and* right before a weekend." Bless you, Nurse Emerson. Considerate as always. "I've asked Sally for some black towels as well."

"*Black towels*? Why would we need black towels, Hollie?" stammers John, nervously. I get the impression he knows the answer to this, though it's not something he wants to willingly acknowledge. "Seems a little... weird."

"You *know* why, John." responds Nurse Emerson, somewhat apprehensively. "It's to do with Isabella's tumours." She now whispers, though I can still make out what she's saying. "If one should sever a vessel in her throat, which is very possible, she could vomit goodness-knows how much blood all over the place. We're talking projectile here." She lowers her voice even quieter, but I can still make out what is being said. You'll have to try harder than that, if you don't want me to hear what's being said, my dear. "Black is a better colour to hide red." Oh, don't be so paranoid. I am quite alright, Nurse Emerson. There is still a sick feeling in my gullet, but it's staying put for now. Well, I think it is. "Me and Sally have kept some black towels in her manager's office, just in case this scenario was ever to rise. The chance of an artery rupturing in her throat is looking more and more likely now, John." sighs my nurse. "When I was doing Isabella's dressing earlier, I noticed there was a small trail of blood coating her tongue. It's an awful thing to think about, but we need to be prepared."

"Jesus, I didn't think of that." I can distinguish John throwing himself into the chair beside me, clearly dismayed by what Nurse Emerson said, and then my eyes open just enough to make out his gaunt expression. "I hope it doesn't happen. No amount of training could prepare any of us for something so bad."

"It's to do with Isabella's dignity, John." interjects Nurse Emerson. "And not to mention the reaction staff may give, like you pointed out, should they see a room full of blood-stained linen. We'll hide the black towels under Isabella's bed – especially out of Caroline's view. Don't say anything to her either, it'll only cause further distress. Caz is going through enough at the minute."

"I wouldn't dare." assures John, as he casts his eyes towards my doorway, perhaps fearing that Caroline might have heard what was being discussed? "I don't think we should mention it at all to Caz." He slowly returns his sight onto me, and for a moment we are looked in one another's gaze. I can sense John's anxiety and, who knows, maybe he can even pick up on mine? "Have you finished putting the medications through her line yet?"

"Yes." replies my nurse, in relief. "The last drop is in now."

There's that cold electricity again. It's slowly running across my stomach like a trickling stream, only then to course throughout my body as if it were a venerable disease. Lord, help me. Focus on Bach, old girl. Focus on being reunited with Robert, for he'll be here soon. My Bobby would never let me down. Hold on a second... where is that funny noise coming from? Nurse Emerson and John don't growl. Oh, it's that ill-gotten lion again. What does *he* want? Close your eyes, Isabella. Make him vanish.

"I *can* hear you, Isabella. You're not ready yet, are you?"

Ready for what, Azrael? Can't you see that I'm busy here? My beloved Caroline has paid me a visit, so your gracious presence is most-certainly not welcome. No offence, dear. I would greatly appreciate some privacy with my daughter, if you so don't mind? We have a lot of catching up to do.

"I am busy as well. I can't lie around here all day, waiting on you. By the way, Isabella... open your eyes."

I'm compelled to do just as Azrael instructs, though goodness knows why. He does seem to have some sort of strange, divine hold over me. I wrench my sticky eyes open, only to find two other strangers lingering over my crippled torso. They're stood beside Nurse Emerson, John, and my Caroline. All of them are staring down on me like I'm part of a bloody sideshow. Can't a woman get any rest around here? At least, good-old Azrael's done a disappearing act. Thank the Lord. That's one good thing.

"Hello, Ms. Appleton. I'm Doctor Hewitson, and this is your mother's Advanced Nurse Practitioner – Melissa Goodheart. Hollie asked for us to come out and see Isabella." This doctor seems to be far-more pleasant than Doctor Kain, though that wouldn't necessarily be a hard thing to accomplish. "We've received a request to amend some of Isabella's palliative medications, to reflect on her deteriorating condition. I'm happy to do this, given your mother's current presentation... bless her." You mean, because I look like I've been dragged through a hedge backwards, Doctor Hewitson? Am I really that ill? "Have the staff here also discussed with you about putting a DNACPR, a Do Not Attempt Resuscitation, authorisation into place? Personally, I believe that it would be in Isabella's best interests to do so. It would be difficult to say what quality of life she would have, should Isabella be brought back."

Here we go again with those nebulous abbreviations and non-sensical terms. Just ply me with more drugs and be done with it. Poor Caroline doesn't need to put up with all this fuss; she has enough on her plate, besides having to dote on me. Anyway, it should be *me* doting on her. I am the parent here, not the other way around.

"Yeah, it's... sorted." replies Caroline, in reluctance. "I verbally consented to one with Nurse Emerson and Doctor Kain." Have you, my darling? Goodness, what an awful decision that must have been for you to make? "I did ask myself if - God forbid - anything should happen to Mam, what quality of life would she have afterwards. It wasn't as hard as I thought it would be, to be honest. Mam's already suffered through enough, and most of it's my fault. You wouldn't let an animal go on like this."

"Caroline..." Nurse Emerson kindly embraces my daughter. That's my job, though. A tremendous and debilitating envy soon riddles me, mostly that I cannot offer the same consolation to my own child. What kind of mother am I? My poor daughter. "Please, stop placing the blame on yourself. Isabella's illnesses are not your fault, not in any way at all. Just you taking the effort to be here for her will be a massive comfort, Caz. Trust me."

"How?!" shrieks Caroline. She then shoves Nurse Emerson away, evidently taking all by surprise (including myself). Calm down, sweetheart. Settle yourself. You never suited that angry look; it contorts your face like Agnes', when she herself is wound up. "Mam doesn't know where she is, who she is, or who I am anymore. *My* mam died a long time ago. I can accept that now." Oh, Caroline. "She's already dead. Look at her! All that's left of my mam now is an empty shell... not the proud and beautiful woman I always knew her to be."

"Don't say that, Caz." interjects John, softly. "Isabella might not be able to speak, but she'll still be able to hear what you're saying. Wouldn't your mam hate to see you upset, like this?"

"It's a load of bollocks!" wails my daughter. "I can't take anymore. I've got to get out of this room." Where are you going, Caroline? Don't leave me! *Please*, don't leave me again. "Call me when 'it' happens." she sobs, in a dazed stupor. "I've phoned around others in our family about Mam's condition, so they'll probably be here soon to keep her company. They can keep a better eye on you than I ever could, can't they, Mam? I'm so sorry. I need to go."

"Caroline - wait!" exclaims Nurse Emerson. "Talk to us! We're here for you, too! I'm so sorry about all this, Doctor Hewitson."

"It's fine, Hollie. Go and see to her. In the meantime, Melissa and I will sort out Isabella's new Kardex. We'll see you downstairs after you've had a chat with Caroline. It's not a problem at all."

"We'll be right back, Isabella." Assures John, as he gently pats at my hands again. "We're just going to check on your Caroline, okay? She'll be fine." You and your lies, John. I'm not stupid. I know my own daughter. Gracious, she's anything but fine. *I* want to help her. Oh, this is simply awful. "I'll put another CD on for you while you're waiting... be back in a tick, sweetheart." "

One by one, my visitors swiftly flee. If only I could. Lord, how I would love to manage that marvellous feat. It must be heading towards evening now, that, or else the lights in my room are playing up? That wouldn't surprise me, given the run of bad luck I've been having today.

Franz Liszt's *La Campanella* begins to play on my stereo, a piece that would usually enchant my senses, yet the fast-paced trills are doing nothing but make me feel worse. It's safe to say, the surrounding atmosphere has become somewhat heavier and foreboding now. You've been so foolish, Isabella. All those perfect chances you could have utilised to repair Caroline's faith and love in you – they're gone. Why aren't you here with me, Robert? Where were you at to put things back into order, like you used to? I do hope you're waiting for me at that lovely cottage in my dreams. I think I'll close my eyes now and go back there. Yes, that's what I'll do. To be with you all again would be truly perfect. It would be wonderful.

OUT OF THE WOODWORK

I had so eagerly desired to revisit that beautiful cottage, to be with my family, again. However, it is clear to see that this is not the case.

I'm sat with my best friend, Joan, in our school playground, and behind us I can hear someone whimpering. I turn to face this sorrowful creature, not knowing at all how to respond, and grimace on discovering that they are in fact my sister – Agnes. She is sobbing into her hands, which wouldn't usually bother me, on account of all the arguments we have, although I feel a sudden urge to offer some much-needed comfort. Agnes and I have our differences but, nevertheless, we are still family – we need to be there for one another; that is how Father and Mother raised us.

Agnes goes on to explain how some so-called 'friends' decided to ostracise her, only because she wouldn't pick on another girl who they didn't like. The girl in question was Maureen Richardson. Poor Maureen had been born with a cleft lip, something which she bravely tried to overcome, particularly at school. Children can be so unkind, but Agnes wasn't innately bad; she was manipulated by the bullies that surrounded her. Maureen was a lovely girl: intelligent, kind, and had a wonderful sense of humour. She also happened to be one of Agnes' oldest friends.

I try consoling my sister and attempt to remind her of how there is nothing wrong with being unique, and that you should treat others as you would wish for them to treat you. Agnes merely scolds me in return. She brushes aside my sympathetic pleas, and with very little decorum. Honestly, how on Earth are we two related? The only thing which Agnes has grown to excel at, is to judge others on their social statuses – their wealth. It's such a pity. I know my sister is better than that. I know that Agnes isn't as cold and heartless as she makes herself out to be. Oh Lord, what a dreadful memory. Why would I want to recall my sister's anguish, her constant struggle to be accepted? I don't know. I'll always be there for her, even if she *does* drive me insane at times.

"Gracious. Look at the sight of her... the poor mite." For pity's sake. Who has come to bother me now? Whoever they are, they sound like an old hag. "She looks terrible, doesn't she? I wouldn't give her long." The very cheek – who *is* this? I've not yet opened my eyes, and I'm starting to think I shouldn't. "Caroline warned us about our Isabella not looking so good. She wasn't lying, was she?"

"Aww, bless her." Not *another* stranger. Heavens, am I not entitled to some privacy away from peeping Tom's today? Both of you, please, just tittle off and leave me be. I just want to sleep, to be free of this awful situation. "She's all skin-and-bones. God, her hair's all over the place. She looks like a drowned rat." *I beg your pardon*? "That's the Cancer, you know? You can see some of her tumours popping out. Look there, at her collarbone." How astonishing. I'm now being subjected to entertain such intellectuals, am I? Gracious me. "It's a nasty illness is Cancer. Doesn't it run in your family?"

"Oh, yes." responds the other woman, somewhat seemingly in a daze. "I've been quite lucky not to have caught it myself... poor Isa." No, it can't be? No-no-no-no-NO! Lordy me, I do recognise *this* voice, and there's only one person who calls me 'Isa'. If it isn't Agnes? My ever-trustworthy and loyal sister has come to pay me a visit. What have I done to deserve such an honour? I must say, Agnes' voice sounds so very old and frail. How queer. Perhaps my ears are playing up, as well as everything else? "Mother died from Lung Cancer, and Father's was the Prostate type - rest their souls. It's such a pity that Isabella has caught it too. Isa would always bleat on about living a 'healthy lifestyle'; it's hardly done her any favours now, has it?" Cancer is not contagious, Agnes. Do you not realise just how daft you sound? I know that you can be simple at times, but *really*? "Isa would often lecture me about how terrible mine was. Life plays its tricks on us all, they say." Agnes. My dear, sweet and naïve, Agnes. For one thing, Mother worked in horrendous conditions. Her illness was caused by an exposure to Asbestos, and you bloody-well know that. Father's illness was simply down to old age. Didn't you listen to a single word their doctors and consultants said? "It's a curse in our family, just as Alzheimer's is. I certainly hope that I don't get that, either. There's not a cat in hells chance *I'd* ever let some stranger wipe my backside for me. Lord no." Thank you for that fantastic reminder, Agnes. I *could* put in a good word with Nurse Emerson, to see if she can maybe offer you this said experience? "I'd rather go quickly in my sleep. I believe that's the best way to go. With how my dicky-ticker is playing up at the minute, there's a bloody good chance that'll happen as well."

"Don't go saying such dreadful things, Aggie." bleats her acquaintance, in a hoarse voice. "You'd out-live the cockroaches, you would."

"Oh you, cheeky so-and-so!" cackles my sister, and then she releases a lengthy sigh. "This is no life for my sister, is this. Isa may as well not be here." For once I agree with you on something, Agnes. But I *am* still here - I'm not dead... not yet. Aren't you even going to talk with me, or am I simply being forced to endure your tedious small-talk? That would be nothing new though, would it? "It's so ghastly to see her in this horrid state. I kept saying to Isa over the years that *getting stressed will do you no good*. She would just laugh back at me... always so stubborn." My sister's tone suddenly seems to darken, and her voice becomes riddled with resentment. "This is all down to Caroline. My niece has a great deal to answer for."

"We both know that fine well, don't we?" insinuates Agnes' companion. "I don't know how that wretched girl can live with her self. I'm just glad I'm not related to her. I feel so sorry for you, Aggie. You haven't a choice on the matter."

"Caroline's not all that bad." interjects Agnes, meekly. "She used to be such a good girl."

"Don't kid yourself, Aggie. You know that you can tell me anything. Your secrets are safe with me."

A few quiet moments follow between us three, with only my Classical music acting as a pleasant distraction. Goodness knows what must be trailing through Agnes' mind? She and Caroline, once over, were so very close. Neither would have had a bad word said against the other. The venom that Agnes and her friend have spouted against my daughter continues to burn away at each of my senses. How *dare* they judge Caroline. No one is perfect. None of us are, no matter how prim and proper we may think ourselves to be.

"Caroline's behaviour *did* put a great strain on Isa and Robert's relationship. I was certain, at one point, that their marriage wasn't going to last." I highly doubt that, Agnes. My Bobby would never forsake me. Don't you remember that dubious occasion when you tried to kiss him? A perfect example of my Robert's loyalty. "I did my best to intervene, but it was no use. They're all stubborn beggars... not at all like me."

Yes, our family was anything but perfect, Agnes. Lord knows how many times I had to sort out *your* problems, had to care for Mother during her illness, had to make the final decision in turning off Father's life-support, had to cope with David's passing with less than a 'sorry' from you. Where were you at during those terrible days? Oh, yes. You were lapping it up in Benidorm, or out with you friends at the Bingo Hall. It was left to yours truly here to deal with all the consequences and lingering grief left behind. My memory has become clouded, though I remember these precise details very well. Calm yourself, Isabella. Blood is thicker than water. Don't be so cross with Agnes, your little sister, as it's not like she can help the way she is. Besides, Agnes was never the wisest, was she? You should pity her, not be angry.

"Have you found out who gets the money from Isabella's house yet, you know, when she croaks it?" How very-dare this individual! The utter nerve of her. I can understand every word you're speaking, regardless of how vile it may be. If my hands weren't glued to my sides, by gum, you'd be in for a good slap or two.

"I haven't particularly wanted to look into it, Audrey." sighs Agnes. "Gracious, Isabella hasn't yet left this world of ours. Why would I even want to look that far ahead?"

"Sorry, love. I'm just being a nosey-parker. Don't mind me." You're a slithering snake, my dear. I'm quite good at telling these things. "Though... won't there be any money made from selling her house? It should go to you, surely?"

"I don't know!" snaps my sister. She was never any good at dealing with confrontations. I would often need to intervene on Agnes' behalf. That's what big sisters are for. "I'm more worried about my Isa's health than her wealth, Audrey. I can think about her finances at another time."

"I'm just thinking about you, dear." assures Audrey, and strangely without an underlying hiss to highlight her serpent-like personality. "The money could be better spent on going towards Isabella's funeral, instead of being spent on her care in this shit hole." Good Scott, this Audrey is relentless! What a vulture, never mind a snake. "It makes my blood boil, Aggie, just how dire the state this country is in now. Isabella should be getting her care for free. Her money should go to you, then perhaps we could go on a nice holiday together, to forget about her passing?" Words are beyond me. I'd hardly class my present surroundings as 'shit', and I am going nowhere. Sorry to disappoint you, Audrey. Yes, this room is quite claustrophobic; however, in a peculiar way, I'm growing accustomed to this dwelling space. I'm being well looked after, which certainly makes up for any lacking possessions. "It's an absolute disgrace. *You* should be getting Isabella's inheritance. Why should the government or Caroline get all her wealth? I mean, half of it *does* rightfully belong to you. You need to stand your ground with Caroline. Show her who is boss!"

"I'm really not that bothered about the money, and I don't wish for another confrontation with Caroline." groans Agnes, wearily. "Honestly, Isa's savings have scarcely crossed my mind."

121

This is a turn for the books. I've never encountered this sympathetic side to Agnes and, in a way, it's considerably disturbing. My sister only ever cared for what money and social status she could gain, so it's a great surprise to see her turning down this vast opportunity. What *has* gotten into you, Agnes, to change your heart and mindset so drastically? Have you rediscovered God? We both know that's unlikely, given how much you detested Sunday School.

"It is still something you should consider, dear." implores Audrey, with some element of desperation. "Just think of what you could do with all the free cash. We could go on that splendid Mediterranean cruise you've always talked about. Wouldn't that be a glorious venture?" You're not giving away your true intentions or anything, are you? For goodness sake, Audrey. "Your Caroline would just drink it all away. You could take it further with Isabella's Solicitor, couldn't you?"

"I only want my sister to be comfortable during her last days, Audrey. Will you please stop going on about her money." snarls Agnes. "We didn't always see eye-to-eye, but we're blood at the end of the day. I just want the best for her. I've not exactly been the best sibling. I hardly deserve to inherit what she has worked so hard for. I'd bet, if Isa could talk, she would have a thing or two to say. My word, it'd be just like old times."

Where do I begin, Agnes? Throughout our childhood you: stole from me, belittled me in front of my friends, convinced Mother and Father that I bullied you, not to mention that failed attempt you made in trying to seduce my Bobby. Lord, we'd be here all day if I had to name every malicious act you've made against me. *Sisters*. Don't take this the wrong way, Agnes, I *do* love you, but you make it so bloody hard at times.

"You have every right to look more into this, Aggie. You've done more for Isabella than Caroline ever has."

122

"No, I haven't." laments Agnes. "It wouldn't be fair to imply such a notion. Caroline has her troubles and addictions, but she has done a lot for Isa... far-more than I have."

"You must be joking, Aggie? After all that horrid girl put your sister and Robert through? Have you been taking your sleeping pills during the day again?"

"Lord no! I don't for one second agree with how Caroline abused her mother over the years, but she has done a great deal since to make up for it." Did I hear you sniffle there, Agnes? Are you... crying? "Caroline was the one who dealt with Isabella's placement here. I wouldn't have known where to start. This care home was the best choice, by far, and I whole-heartedly agree with Caroline's decision to put Isa in here." So, this place is a care home and *not* a hospital. I don't know which is worse. Let that just sink in for a moment, old girl. Perhaps, now might be the time to try and open your eyes. Don't you want to look at Agnes? Don't you want to see your beloved sister? At least, have a think about it. "I've had no excuse not to visit often. I've only ever come to see Isa on her birthdays. That's terrible, isn't it? I should have been there more for her. All those precious years – lost." You're starting to sound so much like me now, Agnes. Do behave yourself.

"Isabella's like a vegetable – look at her." counters Audrey, dismissively. "She's curled up like a helpless, little baby. What's the point in visiting someone who doesn't even know you're there? You could be doing more meaningful things..." Like playing Bingo, or going on a luxurious cruise with my money, Audrey? Let my sister speak. Do us all a favour and stay quiet – even better – tittle off. "Make the most of your life while you can, Aggie. You're not getting any younger. Sort out that money - spend it well. Take us both on that lovely Mediterranean Cruise. Wouldn't that be a blast?"

"*She* is my sister, Audrey. *She* is not a bloody vegetable! I am all that Isabella has left in this world. I didn't see any other names in the visitors' book, when we came in." I am also annoyed by this, Agnes. Why didn't you think to bring Robert along with you, instead of this beastly oaf, Audrey? "I've got to be here for her, more now than ever, especially with how the illnesses are getting worse." Illnesses? My Cancer is a singular disease, is it not? Sorry, but I think you're mistaken here, Agnes. "If only Isabella could see herself. She'd be absolutely mortified, make no mistake of it. I shall have my ten-pence worth with Caroline, one day, that I can promise you. Just you wait and see. It *is* her fault. It's Caroline that made my sister go doo-lally!" Agnes, what is happening to you? Where did all this hatred towards my darling daughter, your niece, come from?

"What goes around comes around, Aggie. Her actions will catch up with Caroline soon enough. I hold no doubt in that." Oh, do shut up. Every word you utter is purely toxic, Audrey. "She wouldn't dare show her face around here, not if she knows what's good for her. How your Isabella ever give birth to that alcoholic waster is well beyond me. They're like chalk and cheese - hardly Mother and Daughter."

One thing I've come to learn in life, is that people are so very eager to judge others – and so wrongfully. Caroline and I have had some difficulties now and then, but that hasn't stopped us loving one another; it hasn't stopped our identical blood flowing through our veins. So, what if I do have Cancer and this other mysterious illness Agnes mentioned? My mind still works the same as it always has done. My emotions still course as strongly as they ever have. Why don't you and Audrey leave me alone to rot in this diseased state, Agnes? Please remember me for who I was; not this broken vessel, this shattered being. Wouldn't that perfect, and also an easy solution to your pressing torment? Leave me be. Go and don't come back. I simply cannot suffer listening to your obvious guilt-trip for another second, not if I can't console you as I used to.

"Oh, Aggie! What is that awful stench?" gasps Audrey. "I do believe our Isabella has had an accident. Can't you smell it?" It's not me! I'm impeccable – pristine! Nurse Emerson and my lovely Carers have seen to that side of things, albeit causing some dire embarrassment to myself. The only foulness I can gather is coming

124

from your sewer-like mouth, Audrey. Leave me alone, for pity's sake. Go away. Let me return to my lovely, little cottage again. "What are these 'Carers' being paid for, eh? Do they get extra for letting Isabella sit in piss? It's a bloody disgrace!"

"Calm down, Audrey. I'll press the call button and get it sorted." I'm an 'it' now, am I? Is that what I've become, an inanimate object, a creature void of any feelings or right to exist? You're overthinking things again, Isabella. Stay positive, old girl. On the plus side, at least that strange lion isn't here. "I admit, the amount of money this care home gets from Isabella's savings *is* scandalous. My sister should be getting the best care there is available, given what she's paying for it. *I'm* not going to let Isa lie in her own filth, not for a moment longer! I haven't seen a single staff member pass by since we arrived. It's appalling, Audrey!

From what point of view would you class my care as 'appalling', Agnes? Who has been tending to my weakened body of late, my constant struggle to rationalise my dire needs, where you couldn't? Beside those two horrid carers, the others have shown nothing but adoration towards me: John, Nurse Emerson, Marius, Zanna - each have bestowed an empathy over me of which I could only ever dream of. I can guarantee that they won't be getting paid much for their exhausting endeavours, either. Surely, they can only be doing this job because they *do* care about those less fortunate? Listen to yourself, Agnes. Listen to your non-sensical ramblings. This, what you are now displaying to Audrey and I, is nothing but sheer guilt. The past is in the past. Leave things the way they are. Wouldn't that be perfect?

"You get them told, Aggie. As soon as one of them turns up; you give them a good telling off."

"I will!" Don't you even think about it, Agnes. "How about we time them? Shall we see how long it takes for one of those so-called carers to answer Isabella's buzzer?" My carers will be undoubtedly busy tending to others, can you not understand that? They are not my personal slaves, regardless of what you may think. Let them get on with their duties and stop stirring the pot, for mercy's sake. "It's been a couple of minutes now, Audrey. I'm not impressed."

"It's absolutely shocking. Isabella could have passed away; she could be lying here stone-cold dead, and *they* obviously don't give a single damn." Thank you for painting such a wonderful picture, as if I don't need reminding of my ailments, Audrey. If Agnes has friends like you to rely on, then why would she ever need any enemies? It's ignorant people like yourself that deterred me away from visiting those coffee mornings at the old folks' centre. Who, in their rightful mind, would want to be associated with nasty, narrow-minded folk - the very likes of you? "I know what they'll be doing, Aggie. Those carers will be sat up that lounge, chatting, drinking coffee, and all the while their poor residents rot away without them giving a toss. I hope the same happens them one day. They all need sacking, in my humblest opinion. Nurse Emerson only looks like a kid. Are you happy with *her* being in charge over Isabella? I wouldn't be."

What consequence does age have over wisdom, on holding practical knowledge? At Nurse Emerson's age I was manufacturing bomb shells and other explosives. Being young held no factor whatsoever in what I achieved back then. Growing old certainly has had little effect on your outlook and sympathy towards others, Audrey. Besides the point, my music has gone silent again. Can't either yourself or Agnes see to this? I'd rather listen to Debussy's dreary compositions, than to put up with you two moaning and whinging on.

"Hi, is there a problem?" Thank goodness you're here, Nurse Emerson. Please, get shot of these two at once. Take pity on me. "I came as soon as I could. How is Isabella?"

"She's *alive*, if that's what you're implying?" snaps Agnes' brutish companion. I peek open an eyelid to look upon her and immediately regret it. Audrey looks to be around seventy years old. Wrinkles are spread across her whole face, and she is forming an expression as one would after sucking on a lemon for too long. What an utterly detestable woman. Agnes was never any good at making nice

126

friends. "We pressed that stupid button ages ago. What took you so long, girl?"

"I was seeing to another resident, who themselves are very ill. I'm sorry if having to wait for me has caused you any distress. I'm the only nurse on shift this afternoon." Don't apologise or explain yourself to these fools, Nurse Emerson. You are doing a terrific job, despite the lack of appreciation currently being shown. Take no notice of them, dear. I understand the predicament you're in. "How can I help?" she groans, clearly trying to remain polite. "What's the matter?"

"*What is the matter?* My girl, Isabella is festering in her own filth! Can't you smell it? It's like standing in a fish market." What have I said before about staying calm, Agnes? You don't cope well with confrontation, so don't even try. "Come on! Quick! QUICK! Do something about it, for goodness sake. I can't have my sister being treated in this undignified way. I'm disgusted by what I'm seeing here."

"I-I'll go get some help." stammers Nurse Emerson. Be brave and defiant. You're worth ten of them. "I Won't be a sec..."

"We're timing you." bleats Audrey, only adding more salt to my nurse's wounds. "Don't think we won't be having words with your manager after this! Your attitude is appalling!"

"Bugger. I need the loo myself, now." mutters Agnes, her words evidently laboured by the exertion required to rant against my nurse. "Can you keep a close eye on Isabella, just while I nip out for a moment? I'm only going for a pee."

"Of course, flower." Assures Audrey. "Isabella is in good hands with me. Take as long as you need. I'd use the public toilet and not Isabella's en-suite, only you don't want that nurse to come back in here and see you with your drawers down, do you?"

"Lord no! Thanks, dear." winces Agnes. "Oh, it's those bloody water tablets Doctor Kain prescribed for me. I can't go ten minutes without needing the loo. Don't you be getting up to any mischief whilst I'm away, Isa. Audrey will tell me if you have."

127

Like *I* would get up to anything? I can't even move my arms. You know, there's a sinister tone lurking within Audrey's voice now, hinting somehow that she's up to no good. I can't quite put my finger on it, but there's something unsettling about how she phrased those last few words. Speaking of fingers, I soon sense an unnerving sensation moving against my own. Audrey's hands quickly delve beneath my bedsheets, and then she places them over where my wedding and engagement rings are situated. What is this swine doing to me?

"This'll be our little secret, Isabella." whispers Audrey, as she painfully twists the metallic bands around my arthritic digits, in an obvious attempt to loosen them. "Caroline will only pawn them off for drink money, should *she* get her rotten hands on them first. I'm doing you a favour. Stay still, Isabella, if you know what's good for you!" What an utter beast! Get off! Get off me, I say! How dare you do this! Robert! Robert, come and stop this monster at once! "Be quiet, Isabella. Stop making those silly noises. No one can hear you, and it's not like you need your rings anymore, is it?" Get your vile hands off me, Audrey! Anybody, *please*, stop her! I can't move my arms to fight back! *"Nearly there... STAY STILL!"*

A sickening grief immediately takes hold over every inch of my body and mind. The reduced weight on my left hand comes as an abhorrent shock, and only clarifies this ghastly act of which Audrey has carried out on me. She didn't manage to get her hands on my wedding ring, thankfully, for I clasped my thumbnail hard against it. However, my sapphire engagement ring can no longer be felt. Robert worked so hard in saving his money for that ring. It is irreplaceable, as is he. You, evil – wicked - creature! How could you do such a malicious thing? Do you have no shame or morals?

"I've always suited blue, Isabella." smirks Audrey. "Thank you, dear. This will stay between you and I. It's a good job you can't talk anymore, isn't it?

My assailant expertly repositions the dishevelled bedsheets, most-likely leaving no evidence of what harrowing ordeal had taken place.

I can hear her laughing away to herself now, the evil witch. Speak, Isabella – SPEAK! Scream at her! Make her regret this heinous crime! Goodness, I feel so sick again. I feel awful.

"Well, *that* was a relief." chuckles Agnes, on her ill-timed return. "Dearie me, Isabella looks terrible! She's sweating all over, and what's wrong with her breathing?"

"I'm not sure, Aggie." gasps Audrey, feigning a surprised reaction. Do you know that your friend here is a thief, Agnes? You need to watch yourself around her. "It's because poor Isabella's had to wait so long for her carers – it's *their* fault! Press the buzzer again, Aggie. Isabella's going a funny colour now... her skin's all blotchy."

"My, dearest Isa. I wish I could end this suffering for you."

To cut a long story short, Zanna and Nurse Emerson swiftly reappear some moments later. What then follows, is the now-familiar routine of being turned over, wiped and dried. They've placed me onto my opposite side this time. I peek through a single eyelid again to find myself facing the room's open doorway. Isn't that a good thing, Isabella? Now you can watch for Bobby. He'll be here soon to save you, to get your ring back. He will. Stop thinking he won't. Why *wouldn't* he visit you?

"I'll be putting in a formal complaint against yourself and that other Carer, by the way." Shut up, Audrey! You've done enough damage today. "Isabella waited far-too long for help there. You're both a disgrace to your profession!"

"I'm really sorry." Don't be, Nurse Emerson. Seriously, do not even acknowledge this abhorrent woman. "We came as soon as possible. There's another lady, a few doors down, who is critically ill. We..."

"*We* don't want your excuses or bad attitude. We want what is right for Isabella, which should also be your highest priority. She pays for all her care, so *she* should be seen first." And you can stay quiet too, Agnes. Really, is there not some company policy to kick these morons out of here? I'd very much appreciate that, if there is.

"Can't you get it through your thick skulls that my sister is critically ill? Never mind telling your manager, I shall be informing the CQC as well about this debacle."

"Again, all I can do is apologise." responds Nurse Emerson, in apparent defeat. "If you wish to put in a formal complaint, you can see our manager, Sally Macintosh, who is in her office downstairs. Sally will address any concerns you might have within twenty-eight days." The professionalism of this girl is truly astounding. Nurse Emerson has a great-deal more patience than I would have in this situation. A good slap around the chops is what these two idiots need. My bed is suddenly knocked, presumably by Audrey and her fat thighs as she moves to stand herself up.

"I'll go and see the manager now, Aggie. You're clearly distressed by the incompetence of this nurse. *We'll* get Isabella the help she rightfully deserves. I'll make sure of it."

"Thank you, flower." Agnes sounds as nervous as Nurse Emerson does. How strange. Only seconds ago, my sister sounded like a raging elephant tearing through a dense jungle. Why the abrupt change? You never used to care so much about me, Agnes. "I'll stay here with Isabella to keep a watchful eye over her. You go ahead, Audrey."

"C-Come on, Zanna." stammers Nurse Emerson. "We'd better go."

Of all the people to be left alone with... Agnes. The last time my sister and I were left in one another's company like this was at our father's funeral. Most of Father's friends were also dead, and what family did come to his funeral party had left due to boredom, or by feeling awkward in our grief-stricken presences. I can recall reaching out to hold onto Agnes' hands, as she sat herself beside me on our parents' sofa. I mean, it felt like the right thing to do at the time. However, it wasn't well-received. We both just sat there, trembling from melancholy, and didn't utter a single word for a good hour or so. In hindsight, we didn't need to speak. We could sense an ease in our pain just by being there for one another. That's what Mother and Father would have wanted, us two getting along for once. This is what it feels like now – right here – and is an unexpected revelation, I might add. Neither Agnes or I are talking, just like then. We're in the same room, the same sombre stalemate, and in total silence. I would attempt to reach out for her hand, but my arms still won't budge, and neither will my head to look upon her. I'm afraid that you'll need to occupy yourself today, Agnes. Good-old Isabella here isn't much use in conversing nowadays.

"Oh, Isa." Agnes knows I despise being referred to by that nickname. "What are we going to do?" Now that my sister has knelt herself closer, I can clearly hear just how frail her voice now sounds. Is it a sign of her permeating sadness, or is it a fickle display of pity towards me? Either way, she sounds like a haggard old woman. "We've had our ups and downs haven't we, petal? We've been through a lot together over our many years." *Many years*? Of what age are you making us out to be? We're only in our sixties, aren't we? Open your eyes, Isabella. Come on, old girl. See for yourself what your sister is rambling on about. "If it wasn't for you and Robert, I don't know how I'd have coped with Mother and Father's deaths. You were always the strongest between us. I never really did thank you for all the help and time you gave me. I just didn't know what to say. I hope that by giving Robert a good send-off, I've made it up to you in some way? That's what a good and decent sister would do. My poor sister."

What did Agnes just say? Surely, my ears are playing tricks on me? This renewed wave of incomprehensible anxiety proves a powerful agent in opening my eyes. Heavens, Agnes looks ancient! My God, in that case, how old am I? What did she mean by giving my Bobby a good send-off? Explain yourself! What do you mean?

"We played that Louis Armstrong song he loved for the procession, Isa. What was it called again... *Wonderful World*? So many people turned up to pay their respects, you know. It broke my heart not to take you along, but you were just so poorly. You wouldn't have understood what was going on. It really did break my heart, Isa." No! This is a dream – a nightmare. This isn't real!

131

"It's all sorted, Aggie." Go away, Audrey! Agnes and have a very urgent matter discuss. You have no right to be here! "The manager was just as useless; she gave me some daft excuses, but promised she'd act on our concerns. Don't hold your hopes up, lovie."

"Thanks again, Audrey. I'm just talking to Isa... about Robert."

"Oh, it was *awful* what that poor man went through." What has happened to my Bobby? Tell me! Just once today, talk directly to me and not over me. I'm *right here.* Explain at once what you're both babbling on about. "Who'd have ever thought that Robert would succumb to Parkinson's disease? I couldn't believe it when you told me, Aggie. It was bloody dreadful watching him go the way he did." Lies! LIES! My Bobby is a bastion of good health. He's barely even suffered with Flu. *Parkinson's*?! I would have been the first to know. I would never have forgotten something like that. "To see him lose his mobility, lose his speech, that PEG feed-thingy he had to eat and drink through..." Oh, I can't take much more of this. Agnes and Audrey have obviously gone mad, or they're just being cruel to me. What have I done to deserve this? Where has that bloody lion gone? *Azrael*?! I could have asked him to gobble up these buffoons. Oh, where is my precious Robert? Come to me, darling. Prove that these foul words are nothing but wicked fibs. I won't believe them. I can't!

"It was the fact he took two weeks to die which got *me* the most. No food. No Water. Robert was nothing but skin and bones in the end, the poor fellow. He looked just like those people he had helped to liberate..." Agnes. Sister. We've had our disagreements, but - this! I don't want to be here, not without my soulmate. It's simply *not* real! Surely, my Bobby can't be... dead? "I felt so bad for our Jessica. She sat by her grandfather's side with me the whole time, before he passed. It's a shame how she can't be here in the same way for Isa. Jessica and Isabella were always so inseparable. Two peas in a pod. I used to get jealous sometimes, you know, over how close they were." My beautiful granddaughter, Jessica. How I could use your pleasant company now. To see your angelic smile, to hear that little giggle of yours, would be most-perfect. It would be...

"Jessica's working down London isn't she, Aggie?"

"Yes. She's a big-time lawyer for a huge corporation. I'm very proud of her. It's still a shame how she can't be here though. Isabella would have liked that."

I would want for nothing more, but to spend some valuable time again with my granddaughter. What has become of me? What evil twist of fate has blocked my knowledge of Robert's passing? I can't believe it – I simply won't! Out of everyone, it should have been *me* that was there to care for him, to tend to his needs, to hold his hand as he died. At least, as some reassurance, he wasn't alone. That's one consolation. Oh, I feel terribly sick. My body's trembling as if it is about to burst like a stretched bubble.

"Isabella? ISABELLA!" Agnes' shrieking cries tear through my ears like a series of nails being dragged along a chalkboard. You're not helping me feel better, dear. Oh, I'm going to be sick. Oh, lord... it's coming! "Why is she coughing up blood, Audrey? Oh, God! Where's that nurse at?"

"*I* don't know!"

"Nurse Emerson! Come Back!" wails Agnes, frantically. "Were you listening to what I was saying, Isa? Is this all *my* fault?"

The proceeding minutes pass by like a vagrant blur. Nurse Emerson and John spring back into action with my 'wonder drugs', administering them with the swiftest of precision. One of them gently cleans my mouth with another sticky swab, and then calmly replaces my blood-soaked pillow as if nothing bad had ever happened. They go to prove that there are some kind-hearted folk in this cold, broken world. Think me foolish, but I'm not concerned at all with my failing health. No. I'm completely consumed with remorse to learn of Robert's passing. My Bobby no longer being here with me is all that transpires throughout these racing thoughts of mine. I should have been there for him. It should have been me to give him the sending-off he deserved. I am his wife, after-all. I love

133

you, Robert James Cunningham. I hope, wherever you may be, that you still know this. Oh, my darling. I simply cannot live without you.

Some merciful angel has kindly put Chopin's music back on for me, which is welcomed more than any medicine my Carers can give. *Nocturne, Opus 9, No.2 in E flat Major* is being performed on an exquisite piano, by the sounds of it. However, I do wish they'd change this track over. It is a beautiful piece which I've always associated with being innately romantic – a lasting reminder of my love and devotion to Robert. Gracious, I'll never see him again, will I? I'll never feel his tender touch, nor hear his enchanting voice. This day has been the worst: I've found myself completely incapacitated, totally dependent on strangers to meet my most-basic of needs, forced to bear witness to my daughter's repentance and, to top it all off, have discovered the love of my life no longer exists. I feel so... isolated. I'm lost. I'm confused. I'm... cast aside. I've been written off by my own family and friends. Will no one take this pain away from me?

"You are not alone, Isabella."

Not that lion again. What do you want, Azrael? I wish to be left alone.

"That's not what you just said. You know, many people go through what you are now experiencing, Isabella - grief."

Yes, but that doesn't exactly ease my sorrow, does it? I'd quite happily fall back asleep, never to awaken again. I couldn't possibly though, could I? Not without my Bobby being there for me, without seeing our little Jessica one more time. However, if I were to fall asleep and never awaken, then I could be reunited with Robert and David.

134

"What about Jessica?"

Didn't you hear what I said, Azrael? I love Jessica more than anything! It's only, Agnes said that she is hundreds of miles away now, in London. It's such a long journey to make. Anyhow, I wouldn't want my granddaughter to see me in this state of affairs. Lord no. I want Jessica to be happy. Seeing me crippled would only hurt her, Azrael. It wouldn't be right.

"Your body is weak, though the love between you and her is not. Don't you want to wait a little while longer, just in case she *does* come to see her grandmother? Who is to say, she won't?"

I'm not at all sure. I can't think straight at all. Jessica must be so busy with her work and own life now? It *would* be wonderful to see just how much she has grown. I've always been proud of her. She is very much like her father, my David: so headstrong and eager to live life to its fullest. I love her immensely, equally as much as I adore her father and grandfather. I can't go on like this for much longer, dear. I'm like a puddle drying up in the midday sun.

"Enough with the metaphors, Isabella. Shall we just wait and see? I don't think that you're ready to journey with me... not yet."

You and your riddles, Azrael. I can't exactly move myself to venture anywhere, can I? I'll close my eyes again, drift off, and then hopefully fall back into that serene Northumbrian landscape. That is all I wish for now. My family are waiting there for me, I *know* they are. I can see them all as clear as crystal. There's a sedating wave creeping back over my body, Azrael. Are those new drugs of mine making me feel like this? My eyes are acting on a will of their own; I can't keep them open, no matter how hard I try.

"Rest, Isabella. You *are* loved dearly by those closest to you and strangers alike. You don't realise this now, but you will. Wouldn't that be perfect? Wouldn't that... be wonderful?"

REMINISCENCE

Lingering within this realm of sedation, quite frankly, hasn't been as unpleasant or terrifying as I had thought it would be. I've been given time to think - to focus on my most-prevalent thoughts, all those nagging doubts and reluctant admissions that I had abstained from dwelling upon. Perhaps I should explain this in greater detail, instead of babbling on about nothing like a demented old woman? Rambling a load of nonsense is certainly becoming a bad habit of mine.

I've realised today that the memories you make through life are, without any argument, its greatest gift - even the ones you might wish to forget. Memories help you to learn, to adapt, to focus on who and what truly matters, or if in fact they don't matter at all. My memories have been like a scattered puzzle over the last few hours, one which has pieces that continue to elude me. I find myself in an unfortunate position of wandering: have all these otherworldly experiences and dreams been but a side-effect of my deteriorating Cancer, and *not* from the drugs coursing through my veins? Surely, these medicines must be a factor? They are a foreign substance, after-all. The drugs in my system are a combination of man-made chemicals - completely unnatural. I mean, if you should dare look into our most-recent history, a lot of creations made by human hands are not always good, if anything, they serve to hinder life... even end it. As a species on whole, where quite a destructive one. I don't believe for a single moment that Nurse Emerson would be giving me these medications for no reason, though. To suggest such a notion would be utterly absurd. Keep on telling yourself this, Isabella. You're being well cared for. You're safe and out of harm's way, aren't you?

"Hi, Isabella." Zanna? What a joy it is to hear your voice again, but how long have you been stood there for? I must have dozed off again. "Look at her toes and her fingertips, mate. They're really starting to go blue."

"Oh, yeah." Marius? My dear, what *has* brought you both back, and why do you speak with such a mournful tone? Lord am I not sick of all this melancholic drama today. I'm don't particularly enjoy being the centre of attention, especially if it causes so much upheaval. Put Chopin's music on and forget about me, my dears. It would be the kindest thing to do for yourselves. "She's getting frailer by the minute."

"We need to get Hollie."

"Why? It's not like she's going to find a cure for Isabella's disease anytime soon, is it? Besides, Isabella's already had three doses of her anticipatory drugs. Can she have anymore?" simpers Marius. "I just hope things don't drag out like they did with poor Malcolm. I wouldn't want to see Isabella end up like he did." Zanna, in response, has fallen silent. This Malcom chap must have undoubtedly met a gruesome end? "It'll haunt me forever how bad his tumours were... and the smell they gave off."

"Please, stop talking about him." pleads Zanna, as she gently rests a hand against my own. "Isabella's not that bad, and her tumours won't get the same chance to grow like Malcolm's did." she sobs, causing some tears to form in my own eyes. I have grown so very fond of this girl. "It's all happening so fast. I really don't want to leave her."

"We'll need to soon though, Zan. Handover starts in half an hour. It's almost home time."

What a wicked disease Cancer is; it robs you of all your strength and, at least in my case, can cloud your precious memories. It's insufferable. It's cruel, unforgiving and merciless. What makes this sorry saga harder to stomach, is the sheer fact I'm totally powerless to do anything about it. My fate is no longer my own to direct. I have no recollection of coming here, or of ever greeting these kind strangers, of whom now dutifully watch over me. I wish you were here, Robert. I wish you could make sense of things for me, my darling. Life isn't fair, that's what they say, and by gosh are they right. I miss you, Bobby. I wonder if you can still hear and see me? I've never been without you before.

"They kept poor Malcolm on those sub-cut fluids right up until the last moment." recounts Zanna, bitterly. "God, it was horrific to watch. I know I shouldn't say this, but it's about time euthanasia was legalised..."

"*Whoa*, Zan!" gasps Marius, clearly taken back by these words. "Be careful with what you're saying." he stutters. "It can get you into a lot of trouble saying things like that. Aren't you being a little... extreme?"

"Seriously? Howay, mate." counters Zanna. "Unlike the politicians who make our laws, who've never cared for people at the end of their lives like *we* have, we've watched those under our care die slowly - and for what – to meet the government's *ethical obligations*? How can dragging out someone's pain and humiliation possibly be humane or ethical? It's wrong, Marius. I don't care what you or they say. It's so wrong."

"I didn't say that I didn't agree with you, Zan. I just don't want you to lose your job." whispers my Greek God. "I wouldn't be so open in telling others how you feel, not if you don't want to end up back on the dole."

"I'm entitled to an opinion, aren't I?" seethes Zanna. Gracious, I'm liking this girl even more now. She's got so much spunk! "A few weeks ago, there was a story on BBC News about a woman who took her husband to a clinic in Switzerland."

"A Suicide Clinic?" replies Marius, reservedly.

"Yeah. He wanted to end it all for his own sake, as well as for those he loved. The poor guy had Motor Neuron Disease. He was a prisoner in his own body." Lord, I know that feeling. Bless him.

"It's still illegal isn't it, to travel to one of those clinics? I'm surprised the guy's wife didn't get into trouble for helping him."

"She did. His wife ended up getting arrested when she flew back. You can't tell me that what they did was not a more dignified choice? The poor bloke knew that he was going to die, and he even wanted to. What's so wrong with skipping the horrible parts in-between? All these *do-gooders* don't know what they're talking about."

"Zan," sighs Marius, "I don't think we should be talking about this. I've never liked getting into politics, anyway."

"I'm just saying..."

"I know, but I don't want to talk about it. I'm Catholic... remember?" Oh, like me! "Life is sacred. No one should play God. Personally, I don't agree with those clinics. Can we change the subject, please?"

Marius, my dear, does Zanna not have a valid argument to debate? Is this not a subject fit for open discussion? Are honest opinions really that controversial nowadays? Dear me. "Maybe, now is the time to set up Isabella's syringe driver? For all we know, she could still be in a lot of pain. Hollie was talking about setting it up before she leaves tonight."

Zanna holds her tongue for a couple of seconds against Marius' diversion, likely exhausted by her tirade. I can sense the girl's boiling temper rise, and it does so with good cause. If I were to have a choice, however unlikely, the option of ending this relentless torment would most-certainly be approved. Oh, if only I could talk.

"I can't believe it's nearly clocking-off time." whimpers Zanna, whilst glancing across to my clock. "I'm dreading it. I just want to stay here with Isabella, to hold her hands and never let go of them. Hollie and John might be able to set up the driver before we go, mightn't they? I hope so." she whispers, as if to hide her words away from my prying ears. Do you not have a home to go to, darling? I can't imagine this boring company of mine being overly-thrilling. My conversation skills have greatly diminished, not that Agnes would complain about that. I was quite happy to let my sister rant on about the world around us, despite if she did talk a load of old cods-wallop. Heavens above, even Agnes has abandoned me now. Go back to sleep, Isabella. Do yourself a favour, old girl. Focus on

Chopin's music and let it take you away from this vicious cycle. "We've looked after Isabella for over six years... that's a long time. She's more like family now, than a client. I'm gonna miss her so much." I haven't gone anywhere yet, flower. Bloody Nora, she's starting to cry again. "I'm sorry." sniffles Zanna.

"You've let yourself get too close." sympathises Marius, mimicking Nurse Emerson's wisdom earlier. "I'm one to talk, though. I've always had a little soft-spot for Isabella. I think you're right, in saying she's been with for six years. It might be even longer."

Six years? I've been trapped in this limbo-state, this crippled body, for six *bloody* years? Good Lord, where has all that time gone? The last thing I can remember, before finding myself stuck in this bed, was going out for some bread and milk one winter's night. It was an unusually-hot, Saturday evening. Robert was very insistent that I shouldn't have gone alone, being it was so dark outside. Bobby was still getting over a bad bout of the flu, so he couldn't accompany me. I don't know why Robert was so concerned. I've always been able to take care of myself. *I* am an Escomb Angel... as tough as they come. Nothing frightens me. Well, not usually.

I got about half-way to the local corner shop when two young children approached me. They only looked to be about fifteen or sixteen years old, and they were wearing those God-awful hoodie clothes. One decided to grab me by the arm, a young girl with rageful eyes, yet I could also sense some fear in them. I can't remember why she was so mad with me, or even if it was I that she was angry at. Heavens above! I wonder where my purse is? I had my bus pass in there and everything. Didn't they take your handbag? Think, Isabella – THINK! They hurt you, didn't they?

"Hollie's doing her handover notes downstairs at the minute. I'll go and give her a shout, Zan." grumbles Marius. "I'm not leaving here until that driver's set up."

What is this 'driver' thing they're talking about? Robert used to enjoy playing Golf, well, before his knees started playing up. One of his clubs was called a Driver. Don't say, I'm going to be treated to one of those? Marius and Zanna wouldn't do such a horrid act to me, not my lovely Carers. Get a grip of yourself, old girl.

"Hold on a minute, Marius. We haven't checked Isabella over yet." chuckles Zanna, as she cautiously removes my warm duvet away from me. "She's due a turn and pad check – remember?"

"It's been a long day. I can't smell anything." That's so very reassuring, Marius. Thank you. "She hasn't drunk anything for ages. It'll be a miracle if Isabella's passed urine."

"She hasn't. Her pad's bone-dry."

"Is it?"

With all the terrible events possibly going on in this world, my lack of pee somehow tops the bill, does it? If I should need the bathroom, I'll make it my duty to inform you both. I'm not one for breaking promises.

"Can you let Hollie know that as well, when you find her?"

"Yeah. Come on, let's get Isabella repositioned."

"Hello, Isabella. Are you glad to see me again?"

Not especially, Azrael. Could you kindly give me a moment, please? My arse is out on full display again and, I dare say, it's hardly a pleasant sight to behold.

"I've seen worse. Anyway, how are you feeling?"

What a question to ask. My engagement ring has been stolen, I've had to endure a visit from Agnes, and I've just discovered that Robert has passed away. Do you expect me to be leaping around with joy? I'm surrounded by complete strangers, Azrael, yet they seem to know every fine detail about me. I've never felt so bloody dreadful in all my life.

"I'm sorry... about Robert. It was his time, Isabella. Life cannot exist without death."

Yes, I understand that, and why should you be apologising for anything? You're not even real, Azrael; a figment of my imagination and sedation, that's what *you* are. If it wasn't for the fact you sound like Roger Moore, I'd be politely telling you to clear off. The saddest thing is, and it pains me to say this, you're the only soul who can hear my voice and comprehend my conflicting emotions. The only other who could claim right to such a privilege was Robert, but he's gone. I should be with him, Azrael. I shouldn't be here.

"Patience, Isabella. Look, I can tell when my company isn't wanted. I'll wait a little longer for when, for when you *are* ready to accompany myself on a greater journey."

Zanna is currently busying herself by slapping some cream across my buttocks, Azrael. Now is not the best time for taking on any adventures. Besides, I'm quite settled where I am, thank you very much. Dare I ask what mischief you've been up to, at least since we last spoke? Have you been harassing anyone else?

"I've been keeping a close eye on your sister, Agnes. She's not too well, either. I do hope Agnes is more welcoming than you have been to me."

Agnes hates cats. I can't imagine her being all-too civil with you, Azrael. Don't say that I didn't give you any warning, my dear. Hold on a tic, how *dare* you insinuate that I've not been welcoming towards you! I believe in doing unto others as they do unto you. *He is without sin shalt cast the first stone*, and all that lark. You have been courteous with me thus far, so I have repaid your kindness by not forcefully ordering you to tittle off. Trust me, I've been tempted.

143

"I do appreciate your cooperation. I'm rarely welcomed by those whom I visit. You have proved to be an unexpected privilege, albeit a feisty one, Isabella Cunningham. I'm even starting to enjoy your company."

I can hear footsteps! You need to leave, Azrael! What's to say these new intruders won't see you?

"Rest assured, no one else can see me. Although, at certain times, they may sense my presence here. I am more than just a simple feline, Isabella."

Thankfully, Zanna speeds up her progress and returns my duvet to its original, more comforting, position in no time. There are numerous footsteps entering my bedroom now, a great deal more than what I've heard previously. Who else has come to cry over me? Is this all I must look forward to nowadays? God, it's so bloody depressing being stuck in this room. I'm not used to any drama. I only want an easy life, one where I can walk and talk again. Is that too much to wish for?

"Shhh... listen to them."

"Hello, Isabella." sniffles Nurse Emerson.

"Hi, sweetheart." sighs John. "Her breathing has definitely changed since we last saw her."

"She's breathing more from her stomach now." states my nurse, sorrowfully. "You can leave now, if you want to?" she hints, possibly to Marius and Zanna? "John and I are going to set up Isabella's syringe driver. If you've got other residents to see..."

"No. We'd prefer to stay, Hollie. The other residents are all settled, and we've finished doing our paperwork." replies Zanna, in a dreadfully solemn tone. Please, just one of you, laugh or smile. Enlighten this shattered heart of mine. Break this depressive

144

atmosphere. "We want to stay with Isabella for as long as possible. I for one don't want to leave her alone... not tonight."

"Okay. It'll be handover soon, mind." says Nurse Emerson, as she leans over me with the greatest of care. I manage to peek open one of my eyes, only to discover a thick syringe is situated within her hands. It's full of some strange, clear fluid of which I can only guess are more medicines. Aren't I drugged up enough already? "This isn't going to hurt, Isabella." I certainly hope not. I told you, I despise needles. "There'll be a little scratch, that's all. I'll remove the sub-cut line and place this new one on the opposite side. Are you all watching, only you might learn something?"

"What's in the syringe, Hollie?" questions Zanna, anxiously. With immediate effect, I share in her apprehension. "Will it make, you know, things happen sooner?"

"There's Midazolam, Morphine and Hyoscine in this. They should help to keep Isabella calm and pain-free. The infusion lasts for twenty-four hours, and it's checked hourly to ensure nothing malfunctions." Nurse Emerson playfully taps away at the syringe to release a series of little bubbles, then lowers it closer towards my skin. "It's what she needs, Zanna, but it is not intended to make 'things' go any quicker. I know where you're coming from, and I'd suggest you keep those thoughts to yourself. There's a reason why these medications are classed as controlled drugs, why you need two people to sign them out; it's to stop them being abused... for malicious purposes. What you might think isn't necessarily legal, Zan. I strongly suggest you don't hint at it anymore, and perhaps read up on those doctors who took life into their own hands."

"Told you so." interjects Marius, in a cautious voice. "I said that you need to be careful, didn't I, Zan?"

"I was only asking." counters Zanna, in a nervous murmur. "I'd never think of doing *that*. Never."

Bless her heart. Zanna is saying what most people, well those with any sort of conscience, would likely be thinking. Why death is such a no-go subject is beyond me. If I had the power to do so, I'd quite willingly accept a pill or injection to end this ongoing plight. Zanna is simply proving, more than any others here present are, that she truly cares about my wellbeing. I believe so, anyway. There's a good girl. Don't let formalities dampen your resolve, for it is what makes you who you are, and your feelings obviously come from a lengthy exposure to such ailments as mine. It's a great pity that this topic is so controversial. Maybe, just maybe, one day it won't be?

"If you said to me this time last month, that Isabella would be needing a syringe driver, I'd have thought you were joking." That's better, Marius. Smile. I want to see that lovely grin of yours. "Why has Isabella's health deteriorated at such a rapid rate? I don't get it."

"It's her Vascular Dementia, mate. Depending on the individual, the deterioration can be fast or slow. It's a very unpredictable disease." comments John. Wait a moment, my boy, *Vascular Dementia*? He's getting all mixed up, surely? I have Cancer - not Dementia! Oh, gracious. Agnes mentioned something about me having a separate illness, didn't she? My sister is terrible for telling lies, but she wouldn't make something like this up. Oh Lord, have mercy. "You'll find that some people with it have a sudden deterioration and then plateau, not always, but a lot of the time. Like any other mental illness, dementias are unique to each person. My Grandpa Murray has it now, so I can see it from both sides of the spectrum... at work *and* at home." I don't have Dementia, John. You're quite mistaken, my dear. "Some days, Grandad has very lucid moments, where he actually remembers who I am. On other days, he hasn't a clue at all and thinks that I'm someone he knows from when he worked down the mines. I try to make the most out of his good days, but they're getting fewer now."

"That's awful, John." sympathises Zanna. "It must be really hard for you?"

"Sometimes it is. Visiting Grandpa Murray is getting harder each time I go to see him; you don't ever know what mood he's going to be in, or if he'll even be awake. All he seems to do now is sleep. In hindsight, Isabella has done well with her Vascular Dementia. In the time that she's been here, she's only had a couple of TIA's."

Dementia. He said it again, so you must have heard him right, old girl. Should I feel relieved or absolutely mortified by this revelation? If I *do* have this wicked disease, then it would explain why my memory has been so blurry, and why I had no knowledge of Robert passing away. I mean, what kind of wife wouldn't know that? Poor Caroline. In a sense, my daughter has lost both her parents. This is intolerable. It's so... demeaning. Thank you, John, for finally shedding light on what is the matter with me. Thank you all for being there to help. I do appreciate you, even if I *have* been aggressive towards yourselves in the past. That is not me. I'd never hurt anyone.

"In this day and age, you'd have thought there would be a cure by now? I hope I never get it." groans Zanna. "You wouldn't wish it on your worst enemies. They can send people to the moon, spend millions on pointless wars, but they can't stop *this*. Our world is so screwed up."

"Research on Alzheimer's and Dementia is making progress, Zan, probably because our government is starting to realise just how much it's costing them." says John, with a subtle roll of his eyes. "Who knows, there might be a cure found in our lifetime? That won't be much use to Isabella though, would it?" Thanks for your lovely input there, John. You know, the name 'Murray' does somewhat ring a bell. I wonder if it is Henry, the chap my Bobby used to play Dominoes with, down the working men's club? He was a funny fellow. "All we can do in the meantime, is to keep our residents as comfortable as possible, to help promote their purpose and grant some quality of life to them. It's not always an easy task to achieve, not when we've been so short-staffed, like today."

"Can we have some quiet now, please? I'm going to start Isabella's infusion. I need to concentrate." ushers Nurse Emerson, to a swift and definitive silence. She is moving that syringe ever-closer towards me, along with a large, clear box in her other hand. What strange technology. It's like a small computer. "That's the needle in. I'll just commence the infusion and..." The needle is already in? I never felt a thing. All I *can* feel is Nurse Emerson patting a small plaster onto my stomach. This is all so very peculiar. "We're done. I'll just check the volume and battery life, then lock it up. Twenty-four hours..." She's gone quiet herself now. Why leave that sentence on such a cliff-hanger, Nurse Emerson? Do you not believe that I will see out those promised hours? I'm going nowhere, dear.

"Take care, Isabella. We're going home in a short while, but we'll be thinking of you tonight." whispers John, tenderly. "You know, I've done this job for nearly ten years. Despite that, this part never gets any easier. It's difficult when you've got a soft-spot..."

"Doesn't that just mean that you care, John?" interrupts Zanna. "It wouldn't be right otherwise. I seriously don't want to leave Isabella alone. We're short-staffed tonight as well, aren't we? Who is going to sit with Isabella, to keep her company?"

"Well," Nurse Emerson exhales heavily, then pats along my bedrails in a nervous manner. "*Apparently*, another family member is due to arrive soon. They might be staying with Isabella overnight. It just depends on how things go."

"Oh, yeah. I heard about that." gleams Marius. "She should have been here by now, from what Sally said to me in the staff room. I've never met this other relative yet."

"I hope they still turn up. I don't want to come in tomorrow to find out they haven't been." says John, glumly. "She's been let down so many times before. Poor Isabella's been let down enough by people who said they'd visit her."

If being truthful, the greatest issue I presently have is my lack of being able to converse with these doting carers of mine. I'm also unsure as to whether being visited by this 'other relative' is going to be a good or bad thing. If it's my cousin, Matilda, then I'd frankly rather be doped up to the eyeballs. Heavens, she's worse than Agnes for trying my patience.

From what I've been able to gather, Nurse Emerson and my Carers have been here for at least ten hours today. All that time spent on looking after me, away from their families, somehow compelled into serving my basic needs. Surely, they can't be doing it for the money? What a humbling thing to witness. I don't know any of you but, know this, I *do* appreciate your company and expertise. Take little notice of Agnes and Audrey, for they don't and shall never understand your roles. I do... now. I am ever-thankful for you all being here. I only wish that Robert was, too.

"Can you remember that time when Isabella set off the fire alarms, so that she could escape down the stairwells?" chuckles John. "She made it half-way down the road before we managed to catch up to her. Even with a walking frame, she was quick." Well, this *is* news to me. I am glad that you find this 'supposed' event amusing, John. However, I don't recall it at all. "Not forgetting the time when she threw a cup of tea over the mayor's head at our Summer Fete. Man, that was class. The other councillors didn't know where to look."

"It was *so* funny!" giggles Nurse Emerson. I do enjoy seeing this side to you both. It's a refreshing breath of air from our current moping, I'll gladly confess. "What about when she threw that casserole over Sally last Christmas. Isabella certainly showed us just what she thought of our meals, didn't she?" Those puréed meals today were utterly disgusting, though only because of their consistency. I'm sorry if I've caused any offence, dears. "I'll never forget those times. *We'll* never forget you, Mrs. Cunningham."

"So many happy memories." Perhaps, Marius? Although they are memories, of which, I can't remember. What you would consider to be joyous reminiscences, I myself can only fathom as being some out of body misdemeanour. I haven't a clue what any of you are talking about. Goodness, I would never act in such an unruly manner. How many times must this point be made? "I miss how Isabella would insist on me sitting in here with her, so that we could listen to Chopin together. To be honest, I can't stand that kind of music, but it was nice to see the smile lift on her face when she'd

149

hear certain songs play." Chopin was and shall always be my first love, Marius. Thank you for putting up with my music, as well as me. "Listening to music was all Isabella had, especially when her visitors didn't turn up, even after they said they would."

"I'll miss the way she used to follow us around all the time, constantly asking for tea and biscuits. God help you, if you forgot to put two sugars in." You can wipe that smirk off your face as well, Zanna. Oh, and by the way, I'm still waiting for a decent cuppa. It must have slipped your mind with being so busy today? "You couldn't walk past Isabella without getting a slap across the back of your legs with that walking frame of hers, or a punch in the arm. I know it was the Dementia, though. She couldn't help doing those things."

"Going off what Isabella's daughter said, she wasn't always like that." Thank the Lord, Marius. Some sense is finally being spoken. "She was kind, caring, and would never lift a finger to anyone. It just seems, we met a different side to old Isabella – the best side." That's very true, Marius, and quite surprising to learn of this complimentary information coming from Caroline. My daughter would only ever see the wrong in me. Besides, I'm no longer prepared to dwell on the past, for where will it lead me to? Usually if someone annoys me, I would simply ignore them back in return. I would *never* resort to violence, I wouldn't even raise my voice to them. Why waste your time on fools? You can't reason with them. Wouldn't you agree with me, Azrael? *Azrael*?! "I'm surprised at Caroline leaving so soon today. What sort of daughter does that to her mother? *Caroline* – that's who."

"We've no right to judge, Marius." There goes Nurse Emerson with her official tone again. "A lot went on between Isabella and Caroline before we met them. To give her some credit, Caroline managed to look after Isabella pretty well at home, before her behaviours got out of control."

"Like - how?!" snaps Zanna. "When Isabella came to us, she wasn't *that* bad. There wasn't that much wrong with her, apart from some poor short-term memory and the odd mood swing."

"Her hallucinations were horrendous, to say the least." jolts Nurse Emerson. "Try to put yourself in Caroline's shoes: your mother is seeing imaginary animals, she's striking out at you constantly, she won't let you help her in any way, and keeps you awake all night because her body clock has been altered. Caroline had no choice but to watch Isabella - her mother - deteriorate every day, and without any breaks or understanding towards Dementia. Could you cope in the same situation?"

"Well, no... but."

"What else was Caroline meant to do? She did her best to look after Isabella, and for as long as possible. Caroline did more than some people would have, given the same circumstances. It is *not* our place to judge. I know I keep saying this, but it's true. We're here to care for Isabella's needs, not to comment on her personal relationships."

Please, all of you, just leave me alone with Chopin. Take your arguments and feelings, take them all away you, and just let these beautiful Nocturnes guide me off into that heavenly realm again. I don't care who it is that will be visiting me... not now. No one can make me feel any better. No one can bring back my Bobby, and there's little chance they will help to alleviate this awful sense that I'm nothing but a burden – a relic only fit for disposal. That's how I feel, Azrael. But, I'm still not ready to venture off anywhere with you... not yet.

"When *will* you be, Isabella? I can't wait forever."

"Sorry." mumbles Zanna, under her breath. "It's just... it just narks me off how Isabella has been treated by her own family. Can't Caroline see how frail she is now? Doesn't she care? I for one wouldn't treat my mam this way."

"Caroline cares a great deal about Isabella." responds Nurse Emerson. "Why else would she keep on visiting her? It would have been easy enough to have just left Isabella in here with us, never to worry about her again, but Caroline hasn't. Look at some of our other residents: a few haven't had visitors in years, and they're nowhere near as poorly as Isabella is. There's still a huge stigma surrounding mental health – Dementia in particular. Even some medical professionals struggle to understand how it works. Caroline has her own problems, but she still makes a considerable effort to see Isabella. We've done our bit. We've kept Isabella safe and tried to make her time here with us meaningful; *that* is our role; *that* is why we do this job. Don't make things personal... it'll only tear away at you."

"It's bull-crap." Language, Zanna! Really, my girl. We ladies should never curse, not unless our husband's have given us good reason to do so. Robert gave me plenty of excuses over the years, therefore, I have every ground to swear. I just choose not too... most of the time. "Someone breaks a leg... they're surrounded by well-wishers and sympathy. Someone gets a mental illness... they're ostracised by society. It makes me sick. It's 2016, for God's sake. You'd have thought people would be less ignorant towards illnesses like Alzheimer's by now?"

Oh, Zanna. You need to understand that the brain is a delicate instrument and, in the same sense, is also a controversial entity. I'm at risk of rambling on again, aren't I? What I mean is, our brains send out millions of signals every day and we don't even realise it. They control our very actions – our very thoughts. Brains, like any other muscle in the body, can become frail too. Mine has obviously, by the looks of it. Maybe one day, society will grow to accept our brain's mysteries, its bountiful gifts, whilst also accepting its horrific diseases. There could come that most-desired of times where illnesses like Cancer and Dementia will finally be cured? To some, like myself, mental health is terrifying mystery, a fearful possibility of which may inflict them. I do hope that, at least during your lifetime, the magnificent scientists in this world do discover such miraculous cures. I honestly do, my dears, with all my heart. As Zanna rightfully stated: if mankind can send people to the moon, then why can't they stop Dementia and Cancer from occurring? Does it come down to money? Lord knows, it shouldn't. Life is too precious to cast aside.

"Goodnight, Isabella." whispers John, while he gently pats a warm hand against my cold wrists. "It'll be over soon, darling... you'll be free. Go back to sleep and listen to Chopin. Get the rest you need, what you deserve. Take care, sweetheart. We'll all be thinking of you tonight."

Chopin's *Nocturne, Opus 48 in C Minor* suddenly plays, coinciding with my guests as they each take their reluctant leave. It is piece which I wouldn't normally listen to, partly because it's quite morbid, dark, lengthy and unnerving. I try to replace this frigid atmosphere with more euphoric thoughts of being reunited with my Bobby. Where is he now, I wonder? Is he waiting for me at Heaven's pearly gates? If so, wouldn't that be perfect? Wouldn't that... be wonderful?

AN UNREQUITED ABSOLUTION

Some many years ago, during our childhood, Mother and Father would vehemently insist on taking Agnes and I to church every Sunday – come rain or shine. It was a routine that none of us could break, not even if we fell ill or simply couldn't be bothered to attend. Why, to make such a blasphemous notion would instantly warrant a hard slap across one's buttocks from Father. By gosh, he had a firm hand, nevertheless he was still very loving towards us. You see, we were raised as staunch Catholics, a devotion which I have sadly come to struggle with over the later years in life. I always doubted that this conflict would be understood by my parents, hence why I never openly talked to them about it. I wouldn't even try to explain my reservations to them, seeing as it would only cause them unnecessary heartache. Gracious, I could never do such a thing to Mother and Father, despite them being so usually open-minded.

There was a specific sermon I can recall that held a truly-profound meaning, one of which I shan't forget in a hurry. Our local priest had just lost his youngest daughter to Scarlett Fever, a terrible illness which almost took Agnes and I as well. Father Brian was his name. He was the tallest chap in Harrogate, and a gentle giant of sorts. You would never see him frown, despite his obvious loss, which is something I always admired him for. Anyone else would have surely crumbled under such a tremendous amount of grief, but Father Brian genuinely believed that, someday, he would be once again reunited with his darling daughter, Emily, and that she was waiting for him in Heaven, herself surrounded by countless loved ones and immortal Angels. Such a lovely fellow.

This very sermon emphasised Father Brian's complete adoration to our religion, its doctrines and assuring messages. I can't remember how the exact words went, mind you, though I can still see the wonderful smile on his face as he talked through the various passages. It was a wonderful sight to behold; it was endearing, humbling, and perfect in every way. For that split moment in time, I continued to believe in God, Yahweh, Jehovah... whomever you may refer to this deity as. I only wish that wonderful feeling lasted. Life is so very strange. Life can also be incredibly confusing and contradictory too, can't it?

Why am I bleating on about these memories? Well, I can smell a faint waft of incense which is also infused with the lingering aroma of strong, fortified wine. The last time I could smell these aromas was in church, during childhood. Therefore, I can only gather that a priest is standing before me now. If I could just open my eyes to take a glance. Mind you, there's not much a priest can do for me in this present state, other than to put a good word in for me when I *do* reach those heavenly plains. I do hope it's the pearly gates and not the fiery ones. Oh, my! Now, wouldn't *that* be something? I've lived a mostly righteous life, I think, although there *was* that time I accidently crashed Robert's new car. The silly devil wouldn't teach me to drive, but I simply had to learn... somehow. Bless him. Robert was never one for being patient, not even with me.

"Thank you for coming, Father Mark. Isabella's family will no-doubt appreciate you performing this service for her. I'm afraid that none of them could make this allotted time." I don't recognise this man's voice at all. He doesn't sound like Marius or John. No. This voice is far-deeper and much more mature. I may grow to like him, however only time will tell. "I'll close the door for you on my way out. If you need me for anything, I'll be waiting just outside."

"Thank you, Nurse Vaughan." responds the priest, in a lovely Irish accent. "I should be okay and won't be too long." The sermons I used to sit through lasted, at the very minimum, a couple of hours. Father Mark's idea of a short period may vastly differ from mine. "Good evening, Mrs. Cunningham. It's a pleasure to meet you." The priest tenderly wraps a set of fingers around mine which are very comforting, I must say. He is being so very carefull with me, as a true Man of God should be. "Let us begin... in the name of the Father, of the Son, and of the Holy Spirit. Amen."

Oh, dear. Should I assume that this passage is going to consist of my *Last Rites*? Things aren't looking good for you, Isabella. I would wager a firm bet that Caroline is the culprit behind this unexpected visit. This is quite ironic, really, given Caroline would blatantly refuse to visit church with Bobby, David and I. Agnes wouldn't have gone through the trouble of arranging such a reading; she is just as critical of our religion as I am, not to mention all the possible sins she would have most-certainly committed during her sordid lifetime. The wily, old minx.

"I commend you, my dear sister, to almighty God..."

"Are you paying attention, Isabella?"

I certainly am, Azrael. And when did *you* come in? This is meant to be a private sitting. What gives you the right to be here?

"I don't have much choice. It is not like I enjoy hearing these verses being spouted off again and again, in different contexts and in different languages. I'm curious, do you not find ease in the salvation your faith offers?"

I have found little to no comfort from words handed down by ancient scholars, seeing that there's been far-too much opportunity for their wisdom to be corrupted. Forgive me for thinking this way, Azrael, only my spiritual beliefs have grown weaker and weaker over the passage of time. How can I possibly be subservient to an almighty being, a deity who so cruelly took away my mother and father, my only son... my beloved husband. Where was God at for those poor souls my Bobby helped to liberate back in the war? They were tortured, starved - women and children - as well! Where was God at... oh, never mind. I'm sick of whinging about things today.

"There is always darkness where light flourishes, as there is always light where darkness dwells. That is the way of life, and that is how it shall remain. You cannot change this, Isabella, no matter how much you would like to. Nothing can."

Please don't take my doubts wrongfully, Azrael. To follow a religion can, arguably, carry many positives with it. Take my Aunt Edith for example: she was putting off a visit to Rome for many years, on account of her ridiculous fear of flying. Funnily enough, the year Aunt Edith chose to travel there just so happened to be when her doctors discovered a blood clot in one of her legs. This would have gone unnoticed, had she not summoned the will to take that very flight. Aunt Edith always claimed that this was an 'Act of God'. Agnes and I would often state to her that this was merely a perfect coincidence. Perhaps I learned my stubbornness from Aunt Edith? We were always so very close.

"A *coincidence*? Are you sure?"

Of course! Aunt Edith had terrible circulation *and* smoked sixty cigarettes a day until the day she died, so this news came at little surprise. She should have seen a doctor sooner. Shouldn't the 'divine powers that be' have intervened more swiftly to ease such distress? Goodness, I do miss her. Aunt Edith was such a funny old soul, and her piano playing was simply exquisite.

"People have a free will of their own, Isabella. Be it good or bad, righteous or sinful. Surely, you understand this? Life would be boring if everyone got along, wouldn't it? You would never learn nor grow."

I have seen both the good and bad in people today, admittedly. I do understand where you are coming from, Azrael, and appreciate your insight. I merely don't like to overthink these sorts of things. It's easier just to lie back and watch the world move on without you... as I am now. That would be the best route to take, especially since I can't move.

"With death comes a new path of discovery, along with grief. Some do not require the teachings of old to overcome their troubles, much like yourself. It is a shame, however, that you do not share in the same devotion as your parents did to their faith. Each to their own, they say."

You're mocking me now, aren't you? You horrid, mangey cat! I don't need faerie stories to tell me how to behave or what to be fearful of. I have a free will - like you said - or at least I did, before this bloody illness took over. Why don't you go and bother some other poor soul? I will happily allow for this priest to carry out his duties, even if I don't necessarily need them. Go on! Leave me be, Azrael! Shoo!

"Stubborn as always. Very well, Isabella. I shall leave."

Why on Earth am I arguing with an imaginary feline? For goodness sake, Isabella. You *have* gone mad, old girl. Maybe, in hindsight, I was a little too-hard on Azrael. When he is around, I do feel much more relaxed, though I can't fathom as to why this is so. I shouldn't have brought Robert into this, either. My Bobby remained very loyal to our faith, despite those evil scenes he had witnessed during the war. Robert would often say: God's will could be witnessed in those aiding the inflicted, the innocent victims, and the dying during that wicked period in human history. I feel so foolish for thinking otherwise. You can come back now if you want to, Azrael. I really don't mind sharing in your company. I don't want to be left alone.

"Bless you, Isabella." announces the priest, suddenly, returning my immediate attention towards him. "Goodbye... and may God's grace be with you."

"Thank you, Father." whispers Nurse Vaughan, from beside me. I've only gone and missed my own prayer reading! Mother and Father would be furious with me. "That was a privilege to witness. I'll contact the family to let them know about your visit. Is there anything else you need?"

"No, thank you." smiles my priest. "Isabella is in good hands... that's clear to see. Goodnight. I'll see myself out."

"Would you agree with Father Mark's statement, Isabella?"

Certainly, Azrael, and... thank you for returning. I'm not usually so rude. It's the drugs – yes, that's what it is.

"Apology accepted. Now, if you would be so kind, please answer the question. I'm a very curious feline, you know."

Well, my Carers are ensuring that I'm comfortable, well sedated and looked after. What more could a girl in my position wish for? Some peace and quiet *would* be welcomed. I'm becoming such a terrible hypocrite. I'm desperate to be left alone, to immerse myself in Chopin's preludes, but I'm also fearful of solitude. I don't know where to put myself anymore.

"It is your choice, Isabella. Would you like for me to stay, or should I wait on your decision a little longer? Not to put any further pressure on you, but I'm rather busy."

It all depends, dear. I am growing to enjoy your company, but I'm also passionate about seeing my beautiful granddaughter again. Mind you, what is the likelihood of *that* happening, hmm? From what I can gather, Jessica is hundreds of miles away from here -

159

wherever *here* is. She's undoubtedly living an adult life now, with countless troubles of her own. Why should Jessica make the effort of visiting a knackered old woman like me, one who can't even forge a single word or smile towards her? It *would* have been blissful to have seen how much she has grown...

"Patience is a virtue. Life can sometimes work in wonderous ways. Love is a strong influence and is something you and your granddaughter share in greatly together. I shall wait, though I don't often grant this opportunity. Unlike yourself, Isabella, I am patient."

I'm patient but also realistic, Azrael. It was a bloody miracle that Caroline came to see me, let alone Agnes. I don't want Jessica to remember me as this frail, elderly woman. I want Jessica to remember all the good times we had; all those summer nights in which we star-gazed; all those lovely, winter mornings when we would walk my Winston along the narrow stream; all those weekends spent away at Whitby, and so on. I couldn't bear for her to see me like this, not even the slightest glimpse. It would only cause her upset. I simply couldn't put my granddaughter through that level of misery.

"You have nothing to be ashamed of. The illnesses that constraint you are not of your own making; they are a mere side-effect of existence. I know this will bring little assurance to you and, if being honest, I don't really care. It is the truth, and the truth can hurt. The sooner you accept... the easier this night will become."

"Hello, Isabella." pipes up Nurse Vaughan, taking me completely off guard. I was about to give Azrael a good telling-off, my dear fellow. "I'm sorry to bother you, but I need to give you some more mouthcare. It's a bit like a lollipop, just think of it that way."

Another of those sticky swabs is then placed into my dried-out mouth. Nurse Vaughan teases the stick along my parched lips, and then onto my sore gums. strangely, it's quite refreshing, although it does leave a lemon aftertaste. I can't stand lemons -Yuck! A cup of Yorkshire tea would have sufficed, Nurse. Lord knows, I've been waiting all day for one.

"How is she doing?" comments another gentleman. I'm sure there's a bloody conveyor belt leading through my doorway, with a never-ending supply of random people. "When's Isabella due another positional turn?"

"Not for another hour or so, Stuart." replies Nurse Vaughan, whilst patting carefully at my nearest bedrail. "What are you doing up here, anyway? I thought Sally based on the ground floor tonight?"

"I am – just wanted to come and see how Isabella is doing, that's all. It was only a few weeks ago when she chased me down the corridor with a packet of biscuits. It's the first time I've been assaulted with food." laughs the other chap, and he is soon joined by Nurse Vaughan in chuckling at my expense. Lord have mercy. I *am not* aggressive! Fair enough, I did help to build bombs during the war, but that was to serve my country. Not even Agnes bore the brunt of my frequent frustrations with her, though she did rightfully deserve them. "Dementia's a horrible disease, isn't it?"

"That it is, mate, that-it-is." sighs Nurse Vaughan, just before he removes the sickly swab away from my lips with a precise popping motion. Thank goodness. I couldn't tolerate a moment longer of having to suck on that god-awful thing. "To be honest, Stuart, I wouldn't bother with carrying out the four-hourly turns anymore. Isabella seems settled enough, and the drugs from her syringe driver should be well in her system by now. Let's give her some peace and quiet, yeah? How would you like two random blokes standing over your bedside?"

"I wouldn't." giggles Stuart, awkwardly. "That's a good point, two male carers aren't allowed in a female resident's room by themselves, are they? Well get into trouble." I don't mind you two being here with me, just so long as I'm not subjected to another bed bath. "See you soon, Isabella. I'll come back up later to see how things are going." he mumbles. "Don't you go anywhere, tonight - you hear me? You'll be getting another visitor soon..."

I am stuck in this foetal position, with a ruddy needle lodged inside my stomach, and a migraine that seems to be only getting worse. Where on Earth do you possibly think I will be venturing to, Stuart? Has Azrael been talking to you about his supposed adventure? It's funny what you take for granted, isn't it? Such as: the ficklest of movements from your fingers, the simple action of opening your eyes, your ability to form a basic word or sound, to breath normally... the freedom to go wherever you want. I am a prisoner and there's no questioning that. I am destined to never leave this forsaken bed of mine, never to laugh or scream again. Where is God at this moment to help me? Where is God to end this futile play which is now my life? Do be quiet, Isabella. For all you know, Mother may be listening, and she won't be happy with you saying such blasphemous words.

"Stop being so melodramatic, Isabella. You're not religious – you confessed that yourself. Are you still moping on in self-pity? I thought you were better than that?"

I am in the middle of an existential crisis here, Azrael, if you don't mind? Anyway, what would a beast know of philosophical concerns? Never mind lecturing me, go find somebody else to annoy. I'm expecting a 'guest', don't you know? It would be so very kind of you to give us some privacy. Saying that, you're not the quickest at taking hints, are you?"

"It does not matter what or who you believe in, Isabella Cunningham. You make your own paths, your own failures and redeeming acts in life. So, what if you do not buy into an invisible force – a mystical shroud that holds control over your

fate and destiny? Many others are in the exact same situation, each lost or defiant in what they cannot rationalise. Does that make them any-less intelligent, less susceptible to the events which take place during this never-ending tale? I think not, and I know you too feel this way. You've done your best to make those you care about feel worthy, loved and their lives meaningful. You are not a bad person, Isabella, just innocent. That isn't necessarily a bad quality to possess."

By innocent, are you insinuating naïve? I'm not stupid, Azrael, despite how I may come across to you. I accept these illnesses of mine aren't going to vanish anytime soon. What I do find difficult to digest, given the chance that once I close my eyes again, is that I'll not be able to open them thereafter. I *must* see Jessica. If there is a God, a higher power who cares about me, then won't they bestow this final wish? Must my life end in this foreign room, with these foreign people?

"You'll just have to wait and see, won't you?"

Oh, that bloody lion! Thankfully, in Azrael's absence, my thoughts are taken back to Father Brian's moving sermon. To be blessed with spiritual needs must be a wonderous gift to possess? Mother and Father both believed in life after death - a place where they would once again be together - and I do pray that this has come true for them, regardless how ironic this statement may sound in coming from me. I also hope that they can forgive my doubts about our faith, and my lacking strength. Maybe, when I do leave this world, I'll be proven wrong? For all I know, my parents could be watching over me, laughing at my futile complaints, and preparing for our eventual reunion together – *right now*. Oh, wouldn't that be perfect? Wouldn't that... be wonderful?

A LIGHT IN THE DARKNESS

Now, let me see. What did Azrael say again: *patience is a virtue*? Oh, Azrael, you're the wiliest of scoundrels! To think, I could have imagined any ridiculous creature up, and you were cream of the crop. Such is my run of bad luck, these days. How often have I heard that utterly pedantic saying spouted off over the years? Patience is a virtue. Funny enough, it was one of Robert's favourites, especially after I had tasked him with doing something for me. My Bobby certainly took his time in doing things; he never rushed into a situation, unlike me.

It's all too easy to repeat those promise-filled words enough times and to a point where you eventually believe their meaning, although it's much harder to make them come into fruition. Besides, what would a make-believe beast, such as Azrael, know about being patient? I mean, aren't cats infamous animals for acting impulsively, without any thought towards the possible consequences of their actions – hence - why they need so many lives? Why even worry over such a ludicrous thought, old girl? Just listen to yourself, Isabella, you're rambling on again like a loonie. Hold on. Someone's knocking at the door.

"Yes, Isabella's in this room now. We had to relocate her to the top floor after she tried to escape a few months ago. Please, make yourself at home." implores Nurse Vaughan, sombrely. From what I can distinguish, he must be still standing at the doorway, because he's certainly not close by. Come in, my dear. YOU make yourself at home. I'll gladly accept your company. For one thing, you can turn my music back on, though please no Debussy this time. "Are you sure you're okay? It's been a while since you've seen her, isn't it? Just... take things slow." Who could he be possibly talking with? Please don't say that more of Agnes' friends have come to pay me a visit, or should I say, her thieving miscreants? I couldn't stomach another moment of their falseness or cheap perfume - ghastly! "How about a nice cup of tea or a sandwich? I don't mind getting them for you."

"I'd *really* appreciate that." sobs a young woman, who herself seems to be also standing a good distance away. I can't for the life of me recognise her voice. Come on, old girl. How many people *have* you recognised today? She does sound uncannily like Caroline, but far younger and less riddled with remorse. Oh, this is so frustrating. All these new voices and faces to take in. "Thanks again, Nurse. Can you give us a moment alone, please? I'll be fine..."

Some hesitant footsteps then saunter towards my incarcerated position, as a separate appear to briskly vanish. The suspense is terrible - excruciating. Who is this person? Quite understandably, I begin to feel a new wave of anxiety trail through my tremoring bones and muscles, each unsure as how to react in wake of this unexpected guest. Should I be fearful, excited, joyful or sad? Choices, choices, choices, Isabella. I notice how Azrael has somewhat lost his influence in these tumultuous surroundings, the little devil. I hate to admit it, but I'm starting to miss that flea-bitten feline.

"I'll come back in ten minutes or so, okay?"

"Yeah. Thanks."

There are more sniffling sounds, and then the phantom footsteps become louder. This person seems to be eerily shifting around my bed now. Lord have mercy. Some wild presumptions soon enter my thoughts of whom this new guest could be: they might be a new Carer, or they could even be another relative who has chosen to peek out the woodwork... only to gaze upon my decaying body as some twisted form of amusement? What a glorious side-show you've become, Isabella. Maybe they'll take the hint to turn around and leave you alone? You've become and expert at giving people the silent treatment, haven't you? The footsteps stop, their sound now replaced by rapid panting. The suspense is terrible.

"Why isn't your music playing? You have all these CD's lying about..." groans the girl, her speech laden with a show of genuine concern for my welfare. How kind and thoughtful of her. She's obviously shuffling through my CD collection, given I can hear the irritating clash of plastic against plastic getting louder beside me. "Bach... No. Mozart... No. You can't stand Mozart, so why's *this* CD here?" Goodness, she's grumbling on like a disenchanted toddler. It was in fact Robert who held an affiliation for Mozart; I always found him to be overrated. How does *she* know what I do and do not like? "Beethoven... Nah. Chopin... *Perfect!*" she shrieks at this discovery with the utmost of delight. The young girl now thankfully begins to settle, as if she too shares in some love towards my darling Frédéric. You have great taste, my dear, there's no questioning it. Please, alight our senses with Chopin's wonderous Etudes. I beg you. "Let's see if I can remember your favourite piece?" She starts sniffling again and at a louder volume. For pity's sake, what in the name of all things holy is upsetting her? "Like I could ever forget your favourite? You drummed it into me so much when I was little. All those nights when we'd sit by your record player, listening to Chopin and Liszt..." It can't be? No, your losing the plot again, Isabella. Surely, she wouldn't have travelled all that way to see you?

By the mercy of whatever divine power watches over us, the first few dulcet notes of Chopin's *Ballade No.1 in G minor, Opus. 23* graciously flow into my ears. The instant surge of release I receive from these passing chords proves more potent than any sedative drug could. I do know who you are, and I'm one-hundred percent certain of it. You are my darling, beautiful, granddaughter. Bless you, Jessica, for coming to visit me. Oh, how I've longed to see you again. You're so very correct about this choice, for I *do* adore this composition. Chopin's masterpiece... our song.

"Isabella loves listening to Chopin, doesn't she?" interjects Nurse Vaughan. Good Lord, it didn't take him long to make that cup of tea and sandwich, did it? "We'd often play this or Bach for Isabella,

seeing as they'd really helped to ease her aggressive outbursts."
Never mind *used to*, I shall continue to enjoy this music and
composer until the end of time itself – until my very last breath. And
for the last time *will* you lot stop saying that I'm aggressive? Really,
I'm growing so bloody tired of hearing it now. "Who knows,
Isabella might still be enjoying her music? They do say, the last
thing to go is your hearing."

"Is that true?" questions Jessica, with some desperation evident in
her voice. "Can she... still hear us?"

"Who knows? When your Great-Aunt Agnes was in earlier,
Isabella apparently squirmed the entire time she spoke, from what
the Carers said when they were in there. I think that's enough
evidence to back up this theory." chuckles my nurse. Jessica remains
silent. If I could, I'd join in with this splendid laughter. Honestly, a
speeding train could be passing by you and you'd still hear Agnes
whinging on about nothing. I had every right to squirm, but
nevertheless I do love the old windbag. "If you're wondering what
that machine is next to your grandma; it's her syringe driver. The
idea is, it'll keep Isabella settled and pain free."

"I've seen one before, when Grandad needed the same medicines. I
can't get over how frail she looks." Sighs Jessica. Chopin,
regrettably, does not have the same settling effect on her as he does
with me. How sad and unfortunate. I had hoped for Jessica to carry
on in sharing my musical tastes. "I can't imagine her ever being
aggressive. Grandma wouldn't hurt a fly, she'd go mad if you were
to kill a spider in front of her. *Every life is sacred*, she'd say. Mind,
in saying that, Grandma would somehow forget that saying when it
came to wasps. I've lost count of how many times she's squashed
those things over the years." Erm... yes, and I'm quite ashamed to
admit it. If truth be told, I took no pleasure in killing those ghastly
insects, although they were a bloody nuisance when we'd visit the
seaside. You couldn't have a jam sandwich in peace without those
wretched things trying to divebomb you. Surely, certain exceptions
can be made? "Caroline used to tell me about Grandma lashing out

and swearing at her. I wouldn't believe a word of it – I couldn't. I'd never heard about Vascular Dementia before, until Grandma got it. Even during the later stages, I didn't dare look into the symptoms; I was too scared to find out what might happen. I couldn't face losing my grandmother, not in that horrible way."

"There's a deal of stigma still surrounding Dementia and Alzheimer's." states Nurse Vaughan, after a short pause. "I didn't know much about illnesses like them until I started my training at University. Even then, there wasn't a lot of information about the impact they have on people, and I mean that in the sense of how they affect both the sufferer and their loved ones."

"Well, not looking into it turned out to be a huge mistake on my part." whimpers Jessica. "I tried to prepare myself mentally on the way here for what I would see tonight, but it's still difficult to take in. You know, I only found out a few days ago about Grandma's Cancer, and that was only because a friend of mine noticed a post Aunt Caroline put on Facebook. In her wisdom, she decided to tell the whole world before me."

"Dementia is a cruel disease, as is Cancer." explains Nurse Vaughan, after taking in a cautious breath. His obvious experience in dealing with these diseases clearly shows through his melancholic grunts. The poor fellow. I'd dread to think of what he's seen. "Diagnostic means and treatments have come a long way over the last few years or so. It's a crying shame that Isabella wasn't diagnosed sooner; she could have maybe been started on some tablets to slow down the impact of her illness. We'll never know."

I've heard them say that dreadful word a few times now, so you'd think I'd be accustomed to it, though to discover I do have Dementia is proving more difficult to accept than my Cancer. I don't want to end up like Mother or Father. I don't want Jessica to go through what Agnes and I did - Lord no. It's undignified, humiliating and insufferable, at least, that's what it was like for my parents. Times have changed, old girl. Most of the care you've received today has been fantastic, bar those two morons and their abhorrent music earlier on. Jessica, my sweetest angel, do yourself a favour and leave this depressive atmosphere. Why should you need to witness me in this state? I don't want you to.

"Didn't the consultants at Darlington Hospital put Gran on Memantine a while back?" responds Jessica, somewhat displaying a level of disappointment in her tone. "I was under the impression that those tablets would stop Grandma's deterioration. Where did *that* go wrong?" I can hear Nurse Vaughan stuttering and spluttering away to himself. He must be trying to concoct a reasonable answer? I don't envy him, not one bit. "Aunt Caroline promised me that the Memantine medicine would stop Grandma's illness. She *promised*."

"Caroline has struggled coming to terms with Isabella's illness, too." My nurse continues to stutter over his lines, bless him. "I think... she was maybe just telling you what you both wanted to hear. It's normal to be in denial when you're faced with such bad news." he tries to implore, though I doubt my nurse has any success in doing so. "There isn't a cure yet for Alzheimer's or any other Dementia, but we're not far-off finding one."

"That's not much use for Grandma at the moment though, is it?" sneers Jessica. Gracious, I hate knowing that she's upset. It's something I've never been able to accustom myself with. "So much for having 'wonder drugs' to help. Caroline's never been reliable."

"Medications like Memantine don't always work for everyone. Dementia impacts the sufferer in a unique way; it's different for each person. Isabella's Memantine helped to curb some of her challenging behaviours, as well as helping to retain her memory for a short while." Nurse Vaughan pauses briefly again. "They can only do so much good, Jess. Isabella has deteriorated faster than any of us anticipated, even her doctors are shocked."

"You might not know about what happened, but Grandma's Dementia crept in not long after the mugging - that's what brought it on." Jessica exhales wearily, as do I in unison. I have an awful feeling about where this conversation is going. "It must've been all the stress or shame of what she went through? We'll never be sure,

169

and there's not much point dwelling on it, is there?" Please, turn my music up a little louder, my dears. Let's change the subject, shall we? "She wouldn't talk about the attack with us, wouldn't leave the house, stopped eating, stopped drinking, all because of some stupid kids trying to act hard. All they took from her was ten pounds – ten quid - which she'd have given to them without a fight, instead of having to go through that ordeal." Another lengthy sigh is performed by Jessica, only adding more concern in me as to where this conversation is heading. "They didn't need to beat her up. They didn't need to humiliate her. That was the day I lost my grandmother, and it's a day I'll never forget." Oh, Jessica. What has happened to your blissful, care-free voice? Knowing that you're upset is far-worse than being stuck in this bed. End this conversation at once. *Please*, put Chopin's wonderful music back up. Why don't you play *Fantaisie Impromptu* to lift your spirits up, as it always used to? "I'll never forgive them for what they did to Grandma, the bastards." Language, young lady! You didn't learn such words from me, perhaps your grandfather, but certainly not me. "I'm sorry for swearing, it just *really* gets to me when I think about what happened that night. I know it was eight years ago, but it's still as raw as it was back then."

"I understand. There's no need at all to apologise, Jess. I didn't know about Isabella being mugged." sympathises Nurse Vaughan, evidently in some shock at this revelation. "No one should ever go through an awful experience like that, especially an elderly woman such as Isabella." A couple of tense seconds follow. "All I *do* know, is that Isabella has Vascular Dementia, which itself was caused by several mini-strokes – TIA's. Were you made aware about these? Only, stress can be a key factor towards strokes and TIA's. It makes some sense, from what you said."

"Aunt Caroline kept me and most of our family out the loop on a lot of things." snarls my (usually) mild-tempered granddaughter. I'm witnessing a side to her never seen before. Jessica's so very much... like me. Calm down, sweetheart. Being angry now won't solve

170

anything. "We don't see eye-to-eye and haven't done for a while now, not after I found out how wicked Caroline was treating Grandma at home. Trust me, it's a sore subject. I can't stand the evil bitch." *Language!* Goodness, my heart's struggling enough as it is. "Sorry, I didn't mean to swear again."

"It's okay." Nurse Vaughan then laughs awkwardly. "The Caroline I know doesn't come across like that. Is it true, what you're saying?" he asks, apprehensively. *I'd* rather not be informed, if you could be so kind as to omit any further details.

"She took most of Gran and Grandad Bobby's savings. I bet she hasn't told any of the staff here about *that*." responds Jessica, abruptly. "No. She's too proud to admit what a greedy cow she is. I'll never forgive her. She was quick to get shot of Grandad in a care home as well, you know." Now, Jessica, your grandfather and I have been on the bones of our backsides for most of our lives. I highly doubt Caroline could have taken much money from us, *if* this accusation is even true? So, Robert also ended up in a care home, just like me? My poor husband. "Caroline spent most of their savings on luxury vodka, cigarettes and holidays abroad. The thought of her doing that makes me want to vomit. What kind of twisted person robs from their own parents? The money should have gone towards Grandma's care, once she got put in here, and not towards my aunt's pathetic lifestyle." Please, Jessica, let go of your resentment, let go of the past, just as your aunt and I have. Life is too short to hold onto such grudges. Didn't you hear a single word of what Nurse Vaughan said about stress? I'd dread to think you could end up like me. "All Caroline *did* say, was that Grandma had gone senile – 'bonkers' – in her words. I never once thought she'd end up this bad." Neither did I, petal. That makes two of us, doesn't it? "Those kids have a lot to answer for. The justice system in this country is a bloody joke."

"Did the police ever catch them?" queries Nurse Vaughan, with an emphasis of hope in his voice and clear determination to shift this chat away from Caroline's misdemeanours. "I hope they did. There's no way they should have been able to get away with doing that to Isabella. If it were up to me, I'd lock them away and throw away the key."

"Nope. There weren't any witnesses, and the CCTV cameras nearby didn't work, which were apparently just for show. It was some random guy walking his dog that found Grandma. She must have been so scared. Those *kids* left her half-clothed and covered in blood, right in the middle of Skipton Road's play-park. Scum. They've given my grandmother this life sentence. It should be those little shits suffering - not her!"

This terrible scene does somewhat ring a bell. Oh, lord. For once, I'd prefer for my memory *not* to work. Why would I wish to recall such an experience? I *can* remember the cold evening air, the initial punch that knocked me off-balance, the freezing ground as I struck it, the feral smile on that child's face as they swung their legs to kick me in the ribs... all far-too grizzly to willingly reminisce. Oh, merciful me. I did try to fight back; I gave them everything I could, but they were simply too strong for me. I never imagined a child so small could be so vicious. Goodness gracious, was *I* mistaken. Why they felt the need to strip me is beyond any reasoning. The damage was already done, and just look at where it has left me. Pardon my language, Jessica, but I do agree with your wayward terminology about those vagabonds. However, I was raised to forgive those who have ever wronged me, which probably comes from my religious upbringing. How my treatment that night must have inflicted Robert as well, I dare not imagine. He'd have fettled those little trouble-makers, make no mistake of it. In a way, I do forgive those children, for that is what they are – children: innocent, impressionable, easily misled. They are nothing but a sad reflection of their parents' failings – of society's failings. That does not justify their actions, but to offer forgiveness is the only way I can cope with remembering all this. Jessica, simply let this memory slip away from your mind like a falling leaf in the breeze. It is not worth dwelling over. Don't make yourself ill, darling.

"Anyhow, I'd best give you and Isabella some time alone." says Nurse Vaughan. I sense that my sorry tale has caused him some great trauma; it's not a story many would want to hear in full, let alone be made aware of. Why did I have to remember it, of all things? "If you need me at all, I'm only down the corridor. Are you sure that you'll be okay, Jess?"

"Yeah." whispers Jessica, reservedly. "We'll be fine, won't we, Grandma?"

Someone then kindly turns my music back up. I can only reason that it was Jessica, and that she is doing this to hide her evident sorrow from me, but why? I've always been there as a shoulder to cry on - for *her* especially. I wish that I could leap out from under these wretched sheets to give her a great-big hug and kiss. Oh, that would be wonderful. Unfortunately, it's not something I can manage now. Open your eyes instead, Isabella. Let your granddaughter see that there *is* some life still left in you, that you're not an empty shell lying here for the sake of merely existing. Open them, old girl. Try your hardest – you must! For pity's sake, Isabella Cunningham! Open these eyes of yours this very instant!

"Grandma?" gasps Jessica. "You're... awake?"

Success! Lord, that took some effort. Opening these tired eyes of mine is like trying to pry open a tin can with your bare hands. I've managed, though only just. As I grind my sight across to look upon Jessica for the first time in many years, it immediately strikes me that her features appear so unrecognisable. She looks older than thirty, I'd say, but Jessica still has her father's beautiful eyes and smile. Now, if only I could speak to her...

"Hi, Grandma." mumbles my granddaughter in a bashful manner, with a lovely underlying tune that ascends through her words. "I'm so sorry that it's been a while since I last saw you. I should have come sooner." Jessica slowly runs a hand along the bedrail towards me and then quickly retreats it, as if to touch me would result in her contracting my cruel diseases. *Why* do you not want to touch me, sweetheart? I'm not contagious. I'm lonely and could really do with your warming touch to cheer me up. "You're so frail now. I might hurt you... I don't want to." That explains it then. Lord, this body of mine is nothing but a bloody nuisance. I can't move, can't speak, and now my grandchild daren't touch me. What's the point of being here?

"Aren't you pleased that Jessica came?"

You stay out of this, Azrael. Nobody invited you back.

"Despite the tears in her eyes, I believe that Jessica is overjoyed to be with you again, Isabella. Don't worry, she can't see me."

"I'm so sorry, Grandma. I'm here now, though." emphasises Jessica, frantically. "I'm here for you. I should never have left Newton Escomb. What the hell was I thinking?"

Please, my darling, stop shaking your head as if you are guilty - because *that* you are not. My word, what an astonishing young woman you've grown to be. You look just like your father, my David: the same piercing eyes; the same wavy locks; the same smile that could warm the coldest of hearts. Oh, how I've longed for this sweet reunion of ours. I'll try my best to cheer up for you. It's the least I can do, given how far you've travelled to visit me.

"I work down London now, Grandma." explains Jessica in a woeful voice, but then her spirits somewhat appear to lift. "I've gotten engaged, since I last visited. Christ, I nearly forgot to tell you." *Engaged*? Well... spill the beans, dear! Who is this lucky person, this blessed fellow to be honoured by your precious love and devotion? "I'm not sure if you'd be at all happy about it, mind." Why, Jessica? Don't say that you've fallen into the hands of some womanising scoundrel? Gracious! If you have done, I'd do everything possible to go and put a stop to them, trust me, my darling. Explain this concern at once! "Only, my fiancé is called Emma... she's a woman. I'm not one for stereotyping, but your

174

generation aren't exactly the most understanding about this kind of relationship, are they? I bet, this'll probably come as a shock to you?" Well, no shit (pardoning my French). However, why would this be an issue for me? My body may be ancient, but my mindset most-certainly is not. So long as this 'Emma' treats you well, and loves you unequivocally, you both have my blessing to wed. Love is love, after-all. So, what *if* you are of the same sex? Just so long as you care for one another and are prepared to take both the good and the bad times, for *that* is all that matters. I'm so very proud of you, Jessica Marie Cunningham. I only wish I could tell you this. "I thought I'd let you know anyway, Gran. It wouldn't be right; I couldn't live with myself, if I didn't. I've always been able to tell you things, haven't I? Although, I wasn't too comfortable with you going over the 'birds and the bees' with me that one time." Keep on laughing the way you are now, sweetheart. I'm so very relieved that you did inform me of this wonderous news. Why, I'm completely ecstatic for you! Why wouldn't I be? My little Jessica, all grown up and getting married. Who'd have thought it? "On top of getting married, Emma and I have adopted a baby girl recently. She's gorgeous. You'd absolutely love her, Grandma, and would have probably spoiled her rotten... like you did with me." Jessica pauses to wipe some tears away from face. What's the matter now? Isn't this good news you're telling me? "We're naming her 'Isabella Rose Cunningham' after her great-grandmother... after you, Grandma."

Seldom are there moments in life that can overwhelm your rational thoughts and senses such as this. If only I could talk but, then again, I'd be utterly speechless. What a humbling gesture to bestow upon me. What an honour to grant, though this is a gift which I do not feel worthy of. You will be a fantastic mother and loving wife, for you have been the greatest grandchild I could have ever wished for. You have brought so much happiness to your grandfather and I, Jessica. *Please*, stop crying my darling. This is a happy occasion, is it not?

Come on Isabella, move yourself! This is your one chance to show Jessica that you and not this demented, cancer-riddled being are still here! Her hand is resting closer now – reach for it! Come on, old girl. Find whatever strength is left inside of your arthritic limbs. Stretch out your aching arms, your crippled fingertips - you simply must! Offer some comfort to your grandchild as you always did, for God's sake! Reach! *Reach*!!

"G-Grandma?" stammers Jessica under her breath, as she motions the resting hand even closer. "Were you listening to what I said? Can you actually hear me?" *Come on*, Isabella! Shift your backside! This is your perfect chance – your only opportunity to make contact with her. Don't give up now. Cast aside all this terrible pain that riddles every inch of your body. There's only a few more inches left. Just... a little... further. "What are you doing, Grandma? I thought you couldn't move anymore?"

The amount of exertion required to slide my twisted fingers along this cushioned bedrail, to place them over Jessica's own far-warmer fingertips, proves to be the most-exhausting of exercises. However, this effort is truly worthwhile. As I run my index finger over Jessica's engagement ring, a surge of euphoric energy courses throughout my body, swiftly depleting any previous agony and torment felt. This is perfect. *This* is wonderful. My darling granddaughter, you have reignited a fire within this plain of darkness, the very likes of which I never thought could ever be managed again. I love you so much. I want to tell you – I want to scream it out aloud so that the heavens above can hear these words coursing through my thoughts: I love you.

"Grandma?" Jessica lowers her jaw to place it on my tremoring digits, in a gentle manner that completely encapsulates her sympathetic nature. Her skin is as soft as it was during childhood – immaculate. Her subtle touch of reassurance brings more comfort to me than any 'miracle drug' ever possibly could. Lord in Heaven, if you're there and do exist, don't let this moment pass. I beg you, with all my might. "I'd do anything to stop your suffering, Grandma. What kind of life is this for you?" Jessica takes in a pained breath, seemingly to prevent her from crying some more. "Why are there

monsters living in this world that lead fantastic lives, yet you –
who've never hurt anyone - had to get Cancer and Dementia?
Having one of those illnesses is bad enough, let alone having them
both at the same time." she sobs, almost uncontrollably now. "What
kind of life is this for you? It's not fair!"

Life is not fair, my dear. Bloody hell, I'm sounding like Azrael
now. Yes, I have these ghastly ailments, but they inflict their evil
upon anyone – righteous *or* sinful. How I would have loved to be
there at your wedding, to have met little Isabella, to laugh with you
just one more time. In your twinkling eyes, I can see the same
wonderous glimmer that my David's had. In your smile, I can see
your grandfather's everlasting hope and determination. Robert
would have been ecstatic to hear these good tidings of yours, without
any doubt. I love you, Jessica. I must tell you this – I simply must!

"I'll make sure our child knows just what an amazing person her
great-grandmother was." whimpers Jessica, discreetly into her free
hand. "Your legacy will live on through us, Grandma. There's not a
day goes by where I don't think about you, or about Dad and
Grandpa Bobby. We've made lots of happy memories together and
gotten up to so much mischief over the years, haven't we?" Yes,
flower, we certainly have. They were jolly times indeed. "I'll never
stop thinking about you. I know you're in there... I can see it in your
eyes."

It's now or never, Isabella Cunningham. Focus. Take in that vital
oxygen. Rekindle those pathetic vocal chords of yours. Brush aside
that awful vomiting sensation and declare what must be said! Blare
out for all the world to hear just what you think about your
grandchild – about your beloved Jessica. Say it! Speak, old girl!
SPEAK!!!

"Love... you."

"Grandma?!" The instant look of surprise on Jessica's face is
easily matched by my own amazement at having formed these

strained, though sincere, words. Goodness, that was so difficult to do. I feel terribly drained now. Merciful me, here comes that dreadful rush of searing vomit again. Oh, Lord. I can hear your panting again, Azrael. Not now, my darling. Come back a little later. I'm doing just fine. "I love you too I love you so much, Grandma. Don't go. Don't you dare leave me."

"Isabella."

I can comprehend that you're there, Azrael. Not now. I'm hardly in the mood for your fun and games. I'm exhausted.

"I cannot wait much longer, and neither can you. What time remains is motioning faster against us."

A rancid stream of bright-red blood suddenly projects from throat, then out from my mouth, without any real warning granted to either myself nor Jessica. My granddaughter recoils away from me in total fright, and a lasting panic then continues to show itself within her forlorn expression. I don't want you to see me this way, sweetheart. Leave me be. Go back to your loving family and new life in London. Oh, I feel so weak. I feel as ill as a dog after chomping on some chocolate. Every breath taken feels like a stabbing wound to my throat and chest. My veins feel as if they are about to burst. Lord, it's insufferable! What is happening to me, Azrael?

"You know fine well what is happening, Isabella. You're still not ready though, are you?"

No. I'm not ready for anything, other than to be granted a proper cup of tea and some more time with Jessica. I wish to see my granddaughter wed, to see her child grow, and all the happy years to follow thereafter. Wherever it is you plan to take me, I am definitely not ready to venture there yet. In all honesty, I don't think I ever will be.

"You can't continue to suffer in this way, Isabella. It is not right. It is not natural. You *must* let go. Close your eyes, for goodness sake. Be free of this torment."

I know what you're saying is correct, Azrael. Regardless of this fact, I'd rather spend some more time with Jessica. We have so much to catch up on. Maybe, if I rest for a short while, then perhaps I can regain my full strength again? My eyes are shutting, despite trying my hardest to keep them open. I must get better. I've never been this ill before. I'm scared. I simply must stay here with my Jessica. Oh, Azrael, wouldn't that be perfect? Wouldn't that be wonderful?

"Isabella... *Isabella?*"

A SYMPHONY DIVINE

My head is throbbing like mad; it feels all fuzzy and strange, unlike anything I've felt before. Am I awake? Goodness, what a peculiar sensation this is.

I dreamt of that lovely cottage again, though this time the ethereal setting felt so much more real: the scents, the sounds, the warm summer's breeze coursing over my skin. I could have stayed there indefinitely, but that would have meant leaving my beloved Jessica behind. I could never do it to her; I couldn't leave my beautiful granddaughter all alone in this god-forsaken room, not with that last image of me bringing up blood. What a ghastly scene to witness for the poor girl. Jessica's still here with me... I know she is. Jessica is holding onto my hand and is breathing ever so gently across it. I never want to let go - never. The only problem is, won't I just become another burden for her to bear? I can't allow for that to happen. Lord no. I'm not that selfish.

"Are you warm enough, Jessica?" questions Nurse Vaughan, from behind me. "You've been here since eleven o'clock. Are you not feeling worn-out?" Some silent seconds of deliberation follow between my observers. Evidently, Jessica *must* be tired – tired enough that she cannot form a response to my nurse. "If you're wanting to stay with Isabella overnight, I can go find a spare mattress and duvet for you? It wouldn't be a problem, given the circumstances."

"I'm fine just sitting here with Grandma, thanks." replies Jessica, clearly exhausted, though with a small hint of humour as a way of compensating it. However, her feigned attempt to lighten the mood in my room swiftly dampens. "By the way, do you know that Grandma's engagement ring is missing? She had it on the last time I visited." Oh my! With everything else going on, I forgot about being robbed. Audrey, you wicked creature. I do hope you are enjoying your new accessory? May those heinous actions long rest on your conscience... for what you did to me.

"*Missing?*" gasps Nurse Vaughan. "I know that Isabella was wearing it last night. I'll have a look in the clinic to see if it's been put in there for safe keeping. Your grandma has lost a lot of weight recently. Maybe the ring slipped off her finger, during one of her checks?"

"Maybe..." says Jessica, dismissively. "I'd really appreciate you looking into it, and I'll let you know if we need anything else. Thanks." I believe Jessica is wanting to spend some more time alone with me, Nurse Vaughan. I would politely take this hint, if I were you, not that we don't like you or anything.

"I'll look for the ring straightaway, Jess." replies Nurse Vaughan, also clearly in concern. "But, if you don't mind, I'd like to check over Isabella's Observations before I go. It shouldn't take a sec."

"Sure, go ahead." groans Jessica, her breaths laden with heavy wave of apprehension. "Do you want me to leave while you do that?"

"No, that won't be necessary." assures my nurse. "I'm just going to check Isabella's pulse and respirations, that's all." Under his breath, I can just make out Nurse Vaughan saying some discerning words that only leave me more anxious. "God, she's freezing. Her skin..."

"I've noticed that myself, especially over the last half-hour or so. Grandma's face and arms are getting waxy as well. Is that normal?" comments Jessica, quite reservedly. "She looks ten years younger because of it. Is it a bad sign, though?"

"I wouldn't like to say, Jess. It's difficult to tell." I've always been good at telling out liars and you're certainly being one now, Nurse Vaughan. Be honest with my granddaughter, it's the least you can do. "I'll quickly check her Ob's over."

As Jessica falls back into a subservient vow of silence, Nurse Vaughan secures his masculine digits around my wasting wrist again. He fumbles across my delicate tendons and veins for a little while, then settles with an audible jolt. Presumably, he isn't best-pleased by the readings. Oh, dear.

"W-What's wrong?" stammers Jessica. Please, darling, don't be so concerned about me. Just go home. I'm quite alright as things currently stand. Who's fibbing now, old girl? "Please, tell me if something is wrong. I promise that it won't upset me... I'd rather know." You don't sound too convincing, sweetheart. You've never been able to lie in a believable fashion, which is another quality that I adore about you. "Is Grandma's condition deteriorating?"

"Isabella's pulse is weaker and faster now compared to the last readings I took." sighs Nurse Vaughan, as he carefully releases his grip from me. "Her respirations are down to eight-a-minute, which *is* bad. I'm reluctant to say this..." I do wish these two would stop it with their awkward bouts of silence in-between talking. My nerves can't stand much more this. It's plain to see that I haven't long left, I mean, only a fool wouldn't see this. Mind you, I've still got some fight left in me. I'm going nowhere. Not even Azrael will shift me. "I don't think Isabella will make it through the night. I'm sorry, Jess. Her body is showing signs that it's starting to shut down."

"Okay." says Jessica quite calmly, although her initial gasp speaks otherwise. "Do you mean, like a computer does?"

"To simplify what I said - yes. The body is just like one of those old computers; the ones that would shut down different parts separately, before not working at all. What is happening to Isabella now is perfectly natural. She won't be in any pain. Honestly." My nurse halts his words for a moment, and I imagine him doing this to comfort Jessica. If only I could. That's *my* job. "Are you okay?"

"Yeah, I'm fine." Again, you are not a good liar, Jessica. I wouldn't bother trying. I don't particularly want you to leave, but maybe now is the time to do so. I don't want you to cry. You're breaking my heart, dear. I just want you to be happy. "You've amazed us all, Grandma. Who'd have ever thought you'd make it to ninety-five years old? I remember you saying, if you made it to seventy, then it'd be a 'bloody miracle'. Well, you proved everyone wrong... even yourself."

Ninety-five?! Gracious! Surely, that can't be correct? I've been walking this Earth of ours for *ninety-five years*? No wonder my skin looks so dry and flaky. I do recall celebrating my seventieth birthday, now *that* was a party to remember: Robert fell asleep after only an hour, given he could never handle his ale, bless him; Caroline completely forgot about it, which wasn't much of a surprise; and not forgetting that Agnes consumed most of my buffet, the greedy so-and-so. Why, with all things sacred, would I recall that ridiculous façade so easily? I believe, in a strange sense, it is because that day summed up my family's chaotic relationship very well. We've been gifted with a great deal of good times, as well as bad. That's how it should be. I think so, anyway. Life would be boring if it were any different. Ninety-five years old...

"I'd best be off now." announces Nurse Vaughan. "Just remember, I'm only down the corridor if you need me for anything."

"Thank you... thanks for everything." I envision Jessica smiling now for some unknown reason, perhaps to rid myself of what guilt has surfaced? There's a certain difference about the tone in her voice now, which is what makes me think this way. "Grandma and I are going to be just fine, we've got each other. I would appreciate that mattress, if you get time." Jessica starts to fumble around beside my bed again. A short while later, she removes her hand away from mine and then pats at my bedrails with an emphasis of glee. "I nearly forgot another thing, Grandma. I've brought a new CD for you. It's by a composer called Ludovico Einaudi, and his music might be a little modern for your tastes. Let's just see, yeah, for old time's sake?"

I've always been one for trying out new things, although I could never get away with the Heavy Metal music my David would often listen to. I used to joke with him that a *good* Catholic should never listen to a band called 'Black Sabbath'. He didn't half give me some grief about saying that. Anyway, I can't admit that I've ever heard of a 'Ludovico Einaudi' before. However, if my Jessica likes him then his music *must* be good – only of the highest standards. Enlighten me, my dear. Chopin needs his rest - as do I - as do you. Let us listen to some wonderful piano music together, just like we used to all those years ago. That would be perfect, simply perfect.

"I'll play my favourite track first if you don't mind, Grandma?" gleams Jessica, as she glances over the CD case. Go ahead by all means, flower. You've engaged my curiosity now. "The song I like most is called *Experience*. It's a lovely track. Who knows, you might like it too?" I'd say it's a fitting piece for the situation we're in. Wouldn't you agree, Jessica? I have ninety-five years of experiences to traipse over, and it's not like I'm going anywhere. Time remains on my side, at least for now. This could be the opportune moment for reminiscing over all my events in life? "This song reminds me so much of you and Grandpa Bobby. I don't know why, but it does. If only we could go back to relive all those happy days together: our holidays to Whitby, our nights-out to the local piano recitals, our nights-in where we'd sit in front of your fireplace with a hot mug of cocoa, when we'd gossip for hours on end about how silly Aunt Agnes was. God, I'd give anything to relive those times." As would I, Jessica. "I won't let go of those memories, and I won't ever let go of you." She sniffles some more. Oh, gracious. I can feel myself welling up. This could be another opportune moment, Isabella. Perhaps, these tears will help to open your eyes once more? "Anyway, I'll pop the CD in now. I bet you're sick of listening to me rabbiting on?" Never. Your voice is as serene to my ears as any Classical masterpiece, Jessica. In fact, I'd rather you kept on talking to me. "I'll make sure that it's not too loud. We don't want to wake up poor Mavis in the room next to us, do we?" Who the bloody hell is Mavis? "There. I hope you can still hear it?"

There's an unexpected creak at my door that annoyingly disturbs this fantastic music, not to mention mine and Jessica's first instance of shared peace with one another. Open your eyes, Isabella. See who it is, old girl. I don't think it's Nurse Vaughan, as you can smell his cologne a mile off. Jessica's anxious panting has returned, which coincides with this incessant knocking. Something isn't right. What's going on now? Why is my granddaughter panting like a dehydrated rottweiler?

"Hello?"

"Caroline?" responds Jessica, scornfully. "What do *you* want? It's two a.m. in the morning, shouldn't you be at the bottom of a bottle?"

"Sorry, Jess. I didn't know you were here. Nurse Vaughan called me to say..." Caroline? So, my daughter has also returned to see me. She sounds as equally distressed as Jessica does. I assume their shared panic must be from seeing one another again? Please, Jessica, try to overcome your differences with Caroline. I can't emphasise this phrase enough, nor its important meaning: life is too short. I of all people realise that now. Forgive and forget. If this saying turns out to be my final wish, and even if it were to be engraved on my headstone, I simply want nothing more than for it to come true. "Mam's not doing well, is she?"

"No, but what would you care of it? Where've *you* been at?"

"Jessica," sighs Caroline, "please... don't start."

"Oh, I'm not starting anything." counters my granddaughter, with a staccato-like precision. So much for having a relaxed evening. "You were the one who robbed her, and who left her to rot in this care home. Where were you at when Grandma needed you most? You'd have thrown her in here without any question - selfish as always!"

"I had no choice!" Caroline's voice shifts between anger and remorse. I don't want any of this fuss, especially over me, seeing as it's so utterly pointless. I don't care if Caroline *did* take that money. My daughter turned to drink for a reason. It was *I* that should have been there for her, not the other way around. I should have done more to help my vulnerable child. Isabella, you're such a fool. "Mam was seeing things that weren't there, Jess. Whenever I tried to change her clothes, or take her to the toilet, she'd either punch, kick or bite me, not to mention she'd randomly scream for hours on end. My neighbours even called the police on me a few times, because of Mam kicking off. God knows, I did my best to care for her..."

"*Really?*"

"Yes! Why would I lie about that?" I believe you, Caroline, and I'm so sorry for doing those terrible things to you. I'm so sorry for becoming this terrible weight on your shoulders. It must have been the Cancer or Dementia making me act that way? That's the only reasonable explanation which I can muster. "It wasn't my decision to have Mam moved into a care home; the social worker made that choice on her behalf. Your Gran didn't have the capacity to consent, and I just couldn't cope anymore. I *did* try my best. You don't need to remind me of how much of a bitch I am. If I could turn back the clock and change how I acted, I'd do it in an instant."

"You can't though, can you?" mutters Jessica, now thankfully in a more settled manner. "None of us can turn back time. I wish that I'd stayed here in Newton Escomb, to be here for Grandma, but I've lost that chance now. I'll never be able to make it up to her." You don't need to do anything for me, darling. I'm only glad that you're here. "Buying this CD was a stupid attempt to make things right. It's not like Grandma can enjoy listening to her music anymore, is it?"

"She still loves her piano music, trust me." responds Caroline, after a few thoughtful moments of contemplation. "Chopin was always her favourite. I could never understand the fascination she had with his music, a bit like Dad." she giggles, softly. "What's this you're playing for her?"

"Ludovico Einaudi. I saw him perform at the Royal Albert Hall with Emma - she's my fiancé by the way - a few months back. I thought that, maybe, Grandma might enjoy his music too."

"Congratulations, Jess." stammers Caroline, evidently in shock. "I didn't know you had a... girlfriend."

"We haven't spoken for so long, *that's* why." simpers Jessica. Do try to remain civil, dear. You and Caroline were doing so well for a moment or two there. "Grandma would be furious with us, wouldn't she? We're going on like a couple of school kids fighting in the playground."

"Yeah." agrees Caroline, after an awkward bout of coughing. "I've been sober for over a year now. That's been my way of trying to make it up to Mam, not that she'd have any clue about me doing that."

"Good for you." remarks Jessica, with a hint of sarcasm. However, her tone changes again immediately. "It must have been hard for you to give up the booze? You've relied on it for so long."

"Torturous, but it was nothing like what Mam is going through at the minute. I made the choice to wreck my liver... she didn't choose this life."

The tense atmosphere in my room gradually begins to ware off. Caroline and Jessica have both fallen silent, which itself can't be good? Open your eyes, Isabella. They can't have left you, surely? Come on, Isabella! you can do it!

"I'm sorry, Caroline."

"I'm sorry, Jess... for everything."

"Having difficulties are we, Isabella?"

I can't open my eyes anymore, Azrael, and *you're* not helping in the slightest. What do you want?

"Why do you wish to open them? Don't you want to go back to that lovely cottage in your dreams?"

I want to see what my daughter and grandchild are getting up to. They're quiet – too quiet – for my liking. Something is going amiss here, Azrael. I'm very concerned for them.

"It's in you, Isabella. You've managed to speak to Jessica. Surely, that was a harder task to achieve than simply opening

187

your eyelids? I can describe this moving scene for you, if you'd like?"

Just you wait until I get my hands on you, Azrael. Can't you see that I'm distressed? I dare to think what is going on beside me. Not even this beautiful music is calming my nerves. Oh Lord. I *must* see with my own eyes what is taking place here. I do hope that I've not been left alone again. Can't you help me?

"Open your eyes, Isabella. Open them. I know you can do it."

Against my diminishing breaths and racing heartbeat, I inhale with a lengthy and ecstatic sensation of purest joy. There, standing right before me, are Caroline and Jessica. Both are held in a loving embrace, dismissing any previous ill-intent felt between them. They are sobbing terribly, but I believe these are tears of happiness – of contentment - and not of anger or sorrow. This is simply wonderful, Azrael. This is all I could wish for, to see my family united again. I pray, particularly when I leave this world, that this loving connection shall endure. Am I being selfish again?

"No. I for one don't think so, Isabella. They do seem a lot happier now, don't they? It *is* a wonderful scene to witness, and sadly one I don't see often."

"Mam's opened her eyes!" screeches Caroline, across Jessica's left shoulder. "*Look!*"

"Hi, Grandma." smiles Jessica, as she turns around to face me. "How are you feeling?" A little worse from the last time you asked me, if being honest. Just to blink involves a tremendous amount of effort, and that's not taking into consideration these persistent waves of numbness, nor this overwhelming cold sensation that's spreading throughout my fingers and toes like rampant wildfire. Maybe it is those drugs that are reeking this havoc upon me? Bloody horrible things, they are. *Is* it the drugs, Azrael? Are they the cause of these peculiar sensations?

"Focus on your children, Isabella. We'll be leaving shortly."

"Her eyes are glazing over, Jess."
"Yeah. I noticed that, but I didn't want to say anything. I wonder what could be going through Grandma's mind, if she even knows what's going on?"
What a morbid curiosity to behold, my precious darlings. Well, around yourself and Caroline, Jessica, motions an ever-enclosing shroud of darkness, one that creeps in nearer and nearer with each passing second. This can't be good, although it somehow doesn't seem bad either. I don't feel frightened by this endless void that now surrounds me. The only way to describe it, is I feel like I'm being pulled into a vat of consuming tar; a place where no air, no light or any warmth can reach me. All the while, I'm slowly entering a euphoric state where I remain aware of certain things – certain emotions - though also slowly shutting down into a needful period of rest. Destiny. Fate. Judgement. Whatever you might wish to name this journey I'm about to take, *that* is what's going through my mind now.

"Isabella."

How many times, Azrael? I'm not ready yet. Who would be? No sane person openly welcomes death; the morbid path which, in its own daunting way, now lingers ahead of me. I might have lost some of my marbles lately, but I do hold enough wits about me not to willingly leave this life... not at this precise moment. Most of all, I don't want to never see my granddaughter's beautiful smile again. Jessica looks so much like my David and Bobby, her father and grandfather. You see, to gaze upon Jessica's eyes ignites a passionate realisation, one where I feel like my entire family is standing right here in front of me – for me. I want this beautiful scene to play out forever. I'm afraid, that lovely Northumbrian cottage will just have to wait... as shall you, Azrael.

"I understand where you are coming from, Isabella. But..."

"Jess! I think she's stopped breathing! Oh, God!" screams Caroline, frantically. I wondered what that funny feeling was; it was my lungs giving up. "Get Nurse Vaughan – QUICK!"

"You've lived a long and blessed life, Isabella. Now comes the time when you must rest, for you have earned it. I assure you, your family will be alright in your absence. Don't be afraid."

There's nothing blessed about my current circumstances, Azrael. The darkness is closing in more rapidly now, despite my firm attempts to keep these old eyes of mine open. It's proving to be an impossible struggle. I just want to look upon Jessica's eyes, those of David and Robert's, for a little while more. *Please*, don't let this serenity end. My family are here. I must not disappoint them. I cannot leave.

"Isabella?" questions Nurse Vaughan in a dire tone, whilst swiftly kneeling himself beside me. "Has her breathing only just stopped?"

"Yes. The colour's almost gone from her skin." sobs Caroline. Sorrow is not an emotion which she would ever usually display, so this must be 'it'. Azrael, you scoundrel, I've worked out your riddles. But I'm still not ready. "Her whole body is freezing. Oh, God. Oh, God! Can you do anything, Nurse? Make her come back. Don't leave us, Mam. You hear me?"

"It's too late, Caroline. I'll still check for a pulse..." says Nurse Vaughan, sympathetically. I can't anything now, Azrael. All I can sense is a growing coldness that sweeps across my entire body from the extremities inwards. It's a peculiar feeling which is difficult to accurately describe. I can't think straight. Is *this* normal? "I'm sorry, but I think Isabella's gone. I'll need to double-check with a stethoscope and find my pencil torch. There's one in Sally's office, I won't be a moment."

"Grandma?!" wails Jessica, whilst looking directly into my darkening eyes. To my dismay, her voice slowly begins to fade, although I don't believe it is of any fault of her own. I'm sinking further into this never-ending void. I'm scared, Azrael. Where are you? "I Love you so much. You can't be dead!" I love you too, my dear, always and forever. "Don't go. *Please*, don't go."

I treasure these last few seconds more than anything else I've encountered in life, where Jessica's features remain visible to me; the features of our family, our heritage, our everlasting connection with one another. Keep on smiling, my beautiful girl. Be happy for me - not sad. The wave of darkness now coats everything around me, cruelly tearing away my daughter and granddaughter from all sight. All that exists now is a small, golden hue that strangely seems to be moving towards my position from within this black abyss. Where am I? Are you there, Azrael? Is *this* the journey you spoke of?

"Please follow me, Isabella. There is nothing to be frightened of. My purpose now is to guide you through this shadowed valley."

The golden light immediately transforms into Azrael's, now familiar, presence. He looks far-too pleased with himself. However, I do have a compelling urge that makes me want to meet up with him, against any rational disagreement. All previous reservations are soon wilfully cast aside, only so that I can confront this magical creature about what his true intentions are.

"This way, Isabella. We're almost there."

There's an overwhelming reassurance about Azrael's presence now which stops me from having a go at him, but I can't quite put my finger on why. Like a lost child, I clasp onto this lion's mane in attempt to create some comfort between us. It's incredibly soft and warm, quite lovely, though in an unusual sense. Azrael and I walk a little further into this endless realm, neither of us uttering a single word to the other for a good while or so. Gracious, I can walk again! I'm no longer constrained in that wretched bed. I can no longer feel the coursing pain which had previously inflicted every inch of my body and mind. I feel free, and freedom is a gift I had long taken for granted, though not anymore. This is wonderful, Azrael. Where is it, where you are taking me?

"Patience, Isabella. Are you feeling more like your old self now, I? They're all waiting for you, by the way, so *do* try to be polite."

Before I have chance to counter Azrael, a blinding flash bursts out from his body that takes me completely by surprise. After the initial shock, I rub at my eyes in thinking that doing so will somehow awaken me from this unthinkable dream, though I'm only to find that they are no longer sticky and sore. How marvellous! I slowly start to open them and what now lies ahead is beyond any attainable words. I'm starting to enjoy this journey you have taken me on, Azrael. I'm sorry for the way I acted towards you, earlier.

"Thank you, Isabella. It's been my pleasure. Farewell."

What a joy! And I don't mean that in the sense of Azrael disappearing. No, it is because I find myself standing at the forefront of that heavenly Northumbrian cottage, the one which had only existed in my wildest fantasies. Every fine detail is crystal clear: the yellow roses that are in full bloom, the warm breeze, the trickling stream nearby, and not to mention the growing smell of Robert's cigar smoke. He must be close? My darling husband - I'm here!

Without further thought, I immediately look across towards the wildflower field in search of my young children, although they are not there to greet me this time. A glimmer of despair sets in, but this is soon replaced by an immense burst of utter marvel and relief. In the corner of my eye, I see David and Robert loitering together within the garden. They both look so youthful and care-free, just as I remember them to be during their prime. I take my first steps toward them and, to my further astonishment, notice just how youthful my own skin now appears. All those ghastly wrinkles and protruding veins have vanished - even my hair has returned to its luscious, auburn colour.

"Hello, Mam." chuckles David playfully, as he opens his arms out wide to welcome me. "It's good to see you again. I've missed you."

"My son... David." I gasp, then swiftly motion towards him. "I have missed you too, my darling boy. This can't be real?"

"Isabella!" Robert suddenly lunges forward, giving myself little chance to comprehend his action, and successfully beats our son to bestow a wantful embrace upon me. Robert then steps back slightly to place a hand around my waist, while the other gently strokes through my hair. Instantly, I fall back in love with my Bobby's piercing eyes, the eyes of our family, the same which have always entranced me. "You look beautiful, sweetheart."

"As do you." I reply, in a timid voice. "You look just as you did when we first met."

"I've never left your side, Isabella - not once." implores Robert, as our eyes lock fully together. "I would never forsake our vows, darling. My love for you has only grown stronger. Even death cannot tear us apart."

"Oh, Bobby." Despite this voice of mine returning to its previous strength, I initially struggle to respond under all the emotions now coursing through it. I can't seem to find the correct words. There's so much I want to say to him. "We're finally back together, just how we should be. I love you, Robert."

"I love you, Isabella." whispers my Bobby. He nestles his face against mine, and all the sorrow from learning of his death then leaves from me. His touch is warm. I can feel him. I *am* here with

Robert. This must be real. "Welcome home. You're safe now, Isabella."

I know I've already said this once today, but there are few moments in life that can equate to how thrilling this reunion makes me feel. Robert, like myself, is no longer inflicted by the passage of time: his arms are packed with muscle again, he no longer bears the scars from war, no longer tremors from shellshock, and has seemingly recovered from going bald. Now isn't *that* something? I squeeze my husband with every ounce of will I can forge, then turn to invite our son into this lovely pact. David graciously accepts, much to my further enjoyment. He's always been such a good boy.

"Are you coming inside or not, Mam?" questions David, with a cheeky grin on his face. "Everyone is waiting. They're really looking forward to seeing you."

I've not yet placed a foot inside this cottage, so I'm quite unsure as to what I'll actually discover. I hope it won't be a disappointment, however unlikely that scenario may be. David unlocks the front door and then directs a hand upwards to guide me in. I obey without question, I mean, why shouldn't I? A rapturous applause greets me as I enter this wonderful domain and in response, for the first time in ages, I laugh. It's a mixture between being nervous and pleasantly surprised. Surrounding me now are relatives and friends, all long-gone. Surely, my eyes are deceiving me?

Mother and Father are both sat upon some pretty boudoir chairs, right next to an open fireplace that radiates with a comforting warmth. I smile at my parents, and they simply smile back. Nothing more needs to be said, given that we're each joyful to be back in one another's company.

My best friend, Joan, is also present. She and some of my fellow Escomb Angels are all stood together, clapping, smirking, and seem just as happy as I am. As I walk towards them, I suddenly feel something hairy brush alongside my legs; it's my little Yorkshire Terrier, Winston, and he too appears excited. I clasp the little devil

194

into my arms, then eagerly turn to greet whoever else is waiting for me.

Aunt Edith soon grabs my attention, as she is leaning against an upright piano beside the living room's farthest corner. She's signalling for me to come over. It would be rude not to oblige, wouldn't it?

"Hello, Isabella." smiles my aunt, whilst lifting the piano's lid up to reveal its pristine keys. "How about a performance? We've been looking forward to hearing you play."

I nod back in acceptance, then enthusiastically motion myself towards this divine instrument. It's a Steinway - perfect! I've always dreamt of owning one of those. Along the short trek towards Aunt Edith, a small mirror hanging above the fireplace momentarily takes my sight away from her. Strangely enough, it doesn't show one's reflection, but instead fleeting images of Caroline and Jessica. They're still holding onto one another in the same position as I had left them. Bless their hearts. They look so sad. I wish I could offer them some comfort.

"They'll be fine." assures Robert, as he lovingly places a hand upon my shoulders. "They've got each other, Isabella. You don't need to worry about them anymore." he then turns me to face the magnificent piano, itself looking evermore inviting. "Go on, old girl, play one of your favourites for us. We've been waiting long enough."

"Okay, darling." I reply, whilst reluctantly taking my eyes away from the mysterious mirror and its sombre reflection. "I'll try to not disappoint you all." I jest. "It's been a while since I've last played."

Aunt Edith winks back, then proceeds to wave her arms more rapidly in motioning me over. As I sit down in front of the piano, on its little stool, further conflicting emotions begin to surface. I genuinely can't remember the last time I played, and I'm not helped much by the fact Winston is wriggling himself all over my lap. Robert again places a tender hand on my shoulder, thankfully diffusing these silly doubts of mine, and in turn I nestle my head against him. I'm no longer feeling nervous, if anything, I'm determined to make this the grandest of performances.

A yearning temptation to play a nostalgic nocturne rises, on account of all I've just been through, although this urge swiftly passes. I instead choose to perform Chopin's *Minute Waltz (Opus 64 No.1)*, in fully utilising my newly-obtained ability to use these supple fingers of mine. It's an energetic piece, completely ideal for this heavenly setting, and one I know Robert enjoys listening to. After Winston settles down, I take in a deep breath and then hover my fingers just above the piano's keys. A powerful wave of euphoria instantly shoots through my body as I perform the starting note. I'm a little rusty at first, which is likely down to the tears of happiness streaming down my face, but I soon get back into the swing of things.

"I'm so sorry..."

Nurse Vaughan? Is that your voice I can faintly hear?

"There's no vital signs. Time of death: Three-Fifteen a.m."

It would be so very wrong for me not to think of what Caroline and Jessica must be going through, after-all, death is such a painful event. However, we must all face this horrible reality at some point. Depending on the circumstances, a loved one's passing can be easy to accept, while on others the grief simply becomes too much to bear. I have lived a long and prosperous life, at least until recently. I don't want my family to spend the rest of their lives dwelling in sorrow, Lord no, but instead only to remember all the good times we had.

Please my darlings, do not weep for me, for I am surrounded by friends and family in a place of pure harmony - a realm where no sadness or any other earthly concerns can thrive. I'm not suffering anymore. I'm not reliant on drugs, those ghastly puréed meals or those insufferable incontinence pads. I'm no longer a slave to Dementia and Cancer. I'm not simply existing. I am back to my usual self – my true self. I am so very grateful for being granted this one day of lucidity. I am grateful for all the help and compassion those lovely people in that care home gave me. I'm even thankful for Azrael being there during those darker moments. Now though, finally, I am at peace. This is perfect. This... is wonderful.

Thank you for reading my novel. I would greatly appreciate it if you could leave an honest review on Amazon and Goodreads. As an independent author, every review matters and ultimately helps towards improving my writing skills.

With kindest regards,
Andrew

OTHER WORKS AVAILABLE ON AMAZON

*** Horror/Supernatural ***

"The Skipton Haunting: Tale of The Red Ribbon Witch"

A disturbing true story the author himself experienced.

In 2016, when John Davidson and his family moved to Skipton Road, they had no idea of what terrors awaited them. Things seemed normal at first, apart from the pungent smell of rotten flesh in their kitchen, recurring scratch marks along the walls, and an overwhelming sense of always being watched by someone or "something".

Overtime, through a series of vivid nightmares and intrusive whispers, the Davidsons came to learn of a malignant menace that still dwelled within their new home – a Witch named Sabina, who sought out vengeance upon those whom had betrayed her in life, along with an ancient demon...her 'Master'. Throughout these horrific events, John struggled against his growing depression, his new reliance on alcohol, and the overall strong desire to keep his family from falling apart – which it was. This terrifying period in their lives would forever haunt the Davidsons, as it did with countless other victims before them.

In reading this book, you will bear witness to an actual haunting that took place, its lasting effect on those involved, and one that many people can verify. Some, including the author, would argue that 'The Red Ribbon Witch/Sabina' and her demon do exist...it's up to you to decide. Set in the North East of England.

"Cerebrante - Book One: The Sacred Balance"

The world of Impartia is falling into chaos. Queen Cera, the tyrannical ruler of Magmorrah, has waged a war between mortals and spirits of the like never seen before. As darkness steadily sweeps across the many lands of Impartia, consuming all within its path, only one light prevails - Cerebrante - the Spirit of Balance, although their whereabouts remain... unknown.

As all hope seems lost, an exiled princess named Cara and her young daughter, Sophilia, are thrown into this apocalyptic conflict, their purpose in finding Cerebrante - shrouded in mystery. On their quest to locate Cerebrante, Cara and Sophilia are unwillingly forced apart, each burdened to fulfil an ancient prophecy, one that would reclaim 'The Sacred Balance', one that could tear them apart... forever. A story of 'Good vs Evil' - with a twist.

The first instalment of the 'Cerebrante' Trilogy/Series is an ideal read for fans of J.R.R Tolkien and the 'Final Fantasy' video game series.

(Watch out for free promotional days on Amazon. I announce when these are available through my Twitter account.)

Coming Soon

"The Skipton Haunting 2: Curse of The Red Ribbon Witch"

"Cerebrante – Book Two: The Forgotten Guardian"

Updates for these will be found on my social media pages.

Printed in Great
Britain
by Amazon

32034761R00121